Karen Alexander lives in Johannesburg, South Africa. Her love of creative arts began at an early age with an interest in writing, painting and music.

She is also the author of the novel "Audience with a Sidewalk Saviour".

DEUS EX

MACHINA

K ALEXANDER

DEUS EX MACHINA

Origin: New Latin, a god from a machine,

translation of Greek theos ek mēchanēs

~ Merriam-Webster online

(http://www.merriam-webster.com)

With sincere thanks to Lynette Mae and Jae Gatsby, for being so generous with their knowledge and time.

The orderly makes a note on his clipboard as he glances up at the serial number printed on the door. He doesn't actually need a reminder – he can recite this number in his sleep – but somehow it provides him with a moment of comfort. Then, hanging the clipboard on the hook at the back of the trolley, he steps to the side and crouches to pull a tray from below. He pulls off the white cloth cover which reveals an unappetizing meal of bland mashed vegetables, a baked potato, and a colorless slab of meat. Straightening up, the tray grasped securely in both hands, he approaches the door.

Through the industrial strength Plexiglas, he can see the woman within on the other side of the small room, her slick muscles defined in harsh relief as she works precisely through a series of slow physical movements. Inadvertently holding his breath, he moves to the solid door and slides open the hatch three quarters down. He slides the tray through without a problem and shuts the hatch somewhat louder than he intends. When he straightens up and glances through the porthole again, she is still in exactly the same place, but her movements have ceased, and her shaved head is tilted at a somehow menacing angle. It's almost as if she is listening to his actions and analyzing the most favorable point of attack.

Taking one step backwards, he puts his hands behind him and presses them against the comforting solidity of the steel trolley.

"Ryan! Lunch!"

She does not respond to his barked words, but he knows that she hears him. He moves to a position behind the trolley, aware of his ... he would not call it fear, never that – uneasiness? – and pushes the cart into motion sharply, very glad to step into the safety of the solitary small elevator at the end of the short hallway.

Noting the faint whir of the elevator, she clenches her fists briefly before stretching them wide open and shaking her hands loosely. Her neck is a little tight and she rotates it thoroughly, following up with a roll of her shoulders and a systematic stretching of her muscles. Once she is satisfied that she is properly cooled down, she turns sharply to stare at the tray sitting on the small ledge. It is unappetizing, as she has come to expect, but she is hungry. It has been twenty-four hours since she has eaten. They have begun taking the tray away after it sits for a while. Though they assume otherwise, she would like to eat what she is given. Her physical workouts exhaust her energy at an alarming rate, and when she does not eat, they up her meds and sometimes tranquilize her, roll her out somewhere and stick needles into her to provide the necessary nutrients. She does not mind needles – she's had worse – but the tranquilizers leave her numb and nauseous, which makes it impossible for her to exercise.

Which is intolerable.

And so, whenever she can, she eats what they give her. But only when she can.

She steps forward, her tread light, and reached out a hand for the tray. She is about to touch its white polystyrene edge when her fingers halt in mid-air and freeze there, motionless. Her green eyes narrow and her pupils contract. Then, her hand retracts rapidly to cup the back of her head fiercely. She presses her head hard into her palm and grimaces, her teeth clenched against whatever it is that has invaded the moment. Her other hand lifts and wraps over her eyes, pressing white-knuckled against the ridges of her eyebrows.

She does not make a sound for a long time. When she finally throws her head back her green eyes are filled with boundless ferocity. The snarl builds in the pit of her stomach and rises up through her throat, roughly bursting from her mouth with the intensity of a wild animal. She scrapes her fingertips jaggedly over her skull in rage, but after yesterday's situation there are no fingernails left, so she does not draw any fresh blood. Her hoarse roaring echoes down the hall and back again, with no other place down here for it to enter. Finally she strikes out in aggression, her fist splitting the tray into pieces and spreading blots of pulverized food against the door. The ledge on which the tray is resting also cracks faintly.

She will be punished for that in some way, she is aware of that, even if it is only to tranquilize her while they come in to repair it. She can't exercise when she's numb.

Which is intolerable.

Her snarling ends unexpectedly as she slides to the floor and presses her forehead to the cool metal surface.

"No. Stop it! I'm not listening to this anymore…"

The food is everywhere. It will be needles for her again. Soon.

Doctor Walsch nods thoughtfully and steeples her fingers together. "And the new Lithium dosage? Any more hallucinations?"

The haggard man opposite her shakes his head. "No, Doc, no more dancing worms or talking heads, thank the Lord. I'm sleeping better too. Is that just me or…"

"One major benefit of being more relaxed and less anxious is a better night's rest." She shoots a quick smile in his direction before she withdraws the pen clipped to her notebook and writes something in the margin. "I'm very happy to hear that, Gerry. If you keep improving at this rate, you'll be in a good position to get a job soon."

He shifts forward and perches nervously on the edge of the faded blue wingback chair. "Does that… do you think it would it be possible for me to see Eloise and the kids?"

She raises her eyebrows and taps the top of the pen against the page. "Gerry, we've spoken about this. It's not a matter of medication and control, as much as you would like it to be. This involves lawyers and regulations, and Eloise's emotions, too. You can't discount them, Gerry – your actions impacted on her in a very serious way. Unfortunately these types of circumstances can take years to resolve."

Gerry smiles wryly. "Do you have any meds in that cabinet of yours for increasing patience?"

"Nope." She flashes her crooked smile again. "If it were that easy, I'd be a millionaire and there would never be war. Unfortunately that's a trait you're going to have to develop on your own."

"You crush me, Doc." He shakes his head solemnly. "And here I believed that you could do anything."

"Mostly." She clips the pen back onto the notebook and rises. When he also rises and hesitantly extends a hand, she grasps it firmly and presses once before releasing it. "Next week, Gerry. And remember to do the breathing exercises. I know that you think they're just new age nonsense, but try to give them a chance."

"All right. If you trust them, then who am I to argue. I suppose all it costs is time, and I have no shortage of that." He shrugs and reaches for the doorknob. "Next week, Doc."

"Goodbye, Gerry."

"Bye." He doesn't open the door all the way, but nervously slips around the edge before pushing it closed behind him. With a slight smile, Doctor Walsch makes one or two more notes before she tosses the pen on the small desk and steps out of the office. Cecily Dawson is perched erectly on her padded computer chair, her brown eyes fixed on her monitor with a fierce scowl as she types noisily. Whenever she strikes the space bar ferociously with her thumb, Doctor Walsch winces in sympathy.

"Cecily."

"Doctor Walsch."

"Don't frown so. You'll end up with furrows in your forehead."

"Frowning provides a great deal more gratification than a smooth forehead." Still scowling, Cecily pauses with her sharply angled eyebrows raised, her fingers poised above the keys. Doctor Walsch suppresses the urge to wince when she notes the thumb hovering ominously right over the spacebar. "If you want me to file Mr. Cook's notes, you should put them down."

Shaking her head, Doctor Walsch places the notebook precisely on the corner of the teak desk. "You're much too quick for me. Gerry says he believes I can do anything – he's got the right office, but the wrong miracle worker."

Cecily appears to agree without saying anything or, in fact, moving a muscle. She commences typing, starting with the predictable whack of her thumb against the spacebar. "I do believe that Doctor Clarke is downstairs in the canteen."

"Good. Thank you." For a moment Doctor Walsch watches the furious typing with muted amusement, before she clears her throat. "I really should give you a raise, Cecily."

"Yes, Doctor."

"If only I didn't have to keep buying new keyboards." As if on cue, Doctor Walsch's sentence is punctuated by the smack of Cecily's thumb against the spacebar.

"Yes, Doctor."

The same sentence. Amazing how inflection changes implication. Grinning to herself, the doctor leaves the reception area and walks down the corridor, briefly greeting colleagues as she passes them by. She presses the elevator button once and glances at the numbers lighting up over the door. Currently the elevator is on the fifth floor. With a sigh Doctor Walsch sends a quiet entreaty out into the universe, but is denied her wish when the elevator doors open on her floor to reveal Nesbitt, the plastic surgeon from five. His bright blue eyes flash when he sees her, and he squares his shoulders rakishly.

"Well, if it isn't the delicious Doctor Walsch."

"Nesbitt." She nods curtly at him and steps into the elevator, turning her back on him quite pointedly.

"Going down for a cup of coffee? I'm buying."

It is less of a question than a statement, and she grinds her teeth together in mute irritation before turning her head slightly in his direction. "No, thank you. I'm meeting somebody."

"Oh." He whistles speculatively. "Professional or personal?"

"None of your business, Jack."

Her tone of voice is acidic, and even he cannot fail to notice this time. "Really, Doctor Walsch, won't you ever put that little incident behind you? I did apologize, after all."

"And you didn't mean a word of it." She blesses the elevator as it opens to reveal the glass-encased security booths and the entrance to the canteen. "If you keep bothering me, I'll have one of the guards remove you. That's a promise. Enjoy your day." With that she leaves the elevator, aware that Nesbitt remains where he is. He is not affected by her comment, but is more likely appreciating the view as she walks away. She knows this, but there is little she can do.

As she passes the glass cubicle, she waves to the massive security guard who is studying one of the numerous small security screens before him. Without glancing up, he lifts his hand in greeting. Reaching into her coat pocket she withdraws her white access card and swipes it across the sensor, then steps through the turnstile as soon as the muted click sounds.

When she rounds the corner, she immediately sees Doctor Clarke at a table at the back, oblivious to the charming water feature visible through the tinted glass behind him as he studies a sheet of densely printed paper. She is almost next to him before he looks up and grins, his bushy pale eyebrows jumping.

"Claire. Coffee?"

"Hmm." She leans down and plants a friendly kiss on his ginger-stubble cheek. "No. I'm giving it up." When his eyes shift past her and he bites the inside of his lip, she knows what he is looking at. "Yeah. I had the dubious fortune of being in the elevator with him for much too long."

His hazel eyes crinkle. "And you still want to give up coffee? I'd ask for quadruple-caf if I were you."

"If they made it I'd sure as hell have it, Art." She pats his shoulder affably. "But you're right – I can't possibly think of giving up my favorite crutch at a time like this."

Watching her go to the counter to get a cup, he smiles to himself. "Always the same intention, always the same result."

"Excuse me?"

"Nothing." He pulls the chair beside him away from the table and pats it. "Sit."

Joining him, she opens the plastic lid of her cup, careful not to spill any liquid. "What are you looking at, Art?"

"File from that private hospital." He grimaces and pushes at the paper exaggeratedly with his forefinger. "Fairwater. I wish I could sort this one out or get rid of it."

"Still the one who speaks to God?"

"Yes." With a shake of his head he picks up his own cup and takes a sip, wrinkling his freckled nose at the coolness of the contents. "Uck. Though, technically, you're wrong. She doesn't speak to Him – He speaks to her."

"Either way, I don't envy you." With a glance at the open file, she lifts her cup to her mouth and attempts a sip, jerking back as it burns her lip. "Damn it."

"They make it with boiling water here." He lifts his expressive eyebrows comically, and then sighs. "I should've followed your example and said no to this case. I'm at my wits' end, Claire. It's infuriating. And all of the red tape doesn't help, either. I can *understand* the measures they take, but they make my job immensely difficult."

Placing the cup on the table, she reaches over and touches the back of his large hand lightly. "Art, why don't you just resign from the case? You wouldn't be the first. What's it been – two years? Three?"

"Three. Give or take a millennium, it sometimes seems." There is a moment of silence and then he sighs. "I don't know, Claire. I just don't know. There's something about the whole situation that bothers me. It stinks, and I can't tell what of." He leans towards her and props his sturdy forearms on the table. "What would it take to get you to consult on this, Claire?"

She begins to shake her head and he seems to anticipate it, reaching over to place his hand on her arm. "Listen, wait... don't say 'no' yet. Just hear me out. I..." He thinks, begins again. "I..." And then throws his hands up in defeat. "Oh hell, who am I kidding? I don't have a thing. No enticements, no tempting facts, just a grown man begging like a little girl." When she smiles, he raises his eyebrows pathetically. "Come on, Claire, don't make me do something even more dismal. Please." Though she is smiling at his antics, he knows it is not a sign of flagging will.

"I'm not interested. If I were..."

"You'd have taken it when they offered. I know." He laces his hands together. "I want your input, Claire, and not because you're the best I know, but because I trust your judgment as a friend."

She sips from her coffee cup, scrutinizing him warmly over the white rim. When she is finished with her drink, she pushes it to one side and places her hands palms down on the table in front of her. "You know my opinion, Art – she's a psychopath. The hallucinations are only a manifestation of her subconscious inclinations. It's not something I'm interested in getting involved with."

"But that's your *personal* opinion." For once he sounds a little piqued. "I'm looking for a professional one. You haven't spoken to her."

"Has she said anything at all to you that would point to a different diagnosis?" He does not answer, but she does not need him to. "She hasn't, has she? Because she doesn't actually speak to you. How could I give *any* sort of consultation when she doesn't speak, Art?" She shakes her head. "The woman's a killing machine. That she has God talking to her seems a minor issue to me, compared to that."

Though Art smiles, he is shaking his head too. "She is a highly trained officer, Claire. There is a difference. You don't become a captain in the Marine Force Recon by being a slavering maniac."

Claire shrugs. "As far as I'm concerned, she got that decoration of hers for behaving like one."

"She got the Medal of Honor for leading an entire platoon of rebels away from her troops and then ambushing them by herself, Claire. Whatever the woman's mental state has turned to, her accomplishments are something to respect. And in any case..." he crunches the empty sugar packet into a small wad and throws it at her, "I'm not getting into this argument with you again. You just love to yank my chain."

"That I do." She picks up the wad of paper and throws it back, her aim poor. "Why do you want me to consult, Art? I mean, you know very well how I feel about the case."

"Well." Sitting back in his chair he seems suddenly hesitant. "It's not her mental state I want you to examine, Claire. At least...not only that. After three very difficult years, I don't think there's anything to be done about that. What I want is..." He sits forward and shoots a nervous glance over her shoulder, drawing a puzzled frown from her. "Claire, I think there's something happening in that place that shouldn't be."

Her scowl deepens. "Like what? What are you saying, Art?"

"See, I'm not sure." He taps one finger on the table between them. "Here's the thing. One day she seems completely lucid, and the next she's... Okay, so her baseline isn't even close to normal, and a lot of people – including you – think she's a lost cause, but she's been cycling between all sorts of meds for the last how many years? With the combination of things in her system, she should either have stabilized by now, or she should be a slavering maniac."

Catching her raised eyebrow, he clarifies. "*Consistently*, I mean. Look, I know it sounds very James Bond, I'm fully aware of that, and I could be having a moment of complete delusion. I'm overworked and under-appreciated. But what if there's something I'm not seeing, and I give up when I shouldn't? I don't like the idea of that, Claire – signing off on somebody who might need help just because I'm *tired*. I suppose that what I'm asking you to do is only to go there and see whether everything seems legitimate. If you can do that for me, you'd put my fears to rest and simplify any decision that I might have to make in the near future." He spreads his hands towards her. "So that's what I'm asking."

Claire heaves a sigh and compresses her lips in thought. "Would they even let me consult?"

"Hah. The esteemed Doctor Walsch, come to reclaim the offer made first to her?"

"The esteemed Doctor Walsch, dying to run as fast as possible in the opposite direction." She grimaces at him. "There goes giving up coffee. I think it would be a very bad idea at this point in time."

"I think you're right." He rises to his feet and forestalls her movement with a wave of his hand. "Sit. I'll get it. I'll get you anything you want."

"Can you get me amnesty from this whole yucky affair?"

"No. How about a banana muffin?"

"I suppose that's the next best thing."

The small elevator makes a strange ticking noise as it descends, and Claire Walsch glances upwards in quiet trepidation. When she drops her gaze again, both Rear Admiral Banks and the short orderly are smiling knowingly at her. Clearing her throat in embarrassment, she shifts the file in her hands and turns to the colonel.

"Her cell is the only one down here?"

He nods. "We prefer to call it a room, Doctor. Captain Ryan isn't a prisoner. She is a very fine Marine, and it is a pity about her condition. We keep her in the most secure area, yes. As a highly trained officer, she has several skills that would facilitate her making an easy escape from the more basic rooms. The military does not want any civilians at risk of being harmed by her in any manner, Doctor, so we have taken stringent measures to prevent that possibility."

"Does she still show signs of harmful behavior?"

The colonel smiles and glances away. "Textbook complex question there, Doctor Walsch. Yes, she does exhibit signs of harmful behavior, but wouldn't you, if you were being invaded by both the medical profession and by what you imagine to be the voice of God?"

Claire keeps her tone even. "Invaded by the medical profession in what manner?"

"Come now, Doctor. Intrusion need not be physical to be intrusion. She has individuals clamoring to get inside her head at all times of the day. I imagine that must be very difficult for someone as private as she is. Or used to be."

"You knew her personally, Colonel?"

"I was with her in Afghanistan in '99."

"Would you say there were any precursors to the delusions?"

He meets her eyes stonily. "I am not qualified to answer that, Doctor."

"I see." She holds his gaze without flinching. "Why exactly is it that you are so reluctant to discuss her condition with me, Colonel?"

"Because a *condition* is all you people see her as!" He snaps his head to one side and quells his sudden outburst before continuing, his voice as smooth as previously. "She is one of the finest people I have ever known, Doctor Walsch. I find it atrocious and reprehensible that this place and that...disease...would strip away all of the good things that she's ever done, and replace them with a case study number."

"You are rather intimately involved with this institution you feel so negative about, Admiral Banks. Or am I wrong?"

His back is straight. "I am here for Captain Ryan. Nothing more."

She considers his observation before she speaks again. "Would I be in any physical danger?"

"No." The Marine has swiftly replaced the distressed comrade in arms. "She has been heavily tranquilized; you should be quite safe. Nevertheless, we would prefer that you don't actually go into the room."

"I will take that under advisement. Thank you."

When the elevator doors slide open the orderly steps out sharply, obviously discomfited by their conversation and eager to move on. He stops at the only door in the hallway and takes a look at the clipboard he has had clamped under his arm, making a note on it before he moves towards the Plexiglas porthole. He glances briefly through the porthole before making a few more notes on the clipboard, which he then hangs onto a hook to the left of the door.

When Banks approaches the door, the orderly moves aside to allow him access to the window. The colonel glances through the clear porthole, his gray eyes inscrutable as he turns to Doctor Walsch.

"She is all yours, Doctor."

He walks away, stiff-backed and elegant, to enter the elevator, and when he turns and presses the button, his eyes meet Claire's. They seem to hold some sort of warning, but she thinks she might only be imagining it, and as the doors close, she turns to the orderly.

"Do you have keys to open this door?"

"No, Ma'am." He shakes his head. "The standard rooms have keys; this one can only be opened from the security center upstairs. But you really shouldn't go in."

"I'm not planning to. But if I wanted to – hypothetically speaking - would you be able to get somebody to open the door for me?"

"Yes, Ma'am." The answer clearly makes him unhappy. "I'd get them on the radio, and if you had proper clearance and they could see you..." he points to the camera tucked into a corner, "they would open the door for you. But you really shouldn't go in there."

"So you said..." She reads his name tag, "Trevor. Thank you. Are you going back up?"

"No, Ma'am. I can't leave you here by yourself."

"All right." She slowly approaches the porthole and then glances through it.

If she did not know for a fact that this is the correct room, she would not connect the person inside with the press clippings she has been scrutinizing. She recalls the photo of Captain Ryan receiving her decoration: An attractive woman with a strong bearing and a healthy bronze hue, her compelling green eyes keen beneath precisely plaited black hair.

The woman inside the small stark room with its padded white walls is slumped with her back against the wall, her arms obviously bound behind her. Her shaven head hangs between the sharp angles of her shoulders, and her skin is unhealthily translucent against the bleakness around her. The paleness is emphasized by the austere white sleeveless vest and cotton pants which drape loosely against her lean frame. When she shifts marginally and draws her legs against her chest, Doctor Walsch catches a glimpse of muscles shifting in her upper arms. There appears not to be a spare inch of fat on Ryan; her frame is lean.

Claire turns to Trevor and finds his eyes fixed on her butt. When she clears her throat, he glances up without remorse or apology.

"Does she do some sort of physical therapy?"

"What? Do you mean with the doctors?" He shakes his head. "Not like that, no, Ma'am. But she's constantly working out in there, doing all sorts of exercises, basic and otherwise. Almost obsessively, if you ask me. I don't know what it's all about – maybe it's just the only thing to do in there. If I didn't start out that way it would make me crazy, I can tell you."

Turning away from the talkative orderly, Claire peers through the porthole again. The woman is sitting in the same position, her head drooping apathetically towards her chest. Leaning towards the sound grid positioned just under the porthole, Claire speaks into it as she has been instructed to by Banks.

"Good afternoon, Captain Ryan. I am Doctor Claire Walsch." There is no response, and when she glances through the porthole again, the Marine has not moved, nor given any sign of acknowledging her presence. Clearing her throat, Claire tries once more. "Captain Ryan? May I speak with you?" Once again there is no response, and the figure does not move. Turning her head slightly, Claire again catches the orderly admiring her butt.

"Stop that, Trevor." When he lifts his shoulders in a minute, not very apologetic shrug, she shakes her head. "Can she hear me?"

"No physical reason why not, Ma'am." He peers through the glass himself. "Maybe she's talking to somebody more important right now."

"Ever seen her do that?"

"Sure." He nods. "She'll be her charming self one moment," he pulls a face to emphasize his sarcasm, "and the next, she's snarling like an animal and smacking her head against things. That's why they padded the walls; they were worried that she'd hurt herself."

"And like this?" She hooks a thumb in the direction of the door. "Docile as a lamb. She just sits there until she wakes up – or God does, whichever comes first."

21

"I see." She thinks for moment. "Does it ever seem strange to you how she goes from one to the next so fast?"

"Strange?" It looks as if Trevor thinks she is joking. "No offense, Doctor, but Captain Ryan here is batshit crazy. She gives strange a whole new meaning. If you mean stranger than usual, I wouldn't even know how to measure that with her. Sorry."

Claire normally hates it when people make snap judgments, but considering that Trevor's just repeating the same thing she's been saying to Art all this time, she decides that it would be hypocritical to take him on about it. She looks through the porthole again at the hunched figure.
"Her hands are bound?"

"Yes and no. There are handcuffs set into the wall."

Claire turns to Trevor and raises her eyebrows coolly. "Isn't that unethical? Surely they must be uncomfortable. How long will she be cuffed for?"

"They are lined, Ma'am, and they only stay on until you leave. For your safety. Then we take them off and let her sleep it off."

The story sounds a little too smooth, but Claire doesn't question it. She is getting less and less interested in getting involved in this case any more than she already is, and now just wants to get the visit over with as soon as possible. Turning away from Trevor, she leans towards the sound grid.

"Ryan."

There is no movement from the crumpled woman. Clenching the file in her hand, Claire bites her lip for a moment and then speaks to Trevor over her shoulder.

"Ask them to open the door."

"But that's not a–"

"Yes." She cuts him short impatiently. "I know. Everybody keeps saying that. Please ask them to open the door."

"Yes ma'am." He is hesitant as he lifts the two-way radio clipped to his waist and speaks into it. There is quite a bit of conversation, very muted and petulant, before he moves the radio away from his mouth and speaks to Claire. "Please step back a little so that the camera can see you." When she complies, he rattles into the two-way radio again before switching it off. "Okay, they're opening it for you now."

As if in confirmation, the door clicks loudly and shifts back from its lock. They both keep a vigilant eye on the figure inside the room, but there is no change in her posture. Stepping closer warily, Trevor braces both arms against the bar on the heavy door and pulls it backwards, allowing Claire Walsch access to the room.

"Please stay out of her reach, Doctor."

She can't resist. "How far exactly *is* her reach with her arms handcuffed behind her, Trevor?"

He glares at her reproachfully. "Don't underestimate her, Ma'am. She's trained to do upsetting things. Stay away from her feet."

Smothering a smile, Claire nods solemnly and steps into the room. The door remains open behind her, ostensibly so that Trevor can come to her rescue should the patient attempt to kick her into submission. When she is inside the small room, she cannot help but feel a twinge of claustrophobia – the walls are close and stark, and beyond the narrow pallet on her right and the basic bathroom ablutions to her left it is completely bare. In here it is easy to understand why Captain Ryan would compulsively give herself over to something as draining as physical exercise. Heeding the orderly's warning, Claire does not approach the woman, but stays close to the exit, her clipboard held in front of her in what she is very aware is a defensive posture.

"Captain Ryan?"

The woman does not respond, though her head drops closer to her chest and comes to rest on her raised knees. In this position, her head pulls away from her arms and her shoulders stand out in lean, sinewy relief.

"Ryan?"

Still there is no response. Frowning, Claire tries to gauge the woman's physical state from a distance, but it is hard to assess.

She is so thin – they did warn her, Ryan does not eat well – and seems so drained at this point that it would be difficult to draw any sort of accurate conclusion. Clutching her clipboard, Claire lowers herself onto the ground and sits down with her back against the wall next to the door, as far away from the shackled patient as the small room allows. The movement seems to draw the Marine's attention. The shaven head lifts slightly and then fierce green eyes ringed with long dark lashes and equally dark circles fix on her intently. The force of the stare is uncomfortable, and Claire falters for a moment before speaking.

"Captain Ryan, my name is Doctor Walsch–"

"I know." The voice is hollow, gritty, drifting into hoarseness from disuse or abuse.

Puzzled by the unexpected response, Claire is only beginning to scowl when the Marine moves. The motion is so unexpected, so controlled and fast, and so belied by her apparent frailness that there is no time to respond. Ryan shoots forward and grabs Claire by her shirt, hauling her up and spinning her around to wrap one arm around her neck from behind. The metal pin to which Ryan's handcuffs have been attached – its pointed end still crusted in cement from her working it patiently from the wall – is held against Claire's throat with the other hand. The doctor's first instinct is to raise her arms and clamp her hands around the forearm pressed so tightly against her throat, but as she shifts, the woman behind her yanks her head back. A sharp gasp escapes Claire's throat, and she swallows with rising panic.

"Keep your hands down. Tell Trevor to step away from the door."

The orderly has been keeping an eye on the good doctor, as ordered, but has been taken by surprise as much as she was. He hesitates, and somehow Ryan seems to know. Tightening her arm around the doctor's throat to an uncomfortable degree, she prods her with the metal pin.

"She's going to get hurt, Trevor. Step back." To punctuate her request, she shifts her arm and twists Claire's head slightly, causing an uneven moan to escape from the doctor's throat. "Hear that, Trevor? I'm hurting her. Step away from the door."

Helpless, he lifts the two-way radio, which is now jabbering uncontrollably, to his mouth.

"I'm going to kill her, Trevor. Put the radio down on the floor and step back against the wall." In her tight grip the doctor's shuddering breath is barely discernible.

After a tense moment Trevor complies. Ryan steps out, keeping the doctor between them. Claire's eyes are wide, terrified, as she stares at Trevor, but he can do nothing but look at the ground, away from her naked fear.

"Get inside."

He complies, and Ryan hauls the doctor towards the door, momentarily moving the pin away from her throat to push at the door. When the doctor shifts, the arm around her throat twitches. "Don't. I'll break your neck."

Almost gagging, she tries to nod, but the restraining arm makes it impossible. When she reaches up to put her hands on the forearm in an effort to ease the pressure, the woman behind her yanks her roughly.

"*Listen*. Don't." Pushing the door closed, Ryan presses the pin to the juncture between Claire's jaw and neck, just below her ear. "Move."

She drags the shorter woman towards the elevator, making a point of keeping the doctor's face toward the camera as they move away from it. Though Claire once long ago completed a self-defense course, she understands that the woman behind her is extremely strong and exceptionally dangerous, and so she concludes that she has no choice but to obey. She does not think that she can move on her own at this point in any case; it is just the sinewy forearm around her neck that keeps her upright. Walking backwards, they move towards the elevator, and when they step inside, the Marine roughly shoves Claire towards the control box. When she speaks her instructions into it, her breath is warm on the doctor's ear.

Captain Lewis is not having a great day. Pompous authority is not something he handles well, and when he is told without preamble by Doctor Balthazar Tilley-Clapham that he is to keep his security cameras firmly pointed at some visiting la-di-dah for the day, his first instinct is to drive the man's artificially perfect teeth into his artificially square jaw. That is not something he can do, however; not because of a high moralistic streak (his is mediocre at best) or physical inability (he has decked men larger than this overstuffed turkey), but simply because he needs the job. Since he took a bullet in the leg and was honorably discharged, he knows what it means to be a hero with no current value. Men will shake his hand ardently and clap him on the shoulder as if they know him, women will simper and bat their eyelashes, but nobody wants to have an aging, wounded officer hanging about. Perhaps they think they are worth less around him.

Either way, his job is the one thing he needs to hang on to with both hands, which means that he cannot afford even to knock one syllable off the honorable doctor's irritating double-barreled surname. And so he has spent the last hour watching the attending la-di-dah mincing about in her neat little suit, her eyes serious as she asks questions which are delivered in a tone barely this side of civil. At least she is something to look at. The moment when the foolish doctor goes in and sits down, rendering herself a nice little parcel, compounded by the idiotic gutless orderly failing to accompany her into the room as ordered, is the worst moment of Captain Lewis's day, his week, his year, and perhaps even his life.

"Christ!" He starts shouting orders. "Wallace, Taylor, Greer, get down there!" The men hurriedly strap on vests and grab their weapons, then move out of the doorway and down the hallway in practiced unison.

Lewis watches on the small screen as Captain Ryan drags the small doctor out of the room and closes the petrified orderly inside. She drags the doctor backwards into the elevator, her eyes fixed on the camera. They are luminous and menacing, too bright for his comfort. In contrast, the doctor's eyes are dilated with pure panic. With another throaty oath, Lewis turns around, wincing as his leg twists uncomfortably beneath him. "Johnston, Smith, to the elevator on this level. Bulley, Simon, one level up. Johnston, check where it's stopping." He watches in exasperation as the men run down the corridors, following them on the monitors as they move quickly towards their destinations.

Johnston's broad serious face tilts towards the camera as he glances up at the elevator lights blinking above him. "Stops at two... four... six... roof."

Lewis turns his gaze back to the screen where he should be seeing Ryan and the doctor in the elevator, and feels remarkably little surprise when all that greets him is static.

"Christ!" If a vengeful lightning bolt doesn't kill him today, he will be surprised. Perhaps he will even appreciate it, depending on how things turn out. "Johnston, Smith, get to two. Bulley, Simon, secure floor four." He lifts his radio and contacts the only remaining security guards in the building. "Markham, take as many of your guys as you can and go to the roof. If she's going to get out, her possibilities are the best up there. Leave two men to make sure that she doesn't come back down."

With a grunt he slides out his firearm and checks the clip before he slides it back into its holster. "You stay at the monitor, Jarvis. Keep me informed when you see her."

Limping, he runs from the security center, down the hallway with its bland cream walls, and turns right just before the boardroom to duck into the emergency staircase. He intends to run out through the front doors to see if he can spot her on top of the building, and when he exits the staircase on the ground floor, he is just in time to see the elevator door open with a lonely ping.

The two waiting security guards tense, their weapons drawn and pointed, but the doors open to an empty elevator. The two creep forward keeping their weapons up, but there is nothing inside beyond the garish striped wallpaper. Just then Lewis's radio bursts into life.

"Captain, Markham here. We've secured the roof. Nothing here. Over."

"Fuck!" Lewis grinds his teeth and then lifts the radio to his mouth. "Johnston?"

"Johnston here. Nothing. Over."

"*Fuck!* Bulley? Tell me you have good news."

"Bulley here. Nothing, Captain. We've secured the level and– What?" He obviously moves the radio away from his mouth to speak to somebody in the background.

"Bulley? Talk to me."

The security guard's voice is too muffled to understand until he brings the radio back up to his mouth in the middle of a discussion. "... you check. Are you sure? Captain..." His attention is now back on the radio and urgent. "We've got a broken grid on four, left of office 7b. Looks like she's gone into the vents."

Lewis refrains from cursing again as he clicks the talk button. "Markham, Wallace, Greer, floor five. Secure the exits, vents, every fucking thing that leads outside. Johnston, Smith, Taylor, three. I don't want her going up or down. Bulley, get Simon in that vent. Now!"

Slotting the radio back into the harness on his belt, he lopes towards the stairs. "McCarthy, four! Elliot, hold the fort. Tell Tilley-Clapham to evacuate his staff."

One of the security guards runs for the stairs as the other steps around the desk and lifts the phone. "Doctor, it's Jack Elliot from the foyer. Captain Lewis– ... No, they haven't found her yet. Captain Lewis wants you to evacuate the staff, Doctor." He winces at the response, which is not a mild one. "I'm sorry, Doctor; I'm just following orders. … Yes, Doctor. All right." He places the phone back on the hook with a disgusted look and sits down in the swivel chair, leaning forward to get a better view of the action on the small security screen as Simon slithers into the damaged vent.

Inside the elevator, something clinks softly before the hatch on the roof is lifted and set aside. A bare head lowers upside down to take in the lobby, and then disappears again, before Ryan silently lowers herself to the carpeted floor. Crouching in the corner with her back flush against the wall, she presses the "open door" button and waits silently as the doors slide open with a groan.

The security guard sitting behind the curved desk is riveted to the little screen on his tabletop, but he glances up when he hears the sound. He sees nothing, and, with a shrug, he leans toward the screen as Bulley and McCarthy flank a door that is marginally open. He does not hear Ryan when she steps from the carpet on to the cold tiled floor; he does not catch sight of her moving form as she slinks below the level of his elaborate desk.

When a figure appears to his side, he glances up in surprise. "Hey, did Doctor Tilley-Cla-" but he gets no further. His eyes open wide in shock at the sight of the shaven-headed woman just before her rigid hand connects with his face and sends him sprawling off his chair, already unconscious.

Leaning over the desk, Ryan studies the fallen body carefully before she steals back to the elevator. She stretches up to grasp the edges of the hatch and pull herself up through it. The bound and gagged woman in the suit shrinks back from her with a muffled sob.

Without a word the Marine reaches forward and drags Claire closer by her arms, roughly thrusting her through the hatch before she lowers herself again, landing gracefully next to the crumpled doctor. Ryan grasps the stockings that binds Claire's hands together, yanks the woman closer and casually wraps an arm around her waist. They approach the security desk, and Ryan leads Claire behind it to the security guard who is lying on his back, his nose a mess of blood. When Claire begins to keen behind the gag, Ryan shakes her.

"Shut up."

She leans closer and, forcing Claire to kneel with her, searches his pockets. His only weapon is an electronic stun gun on his belt. Ryan ignores it, going instead for the security card clipped to his pocket. After she clips it to the bottom hem of her shirt, she lifts Claire to her feet and drags her to the front door, which glides open silently. Glancing around, Ryan notes the camera above her. With a sharp tug, she drags the doctor a few feet down the pavement to where a small red Renault is parked at the curb.

"Yours?"

Tears are running down Claire's ashen face, and she tremblingly shakes her head. With a grunt, Ryan moves toward the car door. Holding Claire with one hand, she methodically works off her shirt and wraps it around the other hand, which she then pounds through the partially open window. She rips the door open, shoves Claire into the passenger seat, and slots in the seatbelt, leaning over her to unlock the driver's door before she vaults over the hood and slides into the driver's seat. Slipping her now slightly worse for wear shirt over her head, she reaches under the steering wheel and rips out a handful of wires, hurriedly stripping two with her teeth.

When Claire raises her head, she notices a shadow against the glass front door. Security is on the way. As the large doors glide open, the car jerks to a start and Ryan drives away from the pursuing guards. A shot rings out and Claire cringes into the corner of her seat, but the bullet thuds harmlessly into the back of the car.

Unperturbed, Ryan hurtles towards the security barrier, and when the guard appears from the guardhouse with his gun drawn, she slides down in the seat and presses her foot down on the accelerator. Unable to shoot because he has orders not to harm the hostage, the guard watches with frustration as the red Renault bursts through the barrier and screeches onto the asphalt, quickly disappearing around a bend in the country road.

"Fuck!" Captain Lewis slams the heel of his hand against his thigh and turns to the tall man to his right. "Did you just shoot, Johnston?"

The man lowers his weapon awkwardly. "Yes, Sir."

"Didn't I tell you *not* to shoot at them? Johnston?"

"Yes, Sir. You did, Sir." The man holsters his pistol. "I'm sorry, Sir."

"Find out whose car that is. Find out where they're going; find out where they're likely to go. Find me any damned thing I can use!" Spinning on his heel, Captain Lewis goes into the foyer where one of the doctors is attending to the fallen security guard behind the desk. Glancing at the man's bloodied nose with disdain, Lewis shoots a longing look at the elevator before he takes the emergency stairs to the first floor. Instead of turning right towards the security center, he turns left, limping along the narrow hallway that ends in a large aluminum door. When he knocks firmly, a voice commands him to enter, and, with an anticipatory grinding of teeth, he enters the office and presses the door closed behind him. Turning to face the man behind the massive desk, Lewis clasps his hands behind his back and stands rigidly.

"Sit, Lewis." He complies. "Have you found her?"

The question is asked in a benign tone, but it does not fool Lewis. When he shakes his head, the doctor explodes. "How the *hell* does she just walk out of here as if she's on some Sunday drive? Were your men even *awake*?"

Lewis grits his teeth. "This is not exactly a maximum security prison, Doctor."

Balthazar Tilley-Clapham slams both hands on the table and leans forward, fixing his eerily pale blue eyes on Lewis. "Isn't that *your* job, Captain? Isn't Security your area of expertise?"

"Yes. But you can't very well expect airtight security when you refuse to implement the measures I request, Doctor."

"Having barbed wire everywhere is not a measure that Fairwater deems necessary, Captain Lewis. Ditto electric laser goodies. We are a private hospital, not a prison. Our patients are free to walk out, should they choose to. Well, the overwhelming majority of them, anyway. ComCor will yank our financing if we turn this into an episode of *Cell Block H*, do you understand me?"

"I understand you. However, under those circumstances, I do not think that–"

"Oh, don't. Don't think." Doctor Tilley-Clapham rests his face in his palms for an exasperated moment. "Go and find her. I have a call to make."

The captain stalks out, stiff-limbed and angry, and the doctor heaves an aggravated sigh before he lifts up the telephone receiver and dials a number from memory.

"May I speak to Colonel Turner, please? It's Doctor Tilley-Clapham phoning from Fairwater. Thank you. ... No, I'll hold. ... All right, thank you." He reaches forward and pokes a perfectly manicured finger into the miniature water feature on the corner of his desk, dabbling half-heartedly with the water. "George. I've got some bad news, I'm afraid. ... Of course you know. I should have expected no less. ... Well, he's the man *you* recommended, George; you can hardly blame me for that decision. ... Yes, they're tracking her now. She's got that Doctor Walsch with her. ... I could hardly tell that moron Clarke that I didn't want her to come in, could I? Well, exactly. What's your next move?"

He listens impatiently for a few minutes. "All right. It's a damned nuisance if you ask me. Funding isn't worth this rigmarole."

He shakes his head at the adamant voice booming loudly on the other end of the line.

"Sure, George. Nothing more I can do; bring her back when you find her. I'm just not going to buy any party hats, okay? ... Yes. Speak to Lewis about that. I have work to do, George. Talk to me when you know anything. Goodbye."

He slams the phone down, then lifts it and slams it down again for the sheer satisfaction. Lifting the abused handset, he glares at it belligerently as he dials another number.

"Garvey?"

"Yes, hello."

"Tilley-Clapham here. About the Ryan case…"

"She was perfectly tranquilized, Doctor Clapham." Garvey typically has a touch of belligerent guilt in his voice, but today it's much worse. "Enough to keep a small calf down. I don't know how she's standing."

"Not just standing, Garvey - scaling walls and flapping an invisibility cloak. Better check your notes. There's sure to be a report coming from this."

Without saying goodbye, Tilley-Clapham slams down the phone again. It is no longer his problem. He will go on as usual.

It is not long before something in the car begins to beep, insistent and high-pitched. With a scowl Ryan leans down and roots around under the dashboard with one hand, managing to stop the sound by manipulating something. She glances in the rearview mirror, and then sideways at her hostage. Claire is crouched in the corner of the seat, as far away as she can shift with the seatbelt around her, her eyes teary and frightened. There is a faint red weal on her cheek where she tried to remove the too-tight gag in the elevator shaft.

Impassively Ryan turns her fierce stare to the road, just as the beeping begins again. She leans forward again, but this time her maneuverings appear to have no results, and one long index finger taps thoughtfully on the steering wheel before she abruptly twists the wheel and drives off the road, careening past trees at a furious pace. Claire gasps behind her gag and scrabbles for her seatbelt latch, but with her hands tied as they are, she has difficulty wrenching her shoulder close enough to release it. Her hands are almost on the lock when the car screeches to a halt, throwing her against the dashboard.

Ryan leaps out and runs around the car to open the passenger door. Leaning over the doctor, who is mutedly sobbing, she clicks open the seatbelt lock and lets it snap back, then grasps the doctor's bound hands and physically hauls her from the car. Horror has turned Claire's legs to jelly, and she almost falls before the other woman hoists her up without any apparent effort. Half-dragging Claire to the nearest tree, Ryan studies the bark before she hooks her fingers under the torn material of the gag and pulls it roughly over Claire's head. Claire almost vomits from fright and the sudden feeling of fresh air rushing in her lungs.

Ryan tilts her head back to study the sky and then turns to Claire. The intensity in her green eyes is chilling. "What year is it?" Her voice is so low that it takes a moment before Claire understands – a moment too long, as Ryan shakes her unceremoniously.

"What *year*?"

"2005." She almost cannot speak, she is so afraid.

The Marine stares at her silently before she finally turns away and studies the country around them. Pine trees line the hills and tower above them, and there are no buildings in sight.

"Please..." Claire almost whimpers.

The woman turns to look at Claire, her eyes unfriendly.

"Please, let me go?"

Without comment Ryan starts to walk briskly away from the car, dragging the doctor with her. Claire's breath stutters, and she stumbles over her own feet as she tries to keep up.

"If you let me go, they'll give you what you want. I'm ... important in my field."

"How wonderful for you." The Marine does not even turn. "I already have what I want."

Ryan leads her to a small clearing where, deliberately, she drops the gag. Then she turns around and leads Claire back past the car and towards the road. Once or twice Ryan freezes and listens. When she is certain that there is nothing that indicates pursuit, she leads Claire across the road. On the other side of the road she makes sure to avoid the long grass, choosing a gravel entry point instead, and turning to the north.

Finally realizing that she will not be let go now that the Marine is free, Claire begins to cry. The hand around her wrist tightens, and then Ryan is staring at her with those mad eyes.

"Please. Please..."

"Run."

As Lewis steps back into the foyer, Simon approaches him. "Sir. The car belongs to a..." he peers at a notepad in his hand, "Mister Chris Langley, an orderly. He stopped at the door today 'cause he was just supposed to run in with the order."

"Do a background check on him. Where did they go, Simon?"

"The gate guard saw them turn left, apparently heading towards Fairfield. We figure she's making for the first town she can find."

"*And?*"

Simon winces at his superior's impatient tone. "Johnston and Bulley are in one car, Markham and Smith in the other, heading towards town."

"All right. ETA?"

"At last report, about fifteen minutes." He glances at his watch. "Make that ten now."

Lewis nods curtly and turns to go back to the security center, but pauses when Simon's radio croaks to life.

The man speaks into it briefly before he addresses the waiting captain. "Sir, Mister Langley neglected to tell us that his car has an immobilizer."

Captain Lewis taps his fingers against his thigh. "Would Ryan have been able to bypass it?"

"I doubt it. She's been out of touch with that sort of thing for quite a while."

"Fuck!" Lewis slaps his hand against his thigh angrily. "Then she's somewhere between us and them, isn't she, Simon? Get on the phone and find out the range of that immobilizer, and then tell us where she is. Hurry, man!"

It is harder than Claire had expected to run with her hands tied tightly in front of her. Ryan has a steel grip around her one wrist and is forging through the undergrowth with no thought for her plight. Claire has stopped crying – it is hard to cry when you're gasping for breath – and is battling to stay upright; the ground is very uneven, and her legs are weak from the cold that has invaded her body. She had already lost her beautiful pair of high-heeled shoes; the woman ripped them off in the elevator and discarded them without a glance. Now she runs in her sheer stockings. The rocks, twigs, and seedpods are bruising her feet, but she cannot very well complain; it has been made crystal clear to her already that Ryan doesn't care.

For the moment, Claire has stopped wondering what will happen to her. She understands what the panic is doing to her, and is trying to remain lucid for that single moment when the right opportunity presents itself. Her mind is under control, but her limbs are exhausted from the shock and the strain, and finally her legs give out beneath her and she stumbles to the ground, clutching her aching midriff.

"Please…"

The woman stops and releases her wrist to avoid being dragged down. She stands glaring down at the collapsed form. "Get up."

"I can't. Please…"

The woman puts her hands on her hips and glances left and right, inspecting the area. For the first time Claire notes that there are smears of blood on her right hand – the shirt had obviously not entirely protected her from damage when she'd smashed the car window. "What is the closest town?"

"I think it's Fairfield." Claire takes strained breaths. "I'm not sure."

"How far?"

"I don't know." At the skeptical gaze that falls on her, she drops her head and gulps in big desperate breaths. "I'm telling you the truth. I'm not from here."

"Slow down your breathing. In which direction?"

"South, I think." Claire glances up at the woman who is studying something in the distance, and tries to edge away marginally, but almost immediately the cold green eyes return to her.

"Don't."

"Please." She repeats the only important word that she can think of. "Please. I'm of no use to you. Let me go."

"No." Ryan glances at the dried blood coating her wrists, before she grasps Claire's wrist again and hauls her up.

"Enough rest. Let's go."

"I can't!" Claire pulls back just a little. "I'm too tired. I need to get my breath back. Please, let me rest. Or..." she turns pleading eyes on her captor, "just leave me here. When they find me, you'll be long gone. I won't say anything, I promise. I promise." Her blue eyes fill with tears she is helpless to stop.

"Sounds like you *have* your breath back."

Ryan yanks her wrist, hard, and begins to walk, dragging her along. At first Claire considers resisting – she is afraid, but has calmed her panic to a manageable level – but she does not know what the woman will do to her if she does resist, or what she is worth to Ryan as a hostage. Taking deep breaths, she follows as quickly and as docilely as she can. When the right moment presents itself she wants to be ready. They are in a pine forest, tall trees swaying about them in the slightly dark sky. Pine needles, cones, and leaves crackle as two sets of bare feet trample them into the cold ground.

Claire cannot tell how long it has been – it feels like forever- before she begins to notice Ryan faltering between steps. The Marine soon recovers her brisk pace and walks another twenty feet before she stops completely, causing Claire to stumble into her. Ryan reaches out a hand and abstractedly rights Claire, and the doctor notes that the Marine is blinking rapidly. Her forehead furrowing, Ryan swallows convulsively and closes her eyes. When she opens them again, they seem a little glazed.

The doctor stands perfectly still, feeling the hand around her wrist tighten its grip, and then loosen. She is preparing herself for action but is still taken aback when the Marine suddenly crumples to the ground, a breathy gasp escaping her lips as she wraps her arms tightly around her stomach and begins to vomit. Abruptly freed, the doctor takes one last glance at the convulsing body before she turns and runs.

Her leg muscles and raw feet complain, but Claire pushes forward without thought for the pain, panting sharply against the burning in her chest. When she hears the crashing and cracking of branches behind her, she tries to speed up, but she is not much of a runner. She twists and turns in desperation, attempting to shake off her pursuer, but the tracking noises draw inevitably closer. With the possibility of escape so close, and clearly about to be dashed, she begins to scream. "No! Help me! Somebody! Please!"

The only result is that it saps her breath and slows her down, and when two lean arms seize her from behind she collapses to the ground in defeat and begins to sob. "Oh God...just let me go...just let me..."

The arms embrace her tightly as she begs breathlessly, until her tears have slowed and she's quiet, taking deep lungs full of air to settle her breathing. Then Ryan gracefully rises, takes one of her arms, and - inexplicably gently - lifts her to her feet.

"Come on, Walsch. Let's go."

In accordance with the captain's terse commands, Markham and Smith continue toward Fairfield to make sure that Ryan has not by some means disabled the immobilizer and gone on to town. Johnston and Bulley turn back toward the hospital, cautioned to begin their search within a five minute radius of Fairwater. They almost miss the car tracks in the grass; it is only Johnston's keen eye that notices something amiss. Carefully – neither of them looks forward to filling out the compulsory forms when there is damage to a company car – Bulley drives off the road and into the long grass, maneuvering between the trees as he listens to Johnston rattle off directions, his head protruding out the window.

When they spot the back of the stationary red Renault, they slow down and stop, casting quick glances about them to ensure that they are alone. A quick once-over determines that there is nothing of consequence in the car. The access card that Ryan took from Jack Elliot lies on the floor, discarded and useless. Whilst Bulley contacts Captain Lewis on his radio, Johnston puts his tracking skills to use and begins to move around, trying to establish the direction of their escape.

"Captain Lewis, come in."

"Lewis. What have you got for me, Bulley?"
"Car went off the road approximately three miles on the left, coming from Fairwater. Veered into the trees. Stationary about five hundred feet further into the cover. No sign of them. Johnston's checking for tracks now." He listens to his colleague and then adds, "Appears she's heading southeast. Fairfield."

"Check. Let Johnston track, and keep your eyes wide open. The woman is dangerous. I'll get Markham and Smith there. Keep me informed."

"Yes, Sir."

Johnston shakes his head. "He sends me right off into the lion's mouth and tells *you* to be careful? What are you, his love child with Liza Minnelli?"

With a grin, Bulley smacks his shoulder. "Move it, Johnston. You heard the captain."

The two men track carefully, both surprised by the clearness of the fugitive's trail.

"Do you think it could be an ambush?"

"I don't know. I suppose we can expect anything of Ryan, but... by all accounts, she's supposed to be doped up. And she's dragging a hostage around with her. I'm sure that the luscious doctor isn't exactly making it easy."

Johnston nods. "Let's slow down a little. But I think you're right."

When they come to a point where there is a small clearing, they pause, but beyond their own sounds and those of the forest, there is nothing to be heard. While Johnston searches the ground for signs of recent passage, Bulley rushes forward to look at the strip of material that has been discarded on the ground.

"Well?"

Johnston looks up with a frown rumpling his forehead. "Nothing." Then he glances back in the direction of the cars. "Aw, crap, Bull, she backtracked."

"Man." Bulley shakes his head. "If I find her, I'm going to have a lot to say to her. And I tend to talk with my hands, y'know?"

Whether in deference to Claire's shorter legs and lesser fitness level or for another reason, Ryan has slowed her steps, but she is still moving at a fast clip. Occasionally she stops to stoop slightly and grimace, but now she keeps her hold on Claire. The doctor has considered trying to hit her over the head when she is bent double, but she is not sure whether she is strong enough to do any actual damage, and to simply antagonize Ryan would not be wise. Claire tries to keep her breathing even as they move through the forest.

Claire has no idea of how much time has passed when they come upon the first house. It is a wooden A-frame, obviously a holiday home. In the back garden, near where they are standing, are a child's swing on a metal frame, and a sandpit. Claire's heart sinks. She does not want this unstable, dangerous woman anywhere near any civilian, but especially not children.

A few feet to their right is a garden shed. Grasping Claire's wrist tightly, Ryan sneaks forward and rounds the corner, keeping an eye out for occupants. None are in view. With one hand she presses open the old wooden door and then drags her captive inside, waiting until her eyes adjust to the dim light before she proceeds. Taking a spade off its hook on the wall, the Marine pulls Claire closer and twists her bonds around the hook.

Realizing that she is located in front of a small open gap, Claire almost lets her glee show before she tries to reassemble her facial expression into one more befitting her predicament. Ryan gives the material around her wrists one final firm twist before she steps back.

"Call for help, and I hurt somebody, Doctor. Run away, and I hurt somebody. You don't want that, do you?"

Claire shakes her head.

Ryan nods. "Good. You can see out through this gap, so you'll be able to see what I'm doing. If you cause trouble, you know what you will see me doing. And it will not be something you'd want on your conscience."

With one last look at Claire, Ryan steps out and closes the door behind her. She has no doubt that the doctor won't endanger other lives to enable her own escape. The curtains in the house are open, but there is no movement. Ryan creeps up to the porch and climbs over the railing, stopping for a moment to quell a bout of nausea before she continues. Dropping to her haunches, she presses her back to the wall and slides over to the screen door where she chances a glance into the house. Apart from the soft sounds of a radio somewhere in the background, there is nothing.

Executing a tight roll past the door, she comes up against the frame and steals a look at the other side of the house. There's a small garage off to the side, from which drifts the sounds of rhythmic hammering and a whistled melody.

Waiting for a moment, Ryan decides that whoever is in there is not coming back to the house, so she returns to the door. Grasping the pin that hangs from the handcuff around her wrist, she inserts it into the lock, wrapping a hand around it at the point of entry to muffle any noise. Without much finesse, she drives the heel of her other hand upwards into the pin. It thrusts into the lock with a muffled thud. Withdrawing the pin, Ryan slips off the porch and back to the shed, where Claire is quietly waiting. While she untangles the doctor's bonds from the hook and then ties her hands together again firmly, the blonde looks at her in confusion.

"What were you doing?"

"Come on." Without bothering to answer, the Marine leads her back into the forest.

It's not long before the Marine's torso once again begins to spasm and she clutches her stomach with her free hand. This time, however, she does not let the doctor out of her grasp. Standing stock still, she takes deep breaths and closes her eyes momentarily before she focuses again. "Come on." With a yank on Claire's wrist, they move forward.

When they come upon the next house, Ryan repeats her previous pattern. This time, after tying Claire to a sturdy branch on a nearby tree, Ryan moves closer to investigate. When she is satisfied as to whatever it is she's looking for, she steals to the back door and performs the same ritual with the pin before she returns to the forest and unties Claire.

The doctor is weary. It feels as if they have been on the move for over an hour, and her raw feet are bleeding and aching. Though the pain is becoming progressively worse, she does not want to alert the Marine to the fact that she is now leaving a very clear trail of their passage. If she cannot escape by her own efforts then she intends to make it as easy as possible for whoever is following them. For a moment she feels panic flood her as she considers the possibility that nobody is looking for them, but then she calms herself by deciding that it is not very likely. She tries to concentrate on the moment, refusing to give in to terror.

When another house appears between the trees, Claire resolves that this time she will not remain silent, even if it puts someone other than her in danger; it is the only immediate option available to her. She is surprised when, instead of tying her up, Ryan stops and scrutinizes the building from the darkness of the trees, and then yanks Claire's arm.

"Let's go."

They approach the house, and the doctor looks around desperately. If somebody would just come outside, she could scream for help.

Ryan glances over her shoulder. "Relax. Nobody home."

Claire is furious – at herself for hoping, at the woman for noticing, at the material that binds her wrists. She grits her teeth and glares fiercely at her captor.

Leading the doctor up the porch steps, Ryan approaches the back door and tries it, but finds it locked. They leave the porch and walk around the right side of the modern house, the Marine trying each window as they pass by. None give. When they reach the front of the house, Ryan finds a window that is open just a crack. Inserting the pin on her handcuff beneath it, she levers it upwards. With a creaking sound, it begins to lift, and she withdraws the pin to slide one hand under the wooden frame.

"Open it."

In response to the command, Claire grudgingly slides her hands beneath and pushes upwards. Finally the catch slips and the window slides up. Claire is startled when she finds Ryan's hands wrapping around her sides and lifting her.

"In."

It is a clumsy affair, and though she is already planning to run once she hits the floor, she doesn't expect it to be so literal. With her hands tied, she struggles to hold her balance as she lands. She staggers into a small table and tumbles to the floor. A hand wraps around her upper arm and hauls her upright.

They are in the dining room area of an open-plan lower level. To their left is an elegant sitting room, with wingback chairs and a sofa arranged around a fireplace. Stairs lead upwards from behind one of the chairs. To the right is the kitchen, a neatly set out space with a tall silver fridge on one side and identical double washbasins on the other. The cupboards are dark wood, to match the shining floor. In front of them is a small oak dining room table decorated with a white silk runner.

Ryan approaches the fridge and opens it, studying the contents before she slides open a drawer and pulls out a flawless red apple.

"Here." She extends it to Claire, who turns her head away.

"I don't want it."

"Eat it."

"No. It's stealing."

Casting a cynical look in the blonde's direction, Ryan shrugs. "Fine." She takes a bite of the apple, chewing slowly as she peruses the variety of foodstuffs. After she swallows the first bite, she blanches and clenches her jaw tightly before carefully setting the apple on the counter. Reaching to another shelf, she selects a blue energy drink, which she also places on the counter before closing the fridge. The apple, a half-moon white crescent jagged in its crimson skin, goes into the dustbin, and then Ryan picks up the bottled drink.

Maneuvering Claire towards the stairs, Ryan leads her to the second level. Beyond the landing, there are three doors – one to the left, which is closed, another directly ahead of them, which appears to be a bathroom, and the third to their right, a bedroom.

A quick glance into the room to the left shows it to be another bedroom, decorated in an ice cream pink theme. Ryan leads Claire forward into the bathroom and closes the door behind them. Finding the key in the lock, she turns it, and then removes it.

"Sit down."

The doctor takes a seat on the edge of the bath as Ryan rifles through the cabinets beneath the basin. When she turns back, she is clasping a small white medical kit. She unlocks the door, grasps Claire's wrist, and leads her into the third room, the main bedroom. It is tastefully decorated in earth tones. Once again finding the key in the door, Ryan locks the door behind them and holds the key loosely in her hand as she motions for Claire to sit on the large double bed. The Marine tosses the first aid kit onto the bed and studies the room for a moment before she moves forward to inspect the dressing table. In the second drawer from the top, she finds a hairpin. Inserting the sharp end into the keyhole of the cuff on her left hand, she probes for a few moments. When Claire shifts closer to the door, Ryan fixes her with an unnerving stare. "Don't."

With a small click, the cuff unclips from her wrist and she begins to work on the right cuff. It takes her a while longer, but finally the cuffs, and the pin attached to them, fall to the floor. Ryan drops the hairpin and, rubbing her left wrist lightly, approaches the bed. Reaching over a cringing Claire, she takes the kit and crouches at her feet, extending a hand towards the blonde's ankle. When

Claire recoils, Ryan glances up at her, the green eyes bright in the light of the window behind them.

"Show me your feet."

Claire has no option but to lift her right foot. Ryan examines the damaged sole before she places it back on the floor and returns to the bathroom to retrieve her drink. When she returns, she places the bottle beside her on the carpet and holds out the towel which she has also brought with her.

"Your foot."

Claire extends her right foot, and the Marine begins to gently clean the debris from the cuts. When she is done with both feet, she rummages in the first aid kit and brings out an ointment, which she applies to the soles of both feet. Claire's toes curl against the ticklish sensation as the long fingers circle over her flesh. When Ryan is finished, she puts the kit down on the bed and cracks open the drink, then takes a long sip.

"Keep your feet off the floor," she advises before she turns around and begins to open closet doors.

Surreptitiously, Claire pulls the kit closer and begins to search through it for needles, scissors, anything that could be useful as a weapon. When she glances up, Ryan is standing in front of the closet door on the right, and has stepped out of her dirty white cotton pants and discarded her shirt. Claire cannot help but notice the fading bruise at the base of her spine and the myriad of scars that mar her skin. From the protruding bones of her shoulders and the bumps of her spinal column, it is clear that she has not been eating well.

Considering her options, Ryan finally pulls on a pair of too-large jeans. She discovers a leather belt and threads it through the loops and then cinches it. Even pulled as tightly as it can be, the jeans still ride low on Ryan's hips. Rifling through the selection of shirts, she pulls out a simple black t-shirt and slips it over her head. Then, from the next cupboard, she removes a thick black wool jacket, which she tosses on the bed. Claire freezes, but Ryan is not looking in her direction. She is searching the bottom of the closet for a pair of shoes on the neatly packed shoe tray. Taking a pair of white trainers for herself, she picks another pair for Claire, then takes a while to come up with socks. Stuffing them inside the shoes, she approaches Claire and crouches to drop the shoes on the floor at her feet.

"Here. Put these on."

Without warning Claire lunges forward, the small pair of scissors flashing in her hand as she drives it towards Ryan. Reacting to the motion, the Marine ducks to her left, the blades barely missing her temple as she catches Claire's hand in her strong fingers and squeezes tightly.

"Let it go."

Driven by fury, and the possibility of escape, Claire attacks, screaming loudly as she kicks out and rakes her fingers towards the other woman's face. Ryan restrains her without a sound, her larger hands covering Claire's as she forces her backwards onto the bed and wraps her legs around the shorter woman's to stop their thrashing. The doctor is restrained by the weight pinning her down. She screams her anguish into the face above hers until her throat is hoarse and the screams give way to sobs.

Once Ryan feels the limbs relax beneath her, she eases off carefully and twists the scissors out of Claire's hand.

"Don't do that again."

After taking the medical kit, Ryan moves to sit on the other end of the bed and begins to clean the dirt from her bloody hands and wrists. When she can clearly see the damage the cuffs have done, she ties the doctor's hands to the elaborate wrought iron headboard and goes into the bathroom to hold her hands beneath the running tap, her expression inscrutable as she watches the rust-colored water drain away. When she returns to the bedroom, the blonde has curled up on her side and is sobbing softly.

There is still a small sliver of glass in one of the cuts on her right hand, which Ryan now removes with the small set of tweezers before she smoothes antibiotic ointment onto the wounds. Covering the cuts with gauze, she winds the narrow white bandage around her right hand and each wrist and then clumsily ties it off before she packs everything back into the kit and zips it up.

Casting a glance at the woman lying quietly on the bed, she slips on the sneakers. They are slightly too big, but she does not care. Pulling the socks from the second pair of sneakers, she sits down near Claire's feet and slides the socks on. Claire takes a shuddering breath but does not resist.

When Ryan slips the shoes onto the treated feet, it is clear that they are much too big for Claire. She puts them back in the closet, then goes to the other bedroom and roots around in the closet, returning with a pair of smaller white sneakers. She's also found a blue baseball cap which is now pulled low over her eyes. The new shoes fit Claire perfectly. After tying the laces swiftly, Ryan stands up and downs the last of her energy drink, and then unties the bonds from the headboard.

"Get up. We're going."

Claire sits up and swipes at the tear tracks on her cheeks, her blue eyes angry. "No."

"It's not a request."

"You don't need me with you. I'm slowing you down. Just leave me here." The blonde eyebrows contract. "Please. You can pull out the telephone line, if there is one. I don't even know where I am. Just leave me. It'll be better for you that way."

"It will be better for *you* that way."

Ryan eyes Claire before she opens the closet again and turns up a dark green fabric belt. Approaching the blonde, who shrinks away from her, Ryan grasps her hands and unties the tatty material around her wrists before she buckles the belt loosely, then slips the loop over Claire's hands and pulls it tight. Picking up the first aid kit Ryan tucks it under one arm.

"Get up." She tugs at the belt, leaving Claire no choice but to get to her feet.

By the time Lewis reaches the site, Bulley and Johnston are already halfway back to the road from the Renault, Johnston's forehead a mass of furrows as he keeps his eyes firmly on the ground. Lewis gets out of his blue Ford Focus and approaches them.

"Well? Where's the car?"

Bulley points in the direction from which they've come. "About three hundred feet in. She—"

Lewis cuts him off impatiently. "If it's about three hundred feet in that direction, what are the two of you doing here?"
Bulley continues calmly, "She made a false track into the forest from there, but doubled back. Johnston thinks she may have crossed the road somewhere."

Lewis shakes his head, either because he knows that he is wrong to have snapped at Bulley, or because he is admiring Ryan's guts. He motions Simon, who has gotten out of the passenger seat and is leaning on the car's roof with a curious look, back into the vehicle.

"I have to take a look at the car. Are you carrying a radio?"

At Bulley's nod, Lewis sniffs. "All right. Keep in contact. We'll catch up." He gets back into the Ford and pulls away.

Johnston tracks the trail to the road, then shoots a quick glance to the left and right to assure himself he is not about to be run over as he crosses. Bulley is right behind him, and when he slows down, the other man steps around him towards the grass on the other side. Johnston's arm shoots out and presses against his chest.

"Stay on the tarmac."

He crouches down and begins to inspect the ground beyond the road.

When Lewis reaches the Renault, he stops the Ford neatly behind Bulley and Johnston's vehicle and climbs out, already scanning the surroundings. Simon gets out with a roll of yellow reflective tape and begins to cordon off the area.

"Are you going to check the car, boss?"

Grimacing at the use of the word that he hates, Lewis shakes his head.

"The boys will already have done that. Langley says that there was nothing in his car beyond sunglasses and chewing gum. Crap like that. If she took that, I don't give a shit."

Patting his side to make sure that his mobile phone is in its holder clipped to his belt, he studies the area beyond the car before he follows in Bulley and Johnston's footsteps, tracking Ryan's first trail. When he comes to the clearing and sees the gag lying on the ground, he chews the inside of his bottom lip as he slides out his phone and makes a call.

"Tilly-Clapham."

"Lewis here."

"Tell me you have her."

"No, not yet."

"Then why are you wasting your time making phone calls?"

Lewis' teeth grind silently before he continues. "We're tracking her now, Doctor, but technically this is out of my jurisdiction. I think it's time to call in the Choteau PD, or the FBI, depending on how big the problem is." His tone is carefully neutral, though he has been kept out of the loop on this situation and resents now having to clean up someone else's mess.

"Technically?" Tilley-Clapham sounds as if he's grinding his teeth, too. *"I don't give a.... I don't* **care** *about technically! Colonel Turner should be calling you any time now with instructions. Beyond that, sit still, don't call anybody, and don't bother me."*

There are few things Lewis likes less than having the phone hung up in his ear, and when it happens, he hurls his own into the forest with a loud curse. Propping his hands on his knees, he takes a few deep breaths and attempts to focus through the red veil of anger that is obscuring his vision. He is still breathing methodically, as the therapist has shown him, when Simon appears in the clearing.

"Captain? Something wrong?"

"Yeah." Taking one last deep breath, he straightens his back and strolls into the trees to retrieve his mobile. "I dropped my phone."

Johnston is struggling to find the point of entry from the road. Where her trail on the other side of the road is rough and clearly visible, this is the point at which she had obviously begun to take more care. He looks left and right, at the grass, which has not been visibly disturbed, and then at the patch of gravel in front of him.

"Move it, Sherlock, before we die by truck."

"Piss off, Bull." He kneels and studies the gravel closely. "She had to go over this." Stepping onto the gravel slowly, he looks down. The patch is about ten feet wide, which does not seem large, but still leaves a number of potential exit points.

"Can I get off the road now?"

"Christ, Bull, you're such a whiner. Get over here." Johnston drops to his haunches and sweeps the possible area with his eyes. "Why don't you try and be helpful for a change?"

"What am I looking for?"

"Broken branches, footsteps, scattered leaves, dropped objects. Anything out of the ordinary, okay?"

"Okay, Liza."

Johnston moves to the left edge of the gravel and begins to search meticulously. Crouching down behind him, Bulley tries to see something other than the scatter of leaves on the ground. They work in silence for a few minutes before Bulley speaks up.

"Hey, Johnston?"

Without turning around, Johnston glances over his shoulder. "I swear, Bull, I'm going to–"

"Would blood count as out of the ordinary?"

Johnston freezes, and then turns slowly. He moves to Bulley's side and peers in the direction of Bulley's extended finger. A leaf lies on its side between a pile of others, only about half of its surface visible. It would have been easy to miss its rust colored pattern amongst the other early fall leaves. Nodding to himself, Johnston rises.

"Okay, let's get cracking."

"What, no 'thank you'?"

"Good girl, Bulley."

Lewis is halfway back to his car when his phone begins to ring. He slips it from its holster and motions for Simon to move ahead. "Lewis."

"Captain Lewis, this is Colonel George Turner. Where are you now?"

"Afternoon, Colonel Turner. I am at the site of the abandoned vehicle, approximately three miles from Fairwater and approximately five hundred feet in from the road. We're heading back towards the road now, so there will be a blue Ford at the side of the road."

"All right." Turner's voice is gruff and authoritative. *"Here's what's going to happen, Lewis. You hold the fort until I send the proper guys to deal with the situation, and then you go back to your post, forget all about this, and get on with your job. Clear? And, Captain, don't mess with the evidence."*

For the second time this day, Lewis has the urge to throw his phone as far as he can, but this time he refrains. It is his personal handset and he does not think it can take the battering. Nevertheless, he does not know anybody who would enjoy being repeatedly stomped into the ground; he most certainly doesn't. Considering the colonel's telephone manner, he wonders what the colonel's conversations with Clapham-Tilley are like.

"Fucking little paper-pushers."

Simon, who has moved ahead and is already waiting in the car, pops his head through the window. "Excuse me, Captain?"

With a sigh, Lewis gets into the Ford. "Nothing, Simon. Nothing."

Ryan leads Claire downstairs, into the kitchen, out the back door – which she leaves open – and towards the garage. The small door into the structure is closed and locked. Striding around the outside of the garage, Ryan finds a small high window and, standing on the tips of her toes, manages to peer into the room. When she drops down to the ground there is a small smile playing around her mouth.

They return to the kitchen where she pulls out drawers and searches through them, whilst Claire looks on in confusion. In a small drawer partially hidden by the bread bin, she finds and retrieves a set of car keys and two unmarked keys. Slipping them into the pocket of the baggy jeans, she takes another energy drink – and, after some hesitation, another apple – from the fridge, and then leads Claire outside again, taking care to close the window by which they had entered and setting the door latch so that it slips closed behind them. As they approach the side door to the garage, Ryan pulls out the two unidentified keys and inserts one into the lock. It turns easily.

The inside of the garage is dark, and she runs one hand against the wall to her right, searching for a light switch. When she finds and flicks it, the sudden flare of light temporarily blinds them both, and then suddenly they can see the large gray Chevrolet Trailblazer parked inside.

Knowing that new transportation will limit any additional opportunities to escape, Claire pulls back, and when Ryan pulls her forward, she begins to yank at her hands, trying to slip them out of their bonds. Impatiently Ryan steps closer and wraps her hand around the doctor's left wrist, wrenching her closer. When the smaller woman still throws her weight backwards, the Marine leans forward and hoists the thrashing woman onto her shoulder.

Ryan unlocks the SUV with the remote and opens the passenger door, depositing Claire into the spacious leather seat before she slides her hand down the edge of the door and adjusts something. Claire is already shifting over the handbrake to reach the other door when her own is slammed behind her and Ryan moves around the car and gets into the driver's seat. Engaging the locks, Ryan glances at the rearview mirror and tilts it slightly upwards, then leans forward to check the cubbyhole. There is a pair of aviator style sunglasses, which she slips on with a ghost of a smile. When Claire tries to open her door, it just clicks.

"Child lock."

Ryan slips the energy drink into the cup holder under the radio and then tosses the small first-aid kit into the cubbyhole. When Claire's eyes fall on it, Ryan turns her head slightly.

"I took out a lot of things. You're welcome to look." She casually tosses the apple onto Claire's lap. "Eat."

The vehicle starts with a roar as the garage door slides upwards.

As Ryan glances over her shoulder to gauge the level of the rising door, a short, sharp breath escapes her lips. Her knuckles tighten on the steering wheel and her hands slowly twist inwards. Ryan turns her head slowly to one side and then to the other, tilting it as if her neck is stiff or aching, before she shudders unexpectedly.

"No."

Her hoarse voice is so soft that Claire almost misses it.

"Ryan?"

The Marine does not reply, her hands tightly wrapped around the steering wheel, until finally she lifts her trembling right hand and lays it carefully against her right temple, after a while shifting it to skim her ear and cup her neck. When she abruptly leans over, reaching towards Claire, the blonde cringes and shifts away. It is with a small measure of embarrassment that she watches as Ryan reaches past her to slip the cubbyhole open and extract the first-aid kit. The Marine unzips it and rifles through the interior, withdrawing a bottle of aspirin before she closes the kit and tosses it onto Claire's lap. Lifting the small bottle, she reads the label before she shakes out four and cracks the lid on her energy drink. Whilst Ryan swallows the pills, Claire puts the kit back into the cubbyhole.

She is still quiet when Ryan reverses out of the garage, pressing the button on the remote to close the door behind them. The Marine glances left and right, gauging direction before she takes the road to the right. They are driving on a small country road, low and narrow between the thinning pines; the vehicle drives smoothly and softly. Ryan's long fingers are searching for an 'on' button on the radio when Claire's voice breaks the silence.

"Ryan?"

It surprises the Marine. It is the first time she can recall the doctor using her name. In lieu of a verbal response, she inclines her head.

Claire notices, but is silent for another moment before she speaks. When she does, her voice is untainted by fear. "Why can't you let me go? Have I done something to you?"

Ryan flashes her a small but genuine smile. A first. With the cap pulled low over her eyes and the large sunglasses above the razor-sharp cheekbones, she almost looks like a model in a trendy magazine.

"It has absolutely nothing to do with you."

"But then–"

"You're completely incidental." Ryan turns her gaze back to the road. "That may be hard to accept, but you're nothing more than collateral. Sorry."

Her voice is husky, as if she has a cold, made more noticeable by what - for her - amounts to a sudden loquaciousness. Claire studies the road with a blank face. She is considering what approach would be most effective with the blank-faced woman, and decides that if she is summing Ryan up correctly, it would probably be honor. Regardless of what Claire thinks of Ryan's actions, it seems that this was what drove her to save her team in Cirez.

"Were you...talking to God back there?"

With that hesitant question, the momentarily casual air about the soldier dissolves. Ryan's jaw bunches and her fingers tighten their grip around the steering wheel.

"I'm sorry. I didn't mean to offend you." There is no answer. Claire picks at an already haggard nail. "Do you get headaches... afterwards?"

Ryan ignores her and takes a slow sip of her drink.

With a sigh, Claire shifts in her seat. "Ryan–"

"Don't."

"Don't what?"

The Marine slips the bottle back into the cup holder with unnecessary force. "Don't speak to me like that."

"I'm sorry. I didn't mean to be rude."

"No." Ryan turns her head to glare at the blonde. "Don't pretend you understand."

Intimidated by the eyes on her, even if they are hidden behind the sunglasses, Claire turns her gaze back to the road. "Don't I?"

"Don't fuck with me." It's an angry hiss, and Claire turns back, if only to keep an eye on the suddenly intense Marine. "You don't think I know what you think about me? You think I'm some homicidal lunatic." Ryan's jaw clamps shut tightly, her mouth set in a bitter line.

Claire tries to smile to diffuse the situation, consciously softens her tone. "What makes you think that that's my opinion, Ryan?"

"I know your type." The declaration is so fervent that the doctor begins to think that she may have made a mistake by trying to engage Ryan. "You're not the first to have thought that, and you won't be the last. I don't care, Doctor Walsch, but do me a favor and *stay out of my fucking head*. It's a little crowded right now."

The fingers on the steering wheel are white with tension.

Claire keeps quiet, looking at the scenery as it speeds by outside her window. When she glances back after a few minutes, the jaw is still set but the hands have relaxed. "Ryan?"

The jaw muscles clench. Bolstering her courage, Claire speaks anyway. "Ryan? I'm sorry if I made you feel as if I'm judging you. I really don't know anything about you. I have no basis on which to form an opinion."

"It's what you do, isn't it?"

Claire sighs. "I'm sorry. I made assumptions."

Ryan nods her head slightly.

"You scare me."

The Marine's eyebrows rise marginally at the blunt admission, but she doesn't respond.

Claire forges on. "It's not because I think you're homicidal or dangerous - it's just that I'm not sure that you have a whole lot of control when you have one of those episodes, and I'm worried that you'll hurt me when you do."

Silence.

"I don't want you to hurt me, Ryan. I don't want to get hurt. And I don't think you want to intentionally hurt me, either. Please just let me go before something happens. You'll be gone before they find me."

More silence, and Claire can almost see the war going on behind the sunglasses as the woman debates with herself. Just as the tense knots in the doctor's stomach begin to ease, Ryan glances over at her.

"I won't hurt you, Doctor. As long as you co-operate." She casts a glance at the rearview mirror before she looks back at Claire, and this time she sounds vaguely amused. "Nice try, by the way. But don't do it again."

Johnston and Bulley are a fair way into the forest when the radio crackles and Captain Lewis commands them to withdraw. To confirm, Bulley has him repeat the order before he signs off.

"What the fuck are they doing? What was the point of sending us this far?"

Johnston spits into the underbrush in disgust. "There's something screwy about this shit, Bull. I wonder what Lewis is up to."

Careful not to disturb the signs they have been tracking, they retreat, to find Captain Lewis on the side of the road, lighting a cigarette. Markham and Smith have arrived and are leaning against their car, staring into the sky. Bulley approaches Lewis sullenly.

"Captain? May I ask you a question?"

Lewis easily matches his irritated tone. "What?"

"What's the point of having us track this far just to pull us off now?"

The captain slips his lighter back into his shirt pocket and takes a forceful drag of his cigarette before he responds. "We've all been pulled off, Bulley, so don't give me crap. I'm getting enough grief over this fucking thing."

"Captain?"

"I don't know, Bulley. I don't know shit. Don't ask me."

They wait in silence. When a black van drives up and pulls over in front of the blue Ford, they all straighten up, glancing at each other perplexedly. A muscular man dressed from head to toe in black gets out of the driver's seat, the side door slides open and another four similarly attired men step into view. The driver studies the group of security guards with something suspiciously akin to amusement before he approaches Lewis.

"Captain Lewis?" When he speaks, he flashes pointy incisors which give him a predatory air.

Lewis steps forward and extends a hand. "Colonel Turner?"

"No." The man returns a brief but firm handshake. "Thank you. I have things under control. You may go."

Lewis is affronted, and atypically brash because of it. "Don't you at least want to know which direction she's moving in?"

The man in black stares at him flatly. "We know. That will be all."

With a frustrated exhalation Captain Lewis jerks his head at his men and gets into the blue Ford. He waits in silence for Simon to close his door before he starts the car and turns around with a roar, heading back to Fairwater.

The man in black does not wait for them to disappear from sight before giving his commands. When he is sure that all avenues are covered, he nods with satisfaction. "Alpha, Bravo, we move. Gear up."

The men slip back into the van. When they appear again, they are suited up in camouflage flak jackets. Small black earpieces anchor communications devices with tubes that curl up from their collars. The man in black casts a rapid glance over them and then nods again.

"Remember – she's not a civilian. Our main objective is to bring her in alive, but if she makes it impossible, we attempt to neutralize the threat. It is in our best interests to retrieve the hostage unharmed, but she is not our main concern." His gaze is impassive. "If she causes complications, eliminate her."

When the men all nod, he reaches down to his belt and unclips a small device, which at first glance appears to be an iPod. Pressing a small button at the upper left corner, he watches in satisfaction as the small screen comes to life. The men wait impassively as he scrolls through the system. When he glances up, they brace to attention and wait for instructions.

"North."

They turn on their heels and slip into the forest, disappearing into the background of foliage almost immediately. Shooting another glance at the device, he slots it back onto his belt and pulls out his mobile phone.

The four men move silently through the forest, stopping occasionally to glance at the chunky black watches strapped to their wrists, or to study the marks in the undergrowth. They are on foot for approximately thirty minutes before they catch sight of the A-frame house between the trees. The closest man raises a fist sharply and the others immediately slow, on guard and alert. They approach the house carefully, tracking the signs that lead towards the shed. Where the trail disappears around the side of the house, the four men stop in the shadows. One of them executes a flurry of gestures and the others all nod before they split into two groups.

Greg McMahon is guiding his lathe firmly over a beautiful piece of wood when a strong forearm slips around his throat and pulls him back from the equipment. A small stocky man in camouflage gear appears in Greg's field of vision and switches off the loud machine. Greg would normally consider himself a brave man, but at this point his body feels alarmingly cold. The small man approaches him, and his flat emotionless face looms in Greg's view.

"Are you alone?"

"No. No." Greg gasps the word. "Please – don't hurt me. My wife... my baby..."

"We are not going to hurt you, sir." The small man nods past his shoulder and the forearm around his neck disappears. "We are here to help you. Where are your wife and baby?"

"Inside." Lifting his hand to his throat uncertainly, Greg turns to keep the man behind him in his sight. "They're inside. What's—"
The small man interrupts him politely. "We need to know if you've seen anything out of place today."

"Out of place?" Glancing from one man to the other, Greg blinks rapidly. "Like what? Oh God. Is my wife in danger?" He moves towards the door, but the large man behind him moves to block the way.

"Sir, have you seen anything out of the ordinary today?"

"I don't...I don't know what you mean! No, there hasn't been any... Are they okay? Are they all right?" He tries to sidestep the man at the door, who meets him inscrutably at every step. The smaller man moves closer.

"Calm down, sir. There's no problem. Please stay here with Rico. I'll be back in a minute." He nods at the big man, who steps aside to let him pass. When Greg attempts to walk with him, Rico shakes his head.

"Please keep calm, sir. We are dealing with the situation."

"Situation? What situation? Oh my God. Who are you?"

The smaller man strides towards the back door, where his associates are studying the door silently. At his arrival, they part, and he instantly spots the damaged lock. He nods to the men, who all noiselessly draw .9mm pistols and step up against the walls, flanking the door. When he kicks it open, a woman's scream splits the air. In the background Greg's voice rises as he helplessly calls his wife's name over and over.

They slink around her where she stands trembling in the middle of the room, her whimpering baby pressed tightly against her chest. They secure all of the rooms before they return. She is frozen to the spot. One of the men notices the phone against the wall and lifts the handset, pulling the long cord as he approaches her and holds it out.

"Phone the local police. You've had a break-in."

The small man retrieves Greg from the garage and leads him into the house, where he immediately wraps his arms around his petrified wife and glares balefully at the intruders.

"What exactly do you want?"

"We're looking for someone."

"Who? Someone dangerous?"

"You're safe. You're alone. Take the phone from your wife and phone the police."

"Why? Who–"

"You've had a break-in." The small man points towards the door. "Report it."

All four men slip their pistols back into their holsters and turn to go. At the door, Rico turns back. "Sorry to have alarmed you folks."

They close the door behind them, and, by the time Greg dials 911 with trembling fingers, they're already deep into the forest.

Crouched in thicket, one of the men grins, his teeth white in the darkness of the forest.

"She's trying to delay us. The woman's got balls."

According to the sign, the next town, Choteau, is nine miles away. When Claire shifts and tries to adjust the leather around her wrists to prevent the inevitable onset of pins and needles, the sunglasses momentarily turn her way. Clenching and unclenching her fingers Claire bites her lip.

"Ryan, could you please loosen this?" There is no response. "Please. My hands are going numb. I can't get out of the car anyway."

The woman smoothly steers the Trailblazer to the side of the road. When she turns, Claire is already offering her hands. Nimbly Ryan slips the belt from her wrists, glances over her shoulder, and pulls back onto the road.

Rubbing one chafed wrist, Claire stares out at the dense foliage rushing past the vehicle.

"What are you going to do with me?" Predictably, the Marine offers no answer. Claire bites the inside of her lip, repeats the question once, and then again.

An irritated scowl appears on Ryan's forehead. "Don't talk to me."

"Why not? What are you going to do to me if I keep talking?" Claire almost smirks as the muscles in Ryan's jaw twitch. Reaching out, the doctor picks up the apple from where she'd tossed it in the storage bin between the seats, and polishes it against her shirt before she takes a bite. When she has finished chewing loudly, she shifts in her seat and looks at the Marine's face.

"Isn't Fairwater a voluntary commitment hospital?"

Ryan frowns, although it isn't clear to Claire whether the Marine is taking exception to her new casual attitude or to the actual question, and it takes a moment for her response. "Yes."

The doctor takes another bite of her apple before she speaks again. "Then why the commotion, Ryan? Why not just sign yourself out?"

"Oh." The Marine's tone is dry. "Gosh. Now why didn't I think of that?"

Claire almost laughs before she manages to curb the whim. "Why didn't you?"

Ryan glances up at the rearview mirror in a motion that seems more habit than necessity. She is silent for a moment before she speaks. "I tried, Doctor. Didn't my file tell you that?"

Claire shakes her head perplexedly. "No. When was this?"

"2004."

"And what happened?"

The Marine shoots a quick glance at her, almost as if she is debating whether to continue the conversation. When she speaks next, her tone is matter-of-fact. "I put in a request for release, which was denied. The next request was also denied. On account of my fragile mental state. The one after that was ignored."

"That can't be right." Claire straightens in her seat. "Who had the authority to keep you committed? Couldn't you contact somebody?"

"I don't have anyone to contact. Besides, I wasn't allowed visitors. Or phone calls."

Claire is frowning, fascinated. "Why not?"
"Because I'm a danger to society, Doctor Walsch." The woman reaches for her energy drink and drains the last of it from the bottle.

Shifting, Claire attempts to catch her eye. "Are you?"

Ryan glances at her. "Yes, Doctor Walsch. I am."

Claire would have preferred a different response. It would have been easier to cope with somebody who at least believes in her own innocence. The indifferent answer chills the blood in her veins. She is in a car on her way to an undisclosed destination with a trained Marine who believes herself to be unsafe to others.

"Did the military have you committed?"

"No. I did."

"Why?"

Though Claire's voice is level and interested, Ryan shoots a puzzled glance at her to see if she is being mocking. The blue eyes that greet her are free of irony. The Marine frowns. "Why? Because I am channeling the voice of God, Doctor. Because I am dangerous." Her eyebrows rise. "Were you not aware of this?"

Claire sits forward, her gaze intense. "You've just forcibly released yourself back into society, Captain Ryan. How sure are you that you've changed?"

The tall woman's jaw clenches tightly and her fingers grip the steering wheel harshly. For a long time there is silence. They approach the outskirts of Choteau. Without turning her head, Ryan speaks.

"Have you got any money on you?"

"No. My handbag is back at Fairwater."

Ryan slips one hand into the pockets of the thick black jacket she is wearing. From the right pocket she pulls two notes, which she studies quickly before she stuffs them back. The ashtray yields a few more coins. At the first gas station on Maine Avenue she pulls over, studying the area before she pulls into the parking lot in front of the small dingy shop. She gets out of the vehicle and takes off the jacket. The black t-shirt is tight across her shoulders and chest. Tossing the jacket into the back seat, she wraps one arm over the top of the open door and the other over the headrest of her seat as she leans closer to Claire.

"I haven't changed at all, Doctor. Not a bit. I am going into the bathroom to get some water. If you get out and run, I will find you. If you involve anybody else, they will get hurt. Do you understand me?" The blonde nods silently. Reaching forward, Ryan grasps the bottle. "If you stay still and quiet, nothing bad will happen."

Straightening up, she closes the door and locks it from the outside, then slips the keys into her pocket. The car door can be opened from the inside, but any delay will count in her favor, should it need to. At the bathroom door, she stops and turns to stare at the blonde woman, whose eyes are fixed on her.

The bathroom is dirty and smells of urinal cake. Her shoe soles make a sticky sound as she lifts them from the floor. Setting her jaw against her disgust, she opens the tap and cups water in her hand, smelling it suspiciously before she fills up her empty bottle. She screws the cap back on and is on her way out, when she abruptly clamps her eyes shut and grasps blindly, wrapping her bandaged right hand convulsively around the top of the cubicle as her legs begin to buckle under her.

Claire sits waiting apprehensively. She imagined that Ryan will only take a moment – too little for her to run - and now the time is ticking by. Her mind keeps whispering, unhelpfully, that if she had left when the Marine entered the bathroom, she would have been long gone. Hovering between her knowledge of what the woman would do if she were to leave and her beliefs of what Ryan would do if Claire were to stay, she calms herself with deep breaths before she clambers over the handbrake and opens the driver's door from the inside. She glances nervously at the bathroom, then turns and begins to walk, as quickly as possible, towards the small shop. She can see the young man inside, but he has his back to her and is talking animatedly on his mobile phone. Just as she thinks she might make it after all, a strong hand wraps around her upper arm and yanks her back against a solid body. A sob pushes from her throat.

The hand around her arm tightens. "You're hurting me," she pleads, but the woman does not ease up.

"Did you not understand what I told you?" The words are a hiss and Ryan shakes her arms slightly. "Do you *want* people to get hurt?"

"No." Claire is sobbing now.

Marching her back to the Trailblazer, Ryan opens the gas cap and slots in the nozzle, watching the numbers carefully until she is has reached the limit of her meagre resources. When she has replaced the cap, she releases Claire's arm and takes her hand instead. "I have to go in and pay. Behave. He's nothing more than a child. Do you want him to get hurt?"

When Claire shakes her head quickly, Ryan leads the way into the shop. The bell above the door dings, and the teenager studies them lazily from the corner of his eye as they walk in. The taller woman in her apparently trendy oversized jeans does not interest him, but he gives the pretty blonde in the suit and trainers a speculative once-over before he turns his back and resumes his phone conversation. Strolling between the aisles, Ryan pulls Claire along, studying the shelves.

"Do you want something to eat?"

The doctor does not answer. Ryan takes a packet of beef jerky and a small plastic mint dispenser, stuffing them unceremoniously in her pocket before she noisily opens the fridge and takes a bottle of water and a carbonated caffeine drink. They approach the till, but the boy is still talking away. When Ryan slams the bottles on the counter, he jerks and turns to face them, a scowl on his spotty face as he speaks to whoever is on the other side of the line.

Pointing to the drinks and then to the gas, Ryan takes out the two notes and tosses them on the counter. He shoots her a filthy look before he stuffs the notes into the till and carelessly tosses her change onto the wooden countertop.

"...yeah, sure, but Rachel went, like, to this guy..."

His story suddenly sputters to a stop as he spots the bandage on Ryan's right hand, now specked with blood and filthy from the grimy surface of the bathroom counter, when she takes the bottles.

Shooting him a skew smile Ryan casually takes Claire's arm and strolls from the shop. When she opens the passenger door and propels the blonde inside, he is still talking on his phone, but he has turned toward them and is watching with low-key interest.

Ryan slips into the driver's seat and takes off the sunglasses. It is late afternoon and the shadows are beginning to lengthen. Setting the carbonated drink in the cup holder, she tosses the bottled water into Claire's lap and then pulls the jerky and mints out of her pocket, dropping them into the space beneath the radio. As they pull away, Claire stares longingly at the brightly lit station.

Ryan cracks open the top of her drink and sips at it slowly. "Drink your water."

Claire does not respond. Shaking her head, Ryan replaces the soda and lifts the jerky packet to her mouth, tearing it open with her teeth. Slipping out a piece, she offers the pack. "Jerky?"

Still no reaction. Ryan replaces the packet and clamps down on the jerky like a cigar as she begins to press buttons on the radio at random. When a country music station suddenly blares, Claire starts. Frowning, Ryan prods the bright blue buttons until the station changes to soft rock on 93.7FM.

In the fading light, Claire turns around and examines Ryan. The woman is chewing her jerky musingly, but a pause in her motions reveals that she notes Claire's scrutiny.

"What?"

The blonde drops her eyes to Ryan's right hand. "Did you hit somebody in the bathroom?"

Flexing the hand, Ryan shakes her head. "No."

"Oh." Claire's eyes move back to her face. "What happened?"
"Nothing." Her voice is inscrutable.

Reaching for the cubbyhole, Claire takes out the first-aid kit and zips it open. "Can I re-bandage that for you?"

With a dubious look in her eyes, Ryan glances at the blonde. "You are aware that there's nothing left in there you can use against me."

"So you said. No hidden motives, Ryan. It looks filthy."

"It's too dark now."

"Switch on the light."

The Marine steals another glance at the woman in the passenger seat before she reaches up and switches on the overhead light, illuminating them abruptly.

"Walsch, if you try anything..."

"Yes. I remember." Claire beckons. "Give me your hand." When Ryan extends her right hand, the doctor dexterously unwinds the bandage, grimacing at the mucky texture of it. Dropping the old bandage in the back, she dabs some antiseptic on the grazes before she neatly wraps a new bandage around the hand and wrist, wrapping until the roll is finished, for lack of scissors. When she has neatly tucked the end in, Ryan draws back her hand and studies the result without comment, reaches up, and switches off the light.

"Thank you."

To her credit, the doctor does not pronounce it a pleasure. She replaces the kit and looks out of the window at the rapidly falling dusk for a while before she straightens in her seat and takes a sip of water. When the jerky packet rustles, Ryan suppresses a smile.

Claire is quiet for a moment, and then, "You stole the jerky."

"Sure. Did you want me to hold up the boy for it instead?" There is silence as Claire chews. Ryan stretches the fingers of her newly bandaged hand contemplatively before she speaks. "Do you know how far the border is from here?"

Claire shifts to look at the Marine. "Canada?" When Ryan nods, she shakes her head at herself. "Of course Canada. You're not taking a northern detour to Mexico. I really can't say for sure. Two hundred miles, perhaps? I'm not that good at distance."

"Closer to a hundred, I think."

Careful not to antagonize the woman, Claire speaks as evenly as she can. "When you get to the border, what are you going to do with me?"

"Drive about another hundred miles and then drop you." The woman's hoarse voice is matter-of-fact. "I've told you before – don't do anything stupid and you'll be fine."

"All right. What will you do then, if I may ask?"

"You may not."

They drive in silence. The area surrounding the road has flattened out, and it is too dark now to see the mountains, which must be within visual range to the left. When Claire begins to talk again, Ryan is not surprised.

"Were you sick recently?"

"Some would say so." Ryan's voice is dry.

"No, I mean have you been ill lately?"

"Why?"

"Your voice. You sound as if you had a cold."

"I didn't."

"Then–"

"No."

Sighing, Claire picks at the label on her water bottle. "Ryan, just tell me. We're going to be in the car for a while."

"You've sure stopped being scared of me fast." Ryan's voice is dry. "I'm not sure I like it."

"I haven't. I'm still scared of you. But you're trying to distract me, so now I want to know why."

There is a heavy silence, and just as Claire thinks that she will have no answer, the Marine speaks.

"It's what your voice sounds like after you've screamed for three days nonstop, Doctor."

"At Fairwater?"

"No. Before."

"Oh." Claire senses by the tone of the answer that this is not an avenue to pursue any further. She changes tack. "I didn't peg you for a screamer." Immediately her face flushes as she realizes the unintended double-entendre, but when Ryan answers it is with no trace of humor.

"Some things are better tolerated that way."

A smooth, soft number by Dido plays on the radio, and Claire lets the soothing tune wash over her as she considers the woman next to her. Much of her panic has disappeared, mostly the doing of her persistent nature. Her captor has turned out to be far less hostile than she would have imagined. If she were to be honest, she would have to admit that this woman could prove to be a brilliant case study, and if she could believe that she would be released without being harmed, the information she could glean from Ryan would be invaluable.

The only matter to decide upon is her approach. She cannot afford to stir up animosity. She sips at her water and allows more silence to creep in before she draws one foot under her and makes herself comfortable in the corner.

"Ryan? When you were trying to get yourself released from Fairwater, why didn't you ask Admiral Banks for help?"

It takes the Marine a moment to respond. "What?"

"He seems to hold you in very high regard. I can't imagine that he wouldn't at least have tried to help you."

"Who?"

"Admiral Banks." Though impatience shows in Claire's tone, Ryan doesn't appear to notice.

"I think you have the wrong name."

Claire purses her lips and frowns. "No, I'm sure that's right. Victor Banks. He said you were in Afghanistan together in '98 or–"

"'99." Ryan draws out the numbers. "What does he look like, Walsch?"

"About five ten, gray hair, gray eyes, beard... What's the matter?"

"*Victor Banks*?" There is definite confusion in her voice. Claire startles when Ryan suddenly pulls to the side of the road and stops.

"Ryan?"

When there is no answer, she switches on the overhead light to find the other woman leaning on the steering wheel with both arms, her eyes distant. Claire repeats her name a second time, and then Ryan's eyes are fixed on her. Leaning forward, Claire carefully reaches out and almost touches her arm before she decides against it. "Ryan?"

"Why was he there?" The woman stares at Claire, her eyes unmoving as she deliberates. "What was he doing there? Did he say?"

"I don't understand. He met me at the front desk and took me through to your cell. Room. I thought it was a given that the military would be keeping you under observation?"

"Yes. But Victor's never been involved in that... We were personal friends. We only served together in Afghanistan and in..." her voice hardens, "Kosovo. Was he in uniform?"

"Yes. I don't understand what the problem is, Ryan. Maybe he was assigned your case after you went in."

Ryan's voice is precise and tight. "Some time last year I was told that Victor retired in 2004." When she starts the Trailblazer again, her jaw is set. Pulling back onto the road, she switches off the overhead light. "May I have some of your water, please?"

"Sure. Here." Claire passes the bottle over. "What's going on, Ryan?"

"I don't know." The Marine unscrews the cap and takes a sip from the bottle before she passes it back. "I'm going to take a small detour."

The men move stealthily through the trees. Finding the same scenario at the second house come upon, they are forced to stop and inspect the property before they can proceed with their tracking. This time the small man is not so amused at Ryan's ruse. They track onwards and when they come upon the third house, they check the perimeter before they begin to inspect the building. If they had been less meticulous, the recently closed window would have escaped their attention. As it is, it takes them a while to note it.

Whilst two men continue to the garage, the other two flank the back door as the fifth picks the lock. Inside, the surfaces are spotless and nothing seems out of place. They secure the downstairs area before moving up the stairs in shadowy sequence, bursting into each room in turn and finding nothing. The man who has just stepped into the bathroom speaks up.

"Blood in the sink, looks like."

A second man joins him in peering at the porcelain and then nods in agreement. At that moment, the third speaks from the bedroom.

"Cuffs."

They congregate around the two separated cuffs lying on the carpet; the pin is still attached to one of them. They move back downstairs and find that one of their crew has come in from outside.

"Bad news. Looks like there was a vehicle in the garage."

The small man nods and lifts his radio to his mouth. "Alpha, come in."

The radio crackles to life. "Alpha here."

"She's taken a vehicle from a residence."

"Right. Give me your GPS co-ordinates." The small man complies. "Get yourselves to the road, Sierra; I'm picking you up in ten."

"Affirmative."

When the van stops and the door slides open, four of the team get into the back. Sierra walks around and gets into the passenger seat. Alpha nods in greeting.

"She's messing us around."

"Not for long." Sierra tilts his chin to indicate the road. "Which way is she going?"

Alpha begins to head back to the main road. "Choteau."

The music gradually changes to a smoother genre, and Claire finds herself nodding off more than once. Each time, as she spirals down, she has flashes of being dragged through the woods, her hands tied, and she startles and sits up in an effort to remain awake. After her head jerks for what feels like the thousandth time, Ryan speaks up, her voice low.

"Go to sleep."

"I'm not tired." Claire stubbornly clings to watchfulness, though the escape and flight have exhausted her, as have the myriad of emotions that still swirl inside her.

Ryan chuckles. "Walsch, every time your head jerks you're diminishing our fuel efficiency by increasing resistance." Her right hand reaches down and feels for the lever at the side of Claire's seat. She pulls it and reclines the chair. "Relax. You'll be fine. Go to sleep."

In spite of her struggle against dropping off, Claire falls into a light slumber as they turn right into Pendroy Road. They pass through Conrad, where – aside from the streetlights – it is dark, and then back onto 15 North, crossing the train tracks.

Between the towns of Conrad and Shelby, Ryan pulls over to the side of the road and studies the sleeping profile of her passenger for some time. She can tell that Claire is genuinely asleep by the regularity and depth of her breathing, and when she has assured herself that the woman will not wake up soon, she lays back and tries to get some rest herself. She has been drinking the caffeinated soda to keep herself from collapsing in exhaustion, and now, ironically, it is working too well. Instead of sleeping, she stares into the dark sky, thoughts and imaginings churning in her mind. She knows that she is definitely being traced, but at this point, she also knows that she cannot drive any further without endangering her own life and that of her passenger. She is a lot of things, but negligent and careless are not among them.

Though it is too dark to see much in the blue reflection of the radio's luminous lights, she turns her head toward Claire. The woman is more resilient than she had expected her to be, especially given that, at first, Claire was mostly whimpering and begging. In fact, the doctor's demeanor has changed from apprehensive and nervous to slightly more self-possessed. Conditions being what they are, Ryan appreciates the strength that takes. Under different circumstances, they would probably have liked one another, she muses.

When Claire wakes up, she stretches as fully as the interior of the vehicle will allow, realizing as she does that she is actually feeling rested and refreshed. Her first glance through the windshield shows a breathtaking sight. The sun rising on the horizon is still at that bright red phase, touching everything around it with a shimmer of crimson. Her second glance catches an image that is not as charming. The Marine is raging outside, a fair distance from the Trailblazer, jacketless in the cold early morning air. From the jerking motions of her bare head – Claire glances to find the cap lying on the seat beside her – Ryan is talking to herself angrily.

Her hands are rigid at her side, though occasionally she teaches up to touch her skull crossly.

Feeling somehow intrusive and suddenly more fearful again at this frantic behavior, Claire turns away just as Ryan folds double and drops to her knees, heaving up the scant contents of her stomach.

The doctor ponders the possibility of escape, but her door is still locked. To climb over the seats to the back door would create a critical delay, and to exit from the driver's seat had certainly not worked for her the last time. Quickly and competently, she weighs the pros and cons of the situation and decides that it would be more dangerous to attempt to flee – and rile the Marine – than it would be to wait for a better opportunity. Panic drives people to take stupid risks, she knows that better than anybody, and so she calmly sucks a mint to remove the fuzzy taste from her mouth, then drinks the last of her water.

When she next glances up, the Marine is at the driver's door and slipping into her seat. Her skin is pale, and the exhaustion in her eyes indicates that she has slept little, if at all. Ryan slips the cap back onto her shaven head, then chews on a mint before she drinks the last of her soda.

"Good morning."

Claire is not expecting a reply as the woman puts on the sunglasses and starts the SUV. When Ryan unexpectedly shuts the engine off again, Claire glances at her curiously.

Ryan clears her throat. "Would you like to stretch your legs before we go?"

Claire can't help but smile as she nods at the unexpected question. "Yes. Please."

Getting out, Ryan walks around to the passenger side. When she opens the door, she leans on it with her forearms. "Will it be necessary to tie your hands?"
"No. It won't." Claire looks into her eyes. "I won't try anything."

"Good. I really don't feel like running." Closing the door behind the doctor with a trace of chivalry that has Claire raising her eyebrows, Ryan strolls to the front of the vehicle and lifts herself onto the hood, stretching out her legs as she leans back on her elbows. "Take your time."

Five minutes later, they are on the road. They pass a sign indicating that they have eight miles to go before they reach Shelby. Feeling revitalized, Claire changes to a radio station with more upbeat music before she speaks.

"Ryan? Why are you getting sick so often? Is something wrong?"

The woman shakes her head. "No. It's the tranquilizers they shot me full of the day before you came. I'm fine. They're just working themselves out of my system."

"Ryan, this morning when—"

"Don't." The Marine shoots her a cool look. "It's not something I want to discuss."

"All right. I'm sorry." Claire is feeling bold, knowing that she is so much more refreshed and alert than the woman beside her. "Will you tell me how you got your medal?"

Frowning, Ryan checks her rearview mirror. "I'm sure that information is in my file."

Claire nods. "It is – whatever is in the articles from the newspapers and magazines. But none of it is very specific. I'd like to hear it from you."

"I don't think you would." Ryan slows down as they enter the perimeter of the town.

"I would like to know." The doctor hazards an opinion that might upset the Marine. "And I think you want to tell me."

"Psychology will get you into trouble, Doctor Walsch."

Between Maple Street and Third Avenue, Ryan pulls into a parking space and takes the coins out of the ashtray, slipping them into her oversized pocket. "I'll tell you later. Right now, I need to make a call." Getting out of the SUV, she walks around to Claire's side and opens the door. "Come on." As Claire gets out of the vehicle, Ryan grips her arm lightly. Claire has to resist twisting her sensitive flesh from the woman's grasp.

"There are a lot of people about, Walsch. Please don't draw attention to yourself."

"I'm sorry. I'm not trying to cause trouble. It's just that my arm's bruised from last night."

The Marine glances down, her sunglasses a solid shield. "I'm sorry." Stepping around to the other side, she grasps Claire's left arm instead. They walk together, the two of them, to the old phone booth that stands in the middle of the sidewalk. Ryan directs Claire inside ahead of her and closes the door behind them, then slots in the coins and dials a number from memory. When she speaks, her voice is pitched much higher.

"Hello, may I speak to LuAnn in Administration? ... Oh? She's not? ... All right, who's available? ... Thank you very much, I'll hold." She waits for a minute and then presses down on the lever to end the call. She dials again, and this time when she speaks her voice is light, with a singsong quality. "Hello, can you put me through to the Records Department, please? Thank you. ... Hello, whom am I speaking with? Anna? ... Hi, Anna, it's Tracy from Admin in Baker. How are you? ... Great, great. Listen, I have a problem here. Postal keeps returning one of yours' mail with an RTS on it. ... Yeah, it's Rear Admiral V. Banks. ... Victor– ... That's right, the scoundrel. ... Well, I did try Edna, but she's not in the office. ... All right." She waits patiently for a moment. "Okay, so that's...67 River Street, Fort Benton. Is that right? ... I sure do hope so. ... Okay, I owe you a box of chocolates, Anna. ... You too, love. Take care."

She puts down the telephone to find Claire staring at her in amazement.

"What? Let's go."

The Marine slips open the door and grips Claire's arm, a little more loosely this time, but when the doctor turns in the direction of the Trailblazer, Ryan steers her down the street instead. She scouts the shops lining the sidewalk and when she sees a coffee shop, she pulls Claire in behind her. The gawky waiter enthusiastically approaches them with menus, but Ryan waves them away. "Two cups of strong coffee, please. Do you have a bathroom?"

The waiter points out a swinging door in the corner, and the Marine leads Claire through it to the bathroom beyond. As Ryan releases her arm, the blonde looks around at her.

"How did you know I needed the bathroom?"

"God told me." At Claire's start, the woman shakes her head. "Joke. Now you know why I don't make them. You're wearing a bra, right?"

"What?" The doctor is certain that she has misheard. "Excuse me?"

"Are you wearing a bra?" Ryan asks again, matter-of-factly, as if it's a stock standard question to ask.

"Um… yes. Why?"

The Marine reclines against the washbasin. "While you're in there, take it off."

"Excuse me?" Now Claire is sure that the woman must be mad.

Raising her eyebrows, Ryan motions her into the stall a touch impatiently. "Go on."

Ryan has just come out of the second cubicle when Claire's voice drifts across the division. "Were you joking about the bra?"
"No." Ryan washes her left hand and adjusts the bandage with the other. "Hurry up. Do you need help?"

"No!" Claire is irritated, and when she steps out of the cubicle, her frown confirms it. Handing over the lacy white bra, she folds her arms defensively over her chest. "What do you want with it?"

Without answering, Ryan holds the bra up and studies the structure for a moment before she raises it to her mouth and begins to gnaw at a seam. With a triumphant expression, she pushes the underwire out and straightens it with her hands. Slipping the wire into an inner pocket of her jacket, she holds the bra out to Claire. "Do you want it back?"

"What for?" Claire is glowering. "It's useless like that."

"Okay." Extending one hand, Ryan grasps Claire's hand instead of her arm then pulls her closer.

"Come on, let's go drink our coffee."

As they exit the bathroom, Ryan is slipping the bra into her pocket when a stern woman in a badly fitted suit walks past. Her forehead furrows in disapproval when she spots the item in Ryan's hand. With a slight smile, the Marine leans in to Claire conspiratorially. "I'm keeping it as a reminder." Her voice is extra husky and the woman's mouth purses into a displeased button as she hurries away from them.

Claire raises her eyebrows. "You take my bra, **and** then you besmirch my reputation? You have a lot of nerve, Marine."

For just a moment they appear to be no more than friends having coffee in a small town on a blue July day. When they sit down, Ryan slips off her sunglasses. Over her cup of coffee, her green eyes are glassy and tired. Claire takes a sip from her own steaming cup.

"Why don't you get yourself something to eat? Have you got enough money?"

Ryan cocks her head. "No."

"Have you even got enough money to pay for this coffee?"

"Yes."

They drink slowly and then Ryan slips her sunglasses back on and takes Claire's upper arm.

"Please." The blonde lifts her arm slightly. "It's a little uncomfortable. I'd prefer it if you took my hand again. If you don't mind."

"I don't mind." Ryan wraps her fingers around Claire's. "Let's go."

They wander down the street and the doctor is beginning to wonder whether they are, in fact, just sightseeing, when Ryan pulls her into a side street. Walking a little closer to the cars parked at the side of the road, the Marine glances casually into each of them before stopping at a white, four-door Mazda. Pulling the blonde closer, she positions her against the door. "Stand right there."

She slips the wire from her pocket and maneuvers it into the rubber gasket that seals the window, shifting it a few times before she lifts it firmly, the door lock rising in response to her manipulations. After opening the door, she leans down and grabs the bag that is lying on the floor of the passenger side. A quick look inside confirms the presence of a purse; shuffling through its contents produces a few bills that Ryan removes and stuffs into her pocket.

"Okay."

She walks Claire back to Main Street and leads her into a small convenience store, where she fills a small basket with a few bottles of water, four packaged sandwiches, and a bottle of aspirin.

"Is there anything you need?" When Claire shakes her head, Ryan takes the items to the checkout and pays, tucking the paper bag under one arm.

As soon as they are back in the Trailblazer, Claire digs into the packet. "May I have a sandwich? I'm starving."

The Marine nods and pulls out of the parking space, slipping into the first gas station to fill the SUV with as much fuel as she can afford. When finally they turn right and drive over the train tracks, Claire frowns over her sandwich. "I'm not that great with direction, but aren't we heading the wrong way?"

"I'm not going to the border just yet." Ryan glances over her shoulder as she takes a cut-off to the right. At the edge of town, a sign announces that Chester is forty-eight miles away.

Chewing pensively, Claire sits up and turns off the radio. "You were going to tell me about the medal." The Marine remains silent. "Come on, Ryan. Surely it's not a state secret or anything. Please? I'm interested."

With a sigh, Ryan opens the aspirin bottle and shakes two tablets into her hand. With a ghost of a smile, she accepts the water Claire offers to her and swallows the pills. "What do you know about Kosovo?"

"Nothing."

The Marine gives a resigned shake of her head. "Okay. I'm not going to bore you with the details. Roughly speaking, there was a power struggle between the KLA - that's the Kosovo Liberation Army - and the Serbians in the late 90's. Government issues resulting in sanctions; the usual sorts of things. The first serious action of the war was when the KLA's attacks on the Drenica Valley area intensified, and the Serbian police pursued a part of the army to Cirez."

Ryan takes a deep breath and looks away for a moment before she resumes.

"We weren't supposed to be there. It was strictly a greenside operation." Catching Claire's frown, she explained. "No direct contact intended. We were doing basic reconnaissance near Cirez when we ran into a retreating faction of the KLA."
The Marine takes a long draught from her water bottle.

"They pinned us in a gully. The best course of action would have been to fall back ourselves, but as we were retreating, the Serbians came from behind and blocked off our escape route. The Serbians thought we were part of the KLA; the KLA thought we were scouts for the Serbian police. We couldn't hold off either of them for long. I crawled down that gully under cover and lured them away."

"How?" Claire's eyes are fixed on Ryan's face, which is drawn and strained.

"If I tell you, you won't ever be able to not know."

The doctor frowns at the odd words. "I *want* to know."

When Ryan continues, her voice is flat. "I ran until I found a Serbian village. It wasn't far. Then, I went so loud with the weapons I had that neither the Serbians nor the KLA could miss it."

"And what happened?"

"The Serbians thought it was the KLA. They came for me. The KLA used the diversion to retreat."
Claire sits forward, absorbed in the story. "And then?"

"And then they captured me, Walsch. My unit escaped and I was shipped off to some hellhole or another."

"Did they keep you as a prisoner of war?"

"If it had happened differently, they almost certainly wouldn't have, but..." Ryan is suddenly hard and remote. "They tortured me for two weeks, until a group of KFOR soldiers found me completely by accident. I don't know why they didn't kill me. I would have if I had been them."

"Why?"

Ryan's jaw clenches "Walsch, you're not hearing me. In that little village... I must have killed about thirty people with whatever I had at hand. Hand grenades, mines, rifle. They were all women and children, Walsch; every single one of them completely defenseless. There were no soldiers, no guns, no terrorists. Just me. I killed them as a means to an end."

Putting her hands to her mouth, Claire closes her eyes against the horror invoked by the words. When Ryan continues, her voice is soft.

"If that had been my village, my women and children, I wouldn't just have done the things they did to me." She turns her head away and continues thickly. "I remember pulling the pin from a grenade. This boy came running towards me from a doorway. He couldn't have been more than seven years old. He was wearing a tattered blue shirt with a big hole over his left shoulder, and he had this big smile on his face. I was already lobbing the grenade by then, and he kind of turned, as if he was going to fetch it for me." She takes a sharp breath, and then exhales slowly. "He thought I was playing a game with him."

Ryan stops talking, and it seems as if she stops breathing, too. In the ensuing silence there is only the hitching sound of Claire's tears, and it is a long time before Ryan speaks again.

"That was the first time the voice in my head told me what to do, Doctor. Auspicious beginning. I got a medal for that. No questions, no details, just a cover-up and a handshake from the President, and a pretty Medal of Honor. So please do excuse me for not being overly enthusiastic about telling the story."

Claire sits with her hands pressed against her mouth, her blue eyes full of tears as she stares silently at the Marine.

Glancing towards her, Ryan shakes her head slightly. "I warned you. Sorry." She shakes two more aspirin into her hand and swallows them, then switches on the radio. This time when country music starts to play, she leaves it on.

It takes Claire a while to gather herself. She is sharply conflicted between her sudden realization of what Ryan is capable of, and her compassion for the effect it has clearly had on her. When Claire has a grip on her emotions – however tenuous - she turns to the tense Marine.

"Do you regret it, Ryan?"

"At the time, I did what I thought I had to do." The Marine turns her head to glance out of her window. "'*Regret*' isn't really a sufficient word." Pulling off the road she stops the car, then takes off the jacket and glasses and opens her door. "I need to take a break."

Before the Marine can walk away, Claire asks, "Ryan, please open my door?"

In silence, the Marine complies, and then turns her back to the car as she searches for a flat piece of ground. Taking a deep breath, she closes her eyes and begins a slow, precise series of stretches, almost like yoga, and even in her oversized jeans and trainers she is exceptionally graceful. Curious, Claire climbs onto the hood of the car and watches as Ryan patiently stretches her muscles. And now, suddenly, the doctor understands why she works out to such extremes, knows the demons that are chasing her so that she feels the need to block them out with movement to the point of exhaustion.

Once Ryan is finished, she returns to the car, the trace of a smile appearing at the corner of her mouth as she sees Claire stretched out against the windshield. "Come on."

They get back into the SUV and Claire studies Ryan critically. "You look like shit, Marine."

"Don't worry," Ryan jokes without a smile, "I look better than I feel."

Claire extends her hand and touches the other woman's bandaged wrist lightly, carefully. "You need to get some rest, Ryan."

"And then?" The woman turns towards her captive. "Will you wait quietly and make sure that nobody bothers me until I wake up?"

She starts the vehicle. "Are you *actually* thinking about going AWOL on me, Doctor Walsch?" Her tone is one of mock surprise.

Claire shakes her head without smiling. "I'm not thinking about running away, no. I'm trying to help somebody who seems to need it."

Letting the car idle, the Marine turns in her seat and slips on her sunglasses, purposely putting distance between her and her passenger. "Listen, Doctor–"

"Call me Claire."

Ryan continues as if she does not hear the interruption. "I am not your patient. I am not in need of help. Not from you, in any case. And I am *not* somebody you want to be on a first-name basis with." Claire begins to speak but the Marine shakes her head. "*Listen* to me. You shouldn't be thinking about my mental or physical state at all. You shouldn't be going anywhere *near* my psyche. You should be thinking about escaping. In a situation of captivity, all you should be thinking about is survival and escape. Do you understand me?"

When Claire nods dumbly, Ryan shifts back in her seat and pulls onto the road. Her voice is businesslike as she continues. "I am not your friend; don't let me fool you into thinking that I am. I know you want to help, but you shouldn't be thinking about me right now. You should be thinking about yourself, and what you can do to not get hurt."

They drive in silence, the Marine serious and Claire pensive. She tries to inject lightness into her voice when she speaks again. "If you so badly want me to escape, why don't you just let me go?"

"You need to get away. I need you to stay. I appreciate both."

Shaking her head, Claire leans down to take out half of a sandwich and then passes it over to Ryan. "BLT. You have to eat something."

Ryan takes it with a dubious look. "It's not for lack of trying." With a small grimace, she takes a bite and chews warily.

Claire watches her until she's sure that the woman won't discard the food. "Ryan? Afterwards, did you tell your commanding officer about the voices?"

"Voice." Ryan raises an eyebrow. "There's only the one, thank God." She purses her lips dryly at her unintended humor. "Or not, as the case may be. I did tell him, of course. With the Force Recon, there're no private issues when it comes to missions. He has to know what's going on to be able to trust me with the lives of my men. I'm not an individual there; I'm just one part of a machine."

"What happened?"

A faint smile curls around Ryan's lips. "And still with the chatting. Were you not here when I was talking to you earlier, Doc?"

"Oh yes. I heard you. But short of climbing through the window and throwing myself onto the highway at seventy miles per hour, I can't exactly escape right at this moment." Claire raises her eyebrows innocently. "Think of it as a familiar action to soothe me enough so that I have a clear head for the escaping-and-surviving bit. Therapy." Ryan shoots her a quick glance and Claire shakes her head, wide-eyed. "Oh no," she demurs. "Therapy for me, not for you. *You* don't need help."

"You're a smart-ass."

The Marine laughs, the first genuine laugh Claire has heard from her, a pleasant low-timbre chuckle that she finds disturbingly appealing. "Yes, I am. So what happened when you told your commanding officer?"

"Persistent." Ryan smiles slightly. "Actually, nothing much. I had a psych evaluation and a few quiet months, and then I went back into the fray."

"So they took you off duty for a while?"

"Not as such." The smile fades. "It was three weeks after I got back from Kosovo. I wasn't physically able to serve for some time, in any event."

Claire thinks about asking, wonders how to do it tactfully, and then decides that there probably isn't any good way. "Ryan, can I ask...what they did to you?"

"Everything they could think of." Ryan is quiet. "It's another of those things I can't untell you, Doctor. Don't invite the nightmares in."

Claire ponders, noting from the corner of her eye that Ryan is finished with the sandwich. "Don't you think it strange that they would put you back on duty with an issue like the one you reported? Surely you would have been considered a hazard to the safety of your peers?"

"I have an excellent record. Colonel Turner told me that that was why they considered it at all."

"Colonel Turner. The same Turner who–"

"Supervises my situation. Yes."

"Hmm." Tapping a finger on her thigh, Claire ponders. "Not to offend you, Ryan, but I think they were incredibly irresponsible to send you back out like that."

"None taken. I was a little surprised myself."

"When did you decide on Fairwater? And why?"

"You know, it isn't too late for you to crawl out of the window and throw yourself onto the highway." Ryan follows her exasperated comment with a sigh. "Late 2001. We were in Chaman, Pakistan, on our way into Afghanistan, and the voice just wouldn't stop. I had these incredible headaches, couldn't concentrate, couldn't even get my eyes to focus properly, so finally I fell back. After that, it was pretty clear to everyone that it was turning into a problem."

"And before that?" Claire frowns. "Wasn't it a problem then?"

"Not really." Ryan glances sideways with a wry smile. "I know, it sounds crazy. Before that, it actually was not so bad, believe it or not. I did hear the voice sporadically when I was in battle, but then it was almost like a separate part of my subconscious, advising me to do things that I probably would have decided on myself."

"You know..." Claire begins gently, her eyes serious as she looks at the Marine, "that's the popular opinion on auditory hallucinations – that they're your subconscious guiding you, commenting, as it were, on your life and your view of yourself."

"I was told that, early on."

"By Art? I mean, Doctor Clarke?"

"No. His predecessor. Doctor Cox, I think it was." She drums her fingers on the steering wheel. "He told me I had to accept that I seemed to be subconsciously guiding myself into activities of my choice. That to evolve it into a different person, so to speak, was taking the strain of my... actions... off my mind."

Claire nods. "It's a common theory."

"It's kind of ironic – that I'm told the only way to get past killing all of those defenseless villagers is to accept that it was my own will."

"Ryan–" Claire begins, but the Marine continues firmly.

"Doctor, do you understand that if I acknowledge that, then I'm saying that it's a part of **me** that kills children? And women?" Ryan shakes her head abruptly. "No. If I give in to that, then I might as well put a gun to my temple. I don't want to be helped if I'm the kind of person who has that capability ingrained in them. I don't want medicines to suppress it, to sanitize it, to hide it away. I do not want to be alive like that. Can you understand that?"

"Okay. Hold on." Claire lays a gentle hand on Ryan's forearm. "It's only one of the theories, not necessarily the right one. If there even is a right one."

"All of them start with me killing innocent people because of a voice in my head." Bitterness saturates the hoarse voice. "I don't care what the current theory is, Doctor Walsch. What I care about is getting far enough away from the rest of the world."

"You'll never get away from it if you don't confront it." The words are strong, but Claire's voice is kind. Ryan glances at her, and then away. "Are there specific times you're more likely to hear it? When you're under stress, or unhappy, maybe?"

"I've heard all of these questions before." Ryan sighs, though she seems to be calmer again. "No, no, and no. It comes and goes."

"What does the voice tell you?"

Ryan chuckles, though it is completely without humor. "Do you believe in God?"

"In an abstract way, yes, I do."

"Then you might not want to hear what the big man has to say."

Claire takes a sip of her water. "Are you feeling okay? Sandwich staying where it should?"

"I'm fine."

"Really?"
"Touch of nausea. Fine."

"Okay." After replacing the bottle, Claire twists in the seat so that she is facing Ryan. "So what does the voice say?"

"You are unrelenting. Should have been a Marine." Ryan clears her throat again. "Different things, most of them unpleasant. In battle, the comments were more geared towards how to approach certain situations."

"And at Fairwater?"

"That I had to kill to escape – doctors, orderlies, no matter, whoever passed me by. When it was just me there were recaps, like running commentary, about things I'd done. Previously."

Claire nods. "And now? Outside?"

"I'm only outside physically, Doctor." The Marine's shoulders tighten. "I've heard a lot of things. Right at the beginning…" a small hesitation as she appears to be considering something, "right at the beginning, it told me to kill you, that you were dragging me down." The blood drains from Claire's face, and Ryan sees it as she glances over. "Sorry. If you believe it's my subconscious knocking on my skull, I've just freaked you out."

Biting her lip, Claire takes some settling breaths. "It was true. I *was* dragging you down."

"Yes. Sure. Because I was dragging you along. It was my own choice." Ryan glances at the radio. "Can we listen to something besides me now?"

"Wait." Claire puts out a pre-emptive hand. "What else?"

The Marine sighs and shakes her head. "What else? You don't want to hear it, Doctor. You really don't. You don't need to know that the person you're sitting next to is being told to blow up schools or churches or gun down civilians on a regular basis. To do atrocious things to people. To you. Is that enough information?" She clenches the steering wheel.

"Ryan, what–"

Suddenly the Marine wraps her hand around Claire's and holds it tightly. "Claire. Please. *Stop.* I have no control over what happens inside my head; let me have some say over what's outside it."

"All right." Claire places her other hand over the bandaged one and rests it there until Ryan pulls her hand away, then she reaches over and switches on the radio. "I'm sorry. I didn't mean to push you so much. I wasn't thinking."

"You were thinking too much."

"That's just silly. There's no such thing." Claire grins to show she is teasing, in hopes that it will lift Ryan's dark mood.

They spend most of the rest of the drive in relative silence, deep in their own thoughts. Given the horrific things she has heard, Claire can only guess what Ryan is thinking about; her own thoughts are convoluted. She knows that she is growing closer to her captor than is wise, that she is investing injudicious emotion in the Marine's situation. That having pushed Ryan so far in an attempt to get her to atone by releasing her captive, she is slipping beyond the bounds of therapy. Ryan is right – she should be thinking about her own survival, but instead she is wondering how Ryan has made it with the burden she is carrying. It is not even two days that they have been together, and it feels like a lifetime. Classic Stockholm Syndrome. She chuckles wryly at herself and is treated to a skewed look from Ryan.

"What?"

"Nothing." She smiles at the raised eyebrows. "Nothing much. Thinking about a lot of things."

They pass through Chester and turn onto Highway 80 towards Fort Benton. It is not long afterwards that Ryan suddenly swings the SUV off the road and stomps on the brakes. Thrown forward hard against her seatbelt, Claire puts out her hands to protect herself, pressing them against the leather dashboard as they come to a halt.

"What..."

She turns to see Ryan crumpling forward against the steering wheel, her face contorted. With a low groan, the Marine fumbles for the button on her seatbelt, her bandaged right hand sluggish and clumsy.

"Ryan?" Claire lays a tentative hand on the woman's back, and then reaches over and unclips her seatbelt. Unexpectedly released from its harness, the Marine finally manages to get the door open and fall out.

"Ryan?"

Unbuckling her own seatbelt, Claire cranes her neck and sees the woman appear in front of the SUV, her eyes clamped tightly shut and her teeth bared in a grimace. She is stumbling forward and as the doctor watches, her legs give beneath her and she goes down hard. She curls up and lies still for a moment before she struggles to all fours, her back arching as she vomits. Claire climbs over the handbrake and out of the vehicle, casting a glance at the convulsing figure before she begins to run in the opposite direction. When she hears the vehicle start behind her, she veers off into the country, struggling through the growth underfoot and falling more than once when snagged by an errant vine or branch. She can hear footsteps following her, but this time she doesn't have a sense of panic, only of inevitability. When the footsteps are almost right behind her, she slows down, causing the Marine to careen into her. Strong arms wrap around her to keep her upright. Ryan's body is warm.

"You should just have taken the car. Are you going to fight me?"

"No."

Claire turns and begins to trudge back to the vehicle. Ryan walks beside her in silence, her hand loose around the blonde's wrist. When they arrive at the car, she leads Claire towards the open driver's door.

"You have to drive for a while."

It is unexpected, the manner in which the doctor suddenly leans back against her hand. "I don't drive."

"You don't? Or you won't?"

Claire's silence verifies the answer. Leading Claire back to the passenger's side, Ryan lets her get in and closes the door before she slips into her own seat and pops two aspirin into her mouth. The blonde's face is rigid, and they drive for about five miles before she relaxes and speaks.

"You can't go on like this."

The Marine glances at her. "Why won't you drive?"

Ignoring the question much as Ryan has ignored hers, Claire lays a hand on the woman's forearm. "You're very warm. Are you sick, Ryan?"

"Tell me why you don't drive."

"This can't still be the tranquilizer, can it?"

"Why not drive, Claire?"

"For God's sake!" It is the first time the blonde raises her voice. "Just *leave* it, will you?"

"What? Don't like your own medicine?" The Marine smiles faintly. "We're talking about this later." When the doctor turns her head to stare out of the window, Ryan raises an eyebrow. "Later."

The radio fills the silence and when Claire finally looks back, the Marine is quiet, her eyes somewhere in the distance. Without the large sunglasses, which she seems to have lost at the last stop, it is hard not to notice how haggard she looks. Her green eyes are glassy and darkly ringed, and there is a faintly waxy sheen to her pale skin. The bandage on her hand is dirty and seeping blood, probably from the fall, and there is a grimy abrasion on the right side of her forehead.

Sighing, Claire slips the first-aid kit from the cubbyhole and takes out a gauze pad, which she moistens with water before she shifts to the edge of her seat and begins to clean the dirt from the injury. Apart from an initial start at the touch against her abraded skin, the Marine is quiet. Claire makes sure that the seeping area is clean before she dabs antiseptic liquid on another pad and presses it against the area, holding it there.

"I'm sorry - it must sting."

Ryan does not answer. The blonde presses the pad to the wound, lifting it every now and then, and when she is satisfied that the bleeding has stopped, she wads up the gauze and discards it.

"Give me your hand."

The Marine complies silently. Claire unwraps the filthy bandage and dabs the bleeding cuts with a piece of gauze. After pressing a pad over the injured area, she wraps her smaller hand over Ryan's to hold it in place. Heat emanates from the other woman's skin.

"How do you feel, Ryan?"

"Hm." The Marine raises a wry eyebrow. "Fantastic."

Claire frowns. "Be serious."

"I haven't slept in a while, I haven't been able to keep anything down for days, and I'm bleeding again." Ryan shoots her passenger a sardonic look. "But apart from that, I'm great."

"Surely the drugs should have worked themselves out of your system by now?"

"I'd imagine so." Ryan gives a minute shrug. "It's fine."

"You're not," Claire argues. "You can't function like this."

"All the better for you. Wait until I fall over and then run."

Lifting the gauze, Claire checks the bleeding, then wads up the stained pad and discards it. "I'm serious, Ryan."

"So am I. You shouldn't be so concerned about me."

"Well, you're driving. If something happens to you while you're behind the wheel, I could get hurt too."

"Hmm. You could have prevented that by driving, Claire."

The blonde folds her arms. "We're not starting this again."

With a slight smile, Ryan flexes her hand and looks at the abraded surface. "Thanks for this, by the way."

"You're welcome."

At the outskirts of Fort Benton, they swing into St Charles Street; Ryan pulls over to ask a pedestrian for directions. Claire waits, willing the man to look in her direction as he speaks to the Marine, but his eyes remain fixed on the Marine's intense gaze until they pull away. They turn left on 14th Street, and then right into River Street. Ryan is looking to her left.

"Look for number 67."

Claire turns her head to the right and peers at the dilapidated mailbox they have just passed. "That's…32 or 38, I can't tell. What are you going to do when you find him?"

"I'm going to have a conversation with him. He's an old friend, after all. 49, 51, 53…"

"It'll be on your side, then."

In silence, Claire watches sunlight sparkle off the river, only glancing over when they pull into a driveway. Getting out, Ryan looks around casually before she walks around and lets Claire out. "Come on."

They walk to the front door and Ryan rings the doorbell once, then twice, with no response from inside. Walking the doctor around the back, Ryan checks the door there and then takes her cap off, gripping it in her hand so that the fabric protects her knuckles. With a firm blow, she shatters the window and reaches inside to open the latch. Claire hopes that there will be an alarm, but after the breaking glass, there is silence. They enter the house and find themselves in a small basic kitchen, the counters spotless and the shelves packed neatly. Pulling Claire with her to the fridge, Ryan then opens the door and peers inside.

"Some leftover mushroom pasta, looks like. Are you hungry?"

Claire folds her arms. "You're stealing someone's food again?"

"He's a friend, Doctor." Taking out the bowl, Ryan lifts the plastic wrap and sniffs tentatively. "Smells good. He probably won't mind." She presses the bowl into Claire's hand and begins to rifle through the drawers, finding a fork that she sticks into the pasta. "Here."

Claire dubiously looks at the food and then back to Ryan, who is checking the remaining drawers at random. Finally she lifts the fork to her mouth and eats the speared macaroni. It is surprisingly good. With an appreciative groan, she chews and swallows.

Turning around, Ryan looks at her. "Good?"

"Mm." She nods, eating another mouthful. With a faint smile, Ryan puts a hand on Claire's back and propels her into the hallway, a narrow affair which leads straight to the front door and is laid with gorgeous mahogany floorboards. On the left there are three doors, two leading to small compact bedrooms and one to a clean blue bathroom. On the right, one doorway leads into a small study, its walls lined with bookshelves, and the second doorway leads to a sizeable dining room with bay windows which look out over the street and the river on the other side. From the other side of the dining room, a door leads to a family room with two leather sofas and a wall unit to match the floor. Pulling out a dining room chair, Ryan motions for Claire to sit, and then she wanders the room studying the surroundings with what the doctor assumes to be approval. Moving towards the hallway, Ryan turns to Claire.

"I'm going to be just down the hall. Don't try anything."

"*Now* I shouldn't be thinking of escaping?" Claire scowls. "Would you like to draw up a schedule for me?"

With a raised eyebrow and a twitch of her mouth, Ryan disappears around the corner. At first the blonde considers trying her luck, but she is not in the best position to do so. There is no escape route from either the dining room or sitting room – both have impressive burglar guards on the windows – so to leave she would have to go down the hallway, which is where Ryan currently is. With a sigh, she eats another bite of pasta. When the colonel comes home there will be more distractions.

Rear Admiral Victor Banks parks behind the SUV and gets out, his eyebrows raised. He glances at his front door and then walks around the unfamiliar vehicle, peering inside it, not seeing anything out of the ordinary. He quietly circles around to the back of his house, where he examines the broken pane on his back door. Resting his hand on the butt of his gun in the holster under his arm, he opens the door stealthily and steps over the shards of glass lying underfoot. The kitchen seems untouched, and he eases down the hallway, stepping over noisy floorboards as he glances right, into his study; then left, into his bedroom; then left again, into the bathroom. A scraping sound in the dining room attracts his attention and he presses his back against the wall, noiselessly moving closer. Dropping to his haunches, he slides the pistol from its holster and prepares himself, chancing a glance into the room.

Captain Ryan is sitting on the window seat, her long legs clad in ridiculously baggy jeans and pulled in under her in a position that seems casual, but to his experienced eyes she is clearly ready to move. One hand is draped over her knee and bouncing up and down slowly. Her face – shaded under a blue baseball cap – is turned towards the street.

Doctor Claire Walsch is sitting on a dining room chair, spooning the remnants of last night's pasta into her mouth. She is exactly as she was when he last saw her – her neat gray suit slightly the worse for wear now, and a pair of incongruous pink trainers on her small feet instead of the heels which she wore... Was it only yesterday morning? He is considering his course of action when

Ryan turns her head and fixes him with those intimidating green eyes.

"Are you going to come in at some point, Victor?"

Shaking his head in amused annoyance, he slides the pistol back into the holster, aware of her eyes on his hands, and gets to his feet.

"Doctor." Extending a hand, he shakes Claire's gently, surreptitiously looking her over for injuries or marks. None are evident, except for a faint red weal on her cheek.

She smiles slightly. "Admiral Banks. Thank you for the late lunch. I hope you don't mind."

"Not at all. It's my pleasure." Turning to Ryan, he nods sharply. "Captain."

"Oh, please." She waves away the formality. "How are you, Victor?"

"I'm fine, Ryan. I'd ask how you are, but you look like death warmed up."

"Thanks. You always were a charmer." She takes a quick look out of the window. "Victor, are we going to have a problem with a security company?"

"No." He shakes his head. "I've already told them it was a false alarm. Been expecting you, Ryan." He pulls out a chair and sits down next to Claire, shooting her a smile.

"Hold on." Ryan gets to her feet and approaches him. "I'd like you to take out your sidearm and pass it to me."

He slips the .9mm pistol out of its holster and places it on the table in front of him. Ryan picks it up and checks the magazine before she slips the safety on and puts the gun behind the cushion of her seat, then sits down again. "Thank you. If you expected me, then you know why I'm here, Victor."

"You want to know what I was doing at Fairwater." He shakes his head with a self-deprecating smile. "That was a mistake; I knew it before it even happened. You always were sharp. But who knew that you'd..." Glancing sideways at Claire, he lays his hands on her arm lightly. "Are you all right, Doctor Walsch?"

"I'm fine, thank you, Admiral Banks."

"I haven't done anything to her. Yet." Ryan's voice is sarcastic. "Talk, Victor; I don't have the rest of the year."

He puts his hands on the table as if to push away from it and then pauses to look at Ryan. "Would you mind if I get myself a whiskey?"

"No." She waves him up. "If that's what you need. But no funny business."

He smiles grimly. "They warned me that you might stop by, Ryan, and they're all on alert for one call from me. If I wanted funny business, I could have set the entire US Navy and Marine Corps on you the moment I saw the car in my driveway."

"And why didn't you?"

"Because I'm a fucking bastard and this what I deserve." He turns to Claire. "Please excuse my language, Doctor. Would you like a drink?"

She glances at Ryan, as if for permission, and the Marine shrugs.

"If you want one, then go ahead. It won't make a difference tonight."

When Claire nods, the gray-haired man turns to Ryan and then shakes his head. "No, of course not for you."

"No."

She watches as he moves into the sitting room and slides out a tray at the bottom of the wall unit, taking two glasses and a bottle of scotch which he places on the dining room table. When he returns from the kitchen, he has a tray of ice cubes, which he neatly cracks into the glasses before he pours a stiff tot into each and passes one glass to Claire.

"*Salut.*" He clinks his glass against hers and takes a healthy sip, before he rests his hand on the edge of the table and looks over at Ryan. "What do you remember about the week before you went into Kosovo? The briefings and medicals and preparations."

She sits forward, her dark eyebrows drawn together in confusion. "What? I remember all of it. What are you asking, Victor?"

"Is there anything unusual that you recall? About the medicals, specifically."

Now she sits on the edge of the seat, her hands splayed tensely against her knees. "Where is this going?"

"Think back, Ryan. *Think.*"

With her eyes unwaveringly on his, she ponders for a moment before she shakes her head. "No. Nothing out of the ordinary..." Yet even as she denies it, a memory is surfacing. Her face impassive, she scrutinizes him. "The seizure during the medical exam."

He slowly rolls the ice around in the glass. "Did they tell you that?"

Ryan stands up uneasily. "I lost consciousness and woke up four days later with a massive headache and a couple of stitches. Not a hell of a story."

"What did the doc say it was?"

He is not looking at her, but is studying the blocks of ice in his drink. Claire's eyes are fixed on the colonel, her expression absorbed as she sips at the scotch.

"Anaphylactic shock. A sudden reaction to the new medication. I seized and hit my head." She folds her arms antagonistically. "Why don't you just say what you have to say, Victor? Don't make me ask."

With a sigh, he puts his glass down on the table and then meets her eyes. "A faction of the Department of Defense has been working on some sort of secret project for the last eleven or twelve years. I don't know exactly what it entails..."

Catching her dark look, he shrugs quickly. "Honestly, I'm not privy to that information; I can't tell you more than I know. From what I've gathered, I think it's some sort of nerve gas that they're engineering to create super-Marines. I can't even tell you precisely what it is that it's supposed to do. As far as I know, it is supposed to alter brain chemistry to achieve a particular effect." He lifts the glass to his mouth and this time drains it before he looks back at Ryan. "I'm sorry. I want to tell you more about it, but I just don't know anything. The security clearance on this thing is extreme. Access is restricted to only the highest levels."

"Hmm." She approaches him and stands so close to him that he has to look up at her. "How is it that you even know about this project, but you don't know details? Surely if you're important enough to know about it *at all,* you wouldn't be in the dark. And if you're not important enough to be told anything, why do you know of its existence in the first place?" She shakes her head. "I don't know where your story is going, Victor, but already I don't like it. Persuade me that you're telling the truth. And just so you know, I'm really crabby right now, so I'd advise you to be very, *very* persuasive."

Moving slowly, so as not to agitate Ryan, he pours himself another drink, this time filling half the glass before shifting the bottle towards Claire, who is still sipping at hers. "Just before we went to Kosovo – I was a Lieutenant Commander, then – I was approached by Lieutenant Colonel Mike Collins on behalf of Colonel George Turner. They were working on this project – they called it DEX, or DAX, something like that – and they needed a test subject in the field."

Ryan interrupts him testily. "They... what? Wanted to inject you with something?"

He gestures at her to calm down. "Wait. They didn't tell me what they would have to do, Ryan; it was too sensitive an issue. All they said was that they needed a subject to test their project on.

According to them, it would help me in the field in some way which they weren't prepared to discuss without my agreeing to the test and signing an indemnity form." He sips at the drink. "I did consider it for a moment. The chance to make history only comes along once in a lifetime, and back then I was still arrogant. But when I asked about side-effects, they were a little vague. Mentioned that it would be interfering with natural brain functions and that it hadn't been completely tested yet, but no specifics."

"What then?"

"Well," he smiles slightly, "history was tempting, but Ingrid was more so. I couldn't choose something like that, knowing that I had no idea what would happen, with her raising Clancy alone at home and none the wiser. I turned them down."

Ryan is motionless. "Out with it. Connect the dots for me, Banks."

He sighs. It is the sigh of a man who is about to do something he truly doesn't want to. "Before I say anything else, I want you to know that they made me sign a gag order, Ryan. I had no choice there." He drains his glass, then sits back squarely and fixes his gaze on Ryan. "After they'd made me sign, they asked who I thought would be the best candidate for something like that. I...I told them it was you." Claire inhales sharply, but Ryan is motionless. "I told them you would be the best option, because you were so dedicated, and such a damned good Marine. I mean, I was just an ordinary paper pusher, but you, you were special." He taps the table with one finger. "But I also told them that you almost certainly wouldn't be interested, that you wouldn't like the idea of being out of control like that."

"What happened then, Victor?" Ryan's hoarse voice is muted.

He shakes his head. "I don't know exactly what happened then, Ryan–"

"There's a lot of not knowing going around."

"Look," his gray eyes are filled with sadness, "I'm sorry. I really want to tell you everything, but there are parts I truly don't know. All I know is that before Kosovo, suddenly you're gone for two weeks. They feed me a story about a seizure of some sort – in a Marine who's in top physical shape – and after you come out of God knows where, two weeks later you disappear again. They said it was because of the..." he glances at Claire, "torture...but something wasn't right. I knew that. For how many months you're in solitary confinement, and then they put you right back into Afghanistan. And then you sign yourself into Fairwater, saying that you're hearing voices, and in '03 they offer me a cushy desk job and a raise, reminding me with a nudge-nudge wink-wink of the agreement I signed–"

"They fucked with my brain and you didn't think to **tell me**?"

Ryan is as livid as he has ever seen her. From the corner of his eye, he notices Claire flinching.

"I couldn't! You *know* what it means to sign something like that, Ryan! I break that agreement and, depending on the importance of the issue, I either find all my bones broken or I come home to find Ingrid raped and killed and the house burnt to a crisp." He is begging for mercy, and he knows it. "Don't you think it killed me to know that what was wrong with you had probably been done to you by your own people? That I had inadvertently been the one to put you in that position? Damn it, Ryan, I thought they'd get your permission first! Until Fairwater, I thought that you *knew*!"

"How sure are you all of it wasn't just coincidence?" It is the first time Claire speaks, wide-eyed but measured, and they are both startled by the interruption.

Victor pours himself another glass of scotch, this time not stopping until he reaches the top. He takes a long drink before he speaks; his voice is almost as hoarse as Ryan's.

"If it were, Doctor Walsch, they wouldn't have been sedating Ryan to check whatever levels they're keeping an eye on every few weeks. If it were just coincidence, they wouldn't have been flying military specialists in to a private hospital instead of using the residents. If it were," he takes another sip, "they wouldn't have gotten me in to make it look like the Marine Corps is simply taking care of their own. Nobly taking responsibility where they really have none, so to speak. She's not officially in the Marine Corps anymore, Doctor. She's a liability, and they've acknowledged that by sending her to a monitored private hospital. Why do you think the military's still sniffing around? Why do you think they were keeping her there? They've done something, Doctor Walsch, and they're still watching, waiting to see what hatches."

In a fury, Ryan kicks at one of the dining room chairs, splintering its back and collapsing it beneath her force. Her face is white, and her eyes are on fire. "Christ! They did that to me? *You* did that to me?!" Helpless with rage, she rips the cap from her head and throws it across the room. "I thought it was me... and all the time... *Fuck!*"

"Ryan..." Claire's voice is conciliatory as she stands up, but when the Marine turns those smoldering eyes on her, she recoils.

"Sit down, Walsch." It is a command, given by a dangerous woman.

Frowning, Claire squares her shoulders. "Don't give me orders."

"*Sit down!*"

This time she obeys, afraid of what the Marine will do if she doesn't. It is clear that Ryan is struggling for control.

Bunching her fists at her sides, the lean woman clenches and unclenches her jaw as she glares at Victor. "Don't you understand what this means? If it were just my own mind, I could take something for it. The fog of medication could let me pretend that it doesn't exist. Now I know it's something far uglier, and I probably don't even know the worst of it! And there's nothing I can do about it!" She snatches his glass and hurls it against the wall, where it shatters. The blonde cringes back in her seat but Victor sits there impassively, his face resigned as he looks at Ryan. Her mouth twists in rage as she fixes her stare on Victor. "Who knows more about this thing? Turner?"

"Yes, Turner, but..." He stops her as she moves for the gun. "You'll never make it that far, Ryan. Wait. One of the specialists who comes in regularly, Mark Grossman, I'll get you his number and address. He's in Helena. He'll talk to you, I'm sure. Wait, will you?" As she throws herself on the seat, her limbs trembling, he gets up. When her gaze falls on him, he lifts his hands. "No funny business, Ryan. I'm getting his address from the study."

Ryan glares at him hotly. "If I find out you know more than you let on... I'll come back for you, Victor. I promise you that."

"I know." He nods silently and walks into the hallway, his shoulders sagging as she slips the gun into her pocket and follows him into the study. Unlocking a drawer, he pulls out a plain brown folder and begins to rifle through it. When the phone suddenly starts to ring, he casts a quick glance at it but Ryan prods him roughly in the back.

"Ignore it."

Following her command, he shuffles through the documents and retrieves a sheet of paper with a series of addresses. Passing it over, he points at the correct entry, just as the ringing phone gives up and the answering machine kicks in.

"You have reached the home of Victor Banks. I am not currently in, but please leave a concise message and your contact details, and I will get back to you as soon as possible."... beep...

"Vic, are you there? Pick up, it's Turner..."

Victor's eyes widen and he turns to speak to Ryan, but she lifts one hand grimly to keep him quiet as she listens to the rest of it.

"Okay, obviously you're not home yet, but I had to share some absolutely exhilarating news with you – that last analysis came back 20% improved."

Ryan's face is pale as she glares at Victor.

"Brilliant, don't you think? Pity the margin wasn't this good with Ryan, but then, as you said, you have to break an egg or two... I think the machine's going to cut me off. Give me a call when you get in. You have my number."

Beep

Victor Banks can feel his muscles begin to tremble as Ryan's ominous green eyes remain focused on him. "I didn't..." he begins, but the words die in his throat as she steps closer, her face almost against his.

"You fucking bastard. You fucking *coward*! You sold me out!"

"No, it wasn't like that..." He tries to step away, but the desk is against his back. "It's not what you think–"

Wrapping her hands in his collar, she pulls him closer, hissing in his ear, "Tell me they set you up, Victor."

"They *did*!" He pulls back, his eyes pleading.

Her hands yank him forward again. "Tell me I'm a friend and you would never sell me out, Victor."

"I *wouldn't*!" His voice is breathless. "I wouldn't!"

She drags him forward, her strength startling, and he stumbles over his own feet, barely held up by his quivering legs. She pushes him out ahead of her and sharply wraps an arm around his throat, pressing her forearm to his windpipe. The other hand grasps his wrist and wrenches it upwards behind his back.

Claire is in the hallway, torn between escaping out of the front door and going to Victor's assistance. She has heard most of the discussion and knows that the Marine is likely to now be completely out of control. But when Ryan appears with him locked in her grip, Claire's shoulders slump.

"Get in the bedroom."

The barked order leaves no room for objection and the doctor complies, her wide eyes locked on Victor's panicked gray ones as the door closes between them and Ryan turns the key, locking Claire inside. Claire glances around helplessly at the posters of sportsmen, the dressing table in the corner, the too-small window, before she sinks down onto the bed, holding her breath as she listens to the sounds from the room next door. Ryan's voice is strident, roaring over Victor's more muffled and beseeching tone, and when suddenly there is a loud thump, Claire closes her eyes and a shocked gasp escapes her mouth. To her relief, Victor's voice starts again, still muffled but louder, and then his pitch rises and rises until a shot rings out and silence suddenly replaces sound.

Claire jerks and a sob escapes her lips. Covering her mouth with both hands, she stares at the closet door in horror, as if she can see through it to what's happening behind it. There is shuffling in the other room and then another thump, and Claire is still staring at the closet when the bedroom door opens unexpectedly and she shrinks back against the wall behind her.

The Marine gazes in, her face set and ashen, a smear of copper beneath her mouth. "Go to sleep." She slams the door closed behind her and turns the key again, leaving Claire curled up and sobbing on the bed until exhaustion and helplessness send her into a dreamless sleep.

When Claire wakes up, for a moment she is confused, her eyes taking in the unfamiliar stars stuck on the unfamiliar ceiling above her. She smiles at the sweetness of it until realization seeps in and her eyes fill with tears. She takes several ragged breaths and rolls into an upright, sitting position, still dazed when the door opens and Ryan enters. Judging by the fresh scent which wafts in with her, the Marine has apparently showered or bathed. Dressed in a pair of camouflage pants – which fit much better than the jeans – and a clean black t-shirt, she looks almost presentable, discounting her unnaturally pale skin and the intense green eyes that burn from her face with something akin to insanity. When she speaks, her voice, hoarser than usual from the shouting the previous evening, is without inflection.

"Here." She holds out a steaming cup of coffee, strong and sweet-smelling, and waits until the doctor takes it with trembling fingers before she steps back. "Do you want to take a shower?" When Claire nods, Ryan walks out into the hallway and waits.

Sipping at her jittering cup, the blonde gets up and walks out into the hall, trying not to look at Ryan's face as they walk to the bathroom. There is a baby blue terrycloth towel folded on the lid of the toilet. Inclining her head towards it, the Marine then closes the door behind her, leaving a shaken Claire to step under the warm, soothing water.

When she is finished and opens the door, the towel wrapped securely around her body, Ryan is waiting, leaning against the wall. Taking her hostage back into the bedroom, Ryan points at the jeans, long-sleeved shirt, and light jacket lying on the bed, and leaves the room to let Claire get dressed. When she returns, she has a small black bag clenched in her hand.

"Come on."

Walking towards the kitchen, they pass Victor's bedroom. Claire tries to glance in, but the door is closed. Ryan's hand on her arm yanks her into the kitchen, and as the Marine passes her a small plate with two pieces of toast with cheese, she glares at the tall woman. "Did you *have* to?" It is a disgusted hiss.

Raising her eyebrows, Ryan stares at her coolly. "Did I have to *what*?"

"You *know*! Did you have to kill him?"

"He's a *bastard*. He betrayed me." The condemnation is vehement.

"And it changes things to kill him?" The doctor shakes her head. "That's the only solution you ever seem to have!"

"You definitely won't understand." With a bitter scowl, Ryan presses the remaining piece of toast into Claire's hand and then puts the plate in the sink. "You're not a monster like me. Courtesy of *him*." Grasping Claire's wrist, she propels her out of the house and towards the SUV.

It is silent in the vehicle as Ryan turns right and then right again, crossing the river and taking them out of Fort Benton. Claire stares at the reflection of the early morning light off the water, and then at the landscape passing them by. When she finally turns her head to look at Ryan, her eyes are brimming with tears.

"You knew him. You knew his daughter. Now you're going to be the reason she wakes up today without a father?"

The Marine's jaw works convulsively. "She'll be fine."

"You think?" Claire raises her eyebrows. "Why, Ryan? Because good troops never cry? Because for you, life just goes on?" She laughs sharply and shakes her head.

"Because Victor's not dead."

There is a second of silence before the words sink in. "What? You shot him! I heard you!"

Ryan shakes her head abruptly. "You heard a shot. When they find him he'll have been unconscious for a few hours and he'll be sporting a good selection of bruises, but he'll be alive."

"But why?"

"I think he *was* set up. He knows more than he's telling but less than they're implying." Her eyebrows draw together. "I may be messed up, confused, my brain fried – but he was a friend and I couldn't kill him."

With a sigh somewhere between hysteria and relief, Claire puts her face in her hands. "Why didn't you tell me earlier? Christ, Ryan..."

"I couldn't tell you earlier because the house is bugged." Ryan adjusts the rearview mirror slightly. "Someone was listening."

"... I think the machine's going to cut me off. Give me a call when you get in. You have my number."

Colonel George Turner puts down the phone quietly and smiles to himself as he picks up the handset and dials again. The man who answers on the other end has a deep, smooth voice.

"Yes?"

"Mahoney, this is Turner. The call has been made."

"Good." There is satisfaction in the voice. *"We're listening."*
"Shouldn't be long." Turner rings off without amenities.

Mahoney – or Sierra, as he identifies himself for this mission – sits in front of the surveillance equipment for about twenty minutes before the sound of a shot rings out in his earphones. With a grim smile, he picks up the satellite phone and dials.

"Turner."

"It's done. She's dealt with Banks."

"Good." There is a shuffling of papers on Turner's end. *"Tomorrow, she'll find Grossman. Get some rest."*

"We want to be waiting."

"If you're dull, you're useless to me, Mahoney. Rest. We know where she's going."

"Understood." Sierra disengages and puts down the phone.

Apart from the muted music that drifts from the radio, it is quiet in the Trailblazer, both women's thoughts far away. They have been driving for almost forty minutes before Claire speaks for the first time.

"Banks said some shocking things last night. Do you want to discuss it?"

"Typical therapist. I hear the worst news of my life, and you want to chat." Though her words are terse, her tone borders on humorous.

Ignoring the obvious evasion, Claire persists. "I'd like to know how you're taking it, Ryan."

"As it comes, Doctor. In my stride. I don't have that many options." She cocks her head. "So, I'm some sort of sci-fi monster now. At least I know it's not just **me**."

"That's an admirable point of view." Claire shakes her head. "I'm not sure I'd be able to do the same if I were in your position."

"I'm not being noble. There's just not much else I can do."

In Belt, Ryan stops at a gas station and fills up the SUV, pulling some notes from a brown leather wallet she retrieves from the black bag. Ryan sees from the corner of her eye that Claire is, for some reason, smiling at her. "What?"

"You stole his wallet?"

"He's alive. That's enough."

"I don't think your problem is the voice in your head, Ryan. I think you're a kleptomaniac."

The Marine almost smiles, and when she speaks, her voice is theatrically grave. "You've caught me out, Doctor Walsch. You're not actually a hostage; I just took you because I thought you looked so damned good." Shaking her head at herself, she grimaces. "Sorry. That came out wrong."

"Hey, a compliment's always nice, even if it's just a joke." Brushing off Ryan's awkwardness, she shrugs. "It's okay."

"You do look good. I wasn't kidding about that." Embarrassed, Ryan clears her throat. "Hey, Doc, want to ask me a personal and intrusive question? Right now? How about it?"

Surprised, Claire can't help chuckling a little. "The only time you ever *offered* that. You must be really mortified." Sitting forward, she turns down the radio. "Ryan? You're not as bad a person as you think you are."

Her jaw muscles clenching, Ryan glances out her window. "I believe you. Millions wouldn't—"

"Hey." Tapping her wrist, Claire waits until the Marine looks at her. "It's not your fault. What happened, it happened *to* you. You're dealing with it a lot better than most people would. It's just a pity about the stealing."

Shaking her head, Ryan raises an eyebrow. "Where's that invasive question I'm waiting for? Can we move on to that now?"

"Hmm." The doctor purses her lips, a ghost of a smile playing around them. "All right. Okay. Next topic. *Why* exactly do you think the voice is God?"

"Oh man." Rolling her eyes, Ryan exhales a loud breath. "You play rough."

"You told me I could. Well?" Claire folds her arms expectantly.

"All right. It told me so." She shrugs. "I may not fully *believe* it when I say it, but most of the times it's a hell of a lot easier to think that I'm being contacted by a divinity than that my own psyche's telling me that it wants to be God. Okay?"

"Okay." Claire nods. "So it basically put up its hand and said, '*Hi, I'm God*'."

"Something like that."

"Oh."

"Yeah. Oh. So how much crazier am I now?" Ryan smirks to herself before she glances at Claire, summarily serious again. "It's my turn to ask something."

"You didn't mention the small print on your offer." The blonde turns her head and stares out of the window, sighing when a warm hand gently touches her knee.

"Claire. Come on. Tell me. In a few days, you'll walk away and never see me again. It's good to share. You know that."

After a moment of hesitation Claire starts to speak, her voice measured, as if she's had to tell the story more than once. "It was four years ago. I was working late at the office, and when I got outside, one of my colleagues was just coming through the front gate. He…"

She stops, and Ryan waits quietly for her to compose herself.

"Sorry. I stopped to chat and he asked me to come into his consultation room to check some information for him. It wasn't unusual for me to help out with cases, so I didn't think anything of it. When he backed me up against his desk and tried to kiss me I pushed him away. So he raped me. There was a pen lying on the desk – I remember how it rolled a little every time he…"

Claire stops abruptly to clear her throat.

"Afterwards he told me he needed a lift home, and he got in my car. I had to drive him home, and he kept his hand on my leg the whole way. In a bizarre way that was the worst part – I was shaking and petrified and torn, and he was so calm and relaxed. It was surreal. He told me he'd had a lovely time as he got out of the car to go back to his wife and three children." She clears her throat roughly again. "After that... It's irrational, but I don't like being behind a steering wheel."

"It's not irrational. But you know that. What happened afterwards?"

Claire looks out of the window again. "Nothing."

"No case against him?"

"No. He was a senior partner at the clinic; I'd just started out." She smiles grimly. "If you think rape was a violation, you can imagine what he would have done to me professionally. I'm a coward."

"Hey." Ryan nudges their shoulders together. "You're not, not at all. It probably seemed like he would be violating you all over again if you stood up to him."

"Huh." Claire's blue eyes take in the Marine's earnest expression. "Did you read my case notes?"

Ryan's smile comes easily. "Speaking of which, did you ever see anybody about it?"

"No. I didn't deal with it well."

"And now?"

The question lies between them for a while before Claire responds. "He left two years ago – rumors about sexual harassment – and I'm still there. I'm fine. Surviving."

"That's not always good enough."

Claire shrugs. "I don't drive. I'm not good with...intimacy. I don't deal well with physical threats. But I get up every morning and I feel stronger every day, and I try to make a difference. That seems good enough to me."

"You shouldn't have to settle for good enough." Ryan hooks a thumb at the back seat. "Please pass me the bag?"

Glad to be done with the exchange, Claire reaches for the bag and sets it on Ryan's lap, watching as the woman scrabbles around in it with one hand and pulls out two energy bars, one of which she passes over. They're tasty, apple and cinnamon, and the two women eat in silent companionship before Ryan glances around her.

"There any water left?"

"Sure." Claire fishes the half-empty bottle out from her feet and frowns as Ryan runs her hand around the space next to her seat. "What are you looking for?"

"Aspirin. Do you know what I did with the bottle?"

Opening the cubbyhole, Claire takes out the small white bottle and pops off the lid. "How many?"

"Three."

She shakes three into her hand and passes them to Ryan, watching the Marine's pale face as she slips them into her mouth and washes them down with tepid water.

"What's wrong?"

"Bit of a headache."

"For three aspirin it must be more than just a bit, Ryan."

Ryan glances towards her. "Weren't we talking about you?"

"Not anymore. Have you eaten this morning?"

"An energy bar." Her tone makes it clear that she expects the line of conversation to end.

Claire frowns and ignores the signals. "Ryan, do you have a...dependency problem?"

A low chuckle fills the car. "Not only a kleptomaniac, now I'm an addict, too?"

"Seriously, if there's a problem you can tell me."

The chuckle abruptly gives way to a sigh as Ryan looks over at Claire. "No. I am not an addict." At the upraised eyebrows, she shakes her head in exasperation. "Seriously. I've been having more headaches lately. I'm not sure if it's the meds, or what."

"Did you have them when you were at Fairwater?"

"A few times. But the instances were spread out over a period of time. Now it's a constant bombardment."

"You don't think," Claire begins tentatively, "that it has to do with not eating or sleeping properly? Exhaustion does take its toll."

"No. I've been tired and hungry before."

"Okay."

While Claire is thinking, Ryan glances over at her once, and then again. "Doctor, did you just accuse me of something so that I would have to discuss it to defend myself? And in the process deflect a conversation we were having about you?"

"Maybe." The doctor shrugs her shoulders. "I'm full of surprises."

"Wow. You're sneaky."

"Some would call it that. Some would call me cunningly gifted." Abandoning the light tone, she cocks her head. "You must be exhausted."

"I'm fine."

"Did you ever take a bullet?"

At the incongruous question, Ryan glances over, her green eyes puzzled. "What? Where did that come from?"

Claire shrugs. "I'm interested."

"That's for sure." Ryan shakes her head and taps her fingers against the steering wheel. "Okay. Well, Bosnia in '93, I got a bullet in my chest. I was doing an Intelligence recon, and we got caught in the wrong place at the wrong time." She reaches up with her left hand and rubs reflexively at the concave area just under her collarbone. "Then there was Somalia, late '95. A Somali put one right in my thigh. That was a bad one – hit an artery. If the medevac helicopter hadn't arrived when it did..." Her lips curve just a little. "Military service hasn't been kind to me. It must say something about me that I can't stay away."

"In those situations, it must have helped that your pain threshold is so high."

Ryan considers her words for a moment. "No, not really. Nobody in my squad would have fussed over most things, but a bullet hurts, whichever way you look at it. It's not like in the movies where you take one in the leg and drag yourself forward, still shooting baddies. Falling down and bleeding to death would probably be a much less heroic scene, but it's a lot more accurate. Even just getting clipped hurts like shit. Besides, being in the military doesn't mean you can simply keep going until you die. We're more focused and better prepared for pain, but we still feel it like anybody else."

"Right." Claire nods. "So, right now, for instance, not having slept for a long time and not having eaten for a while, and I think being slightly sick, you're feeling like a normal person would under those circumstances? Which would be not very fine at all."

The dark eyebrows lift in a sharp arch and Ryan purses her lips as she glares over at the blonde. "Sneaky. And twice in one day."

"Gifted." Claire shrugs. "All I'm trying to point out is that you *are* a 'normal person', Ryan. You can admit it when you hurt. Talking about things doesn't do any damage."

"It doesn't do any good, either, Walsch. If I tell you I'm tired, what does that change? I'll still be tired afterwards."

"It'll change *my* awareness of the fact. And it might allow me to help you somehow."

"Like what?"

"Like offer to drive, if I could. Theoretically."

"But you won't, so it's a moot point." Ryan is almost gloating. "Why would you want to help me, Claire? You're a hostage."

"I know. I remember." The blue eyes reflect a wry humor. "I'd help you because you're not as bad a person as you think you are."

"We've had this conversation, and I'm not going–"

Even before her words come to an abrupt halt, Claire can tell by the way her eyes glass over and her pupils dilate that something is very wrong. "Pull over! Pull over, Ryan!"

The blonde grabs the steering wheel and turns it in the unresponsive hands. They skid off the road and come to a screeching stop as Ryan slams her foot on the brake. The suddenness and force of the stop throw them both forward against their seatbelts, and Claire is gasping for breath and slightly dazed as she turns her head to look at Ryan.

The Marine's eyes are tightly closed and she's arched in her seat, her head thrown back. When a muffled growl escapes from between her clenched teeth, Claire fumbles for the seatbelt and undoes Ryan's. She waits for her to get out of the vehicle, but the woman's body is stretched tautly and her muscles strain against her shirt as she tenses against the backrest of the seat.

Gritting her own teeth, the blonde leans across to reach for the door handle, but Ryan's hand wraps around her wrist, shaking wildly. Staring down at it with vacant eyes for a moment, Ryan finally pushes Claire away and stumbles out of the SUV, falling to her knees on the ground. Claire considers getting out and running; she considers – briefly – the option of getting behind the wheel and driving off; she even considers hitting Ryan with something, but as she methodically sorts through the options, she already knows that at this moment she's in too deep to do any of those things. Instead she climbs over the handbrake and into the driver's seat before she slips out of the vehicle and cautiously approaches the crumpled figure.

"Ryan?"

At the sound of her name, the woman heaves a ragged sigh and struggles to her feet, almost collapsing again as she rises, and then obstinately pushes herself up off the ground. When she stands, she is weaving, her jaw tightly clenched as she walks around the Trailblazer. Claire follows her, watching her faltering movements with alarm.

"Ryan?"

Ryan pauses a few feet from the car, and Claire leans against the passenger door, her legs trembling, as fierce green eyes fix on her. When Ryan moves forward the action is not nearly as smooth as usual, but she is still fast, and when her left hand shoots up and wraps around Claire's throat, the doctor lets out a yelp and wraps both hands around Ryan's wrist.

"Ryan. Please. Don't."

The grip is ferocious, unrelenting. It is not this that scares Claire, however, but the blazing violence in the stark face. For a moment Ryan's mouth tightens, and then, unexpectedly, she yanks her hand away, pulling the doctor away from the car in the process.

"Move!"

The command is a roar and Claire darts backwards, her hands now rubbing at her own throat protectively. She is not looking back when the sharp sound of imploding glass blasts behind her, and when she turns, it is to see Ryan laying into the passenger seat window with her right fist, breaking every last bit of glass before she switches to her left hand and destroys the backseat window. When both windows are completely shattered, not a shard remaining in the frame, she moves on to the door, beating her fists against it until her movements begin to slow. It looks garish – the gray of the SUV decorated with smears and spatters of blood. Finally exhausted, she slumps forward against the Trailblazer. Claire wants to go to her, place a hand on her back, but the angle of her shoulders is sharp with tension, and so the doctor stays back and remains quiet.

With an almost inaudible sigh, Ryan presses herself away from the car and reaches inside to unlock the passenger door, then opens it from the outside. Claire is not sure what Ryan intends to do until she sees the Marine beginning to scoop the broken glass off the passenger seat with her bloody hands. Rushing forward, she lays a hand on Ryan's shoulder and pulls her back.

"Ryan, no. Stop."

The lean shoulder shrugs her hand off, but the sweeping motions cease and Ryan turns around. "What?" Her voice is thick.

"You're hurting yourself. Stop."

"You can't sit in the seat like this. Glass."

She reaches forward again and Claire pulls her away. "Wait." Slipping her jacket off, Claire wads it up into a ball and begins to brush the glass and blood from the leather seat, only stopping when there are no further shards of glass visible.

"See? That's fine." When she glances down at Ryan's injured hands, the blood is running freely down her fingers to drip on the ground. With a sympathetic wince, Claire remembers the first-aid kit and its dearth of bandages. She is about to speak when Ryan addresses her dazedly.

"Did I hurt you, Claire?"

"No, you didn't. I'm okay." Ryan raises her hands to Claire's face and Claire flinches, realizing too late how Ryan will interpret the action. When her hands drop, Claire steps closer and carefully touches the blood spattered arm. "Ryan?"

"It's okay."

"Yes, it is, actually. I'm not scared, Ryan, it's just...look at your hands. I don't want to get covered in blood."

Lifting her hands, Ryan studies them without comment. Claire almost chokes. At this level she can properly see the damage: the white of the bone showing through the flesh over the swollen knuckles in several places, the deep cuts, and the blood now trickling down Ryan's arms.

"Oh God. Ryan..."

"Don't faint, Claire. I can't catch you."

"No." Taking a deep breath, she puts a hand on Ryan's waist and gently pushes her towards the passenger seat. "Please, sit down."

The seat is relatively clean and Ryan obediently perches on the edge. Gingerly taking the still bandaged wrists in her hands, Claire grimly examines the battered hands, alarmed by the rate at which the Marine seems to be losing blood. "This is a bit of a mess, Ryan.

You still have glass in your hands, you've probably removed anything in the kit I could use for getting it out, and we used up all of the bandages yesterday. Any bright ideas?"

"Check at the foot of the back seat. I took Victor's kit this morning."

Exhaling in relief, Claire shakes her head at Ryan. "Sheer luck is on your side."

"I think what you mean is that I'm gifted."

With a raised eyebrow, Claire opens the back door, careful not to cut herself on the glass, and pulls out the bigger first-aid kit, shaking it to disperse the small pieces of glass before she zips it open. She removes a pair of clumsy tweezers from the bottom and then discards the kit on the floor of the passenger side. She reaches for the full bottle of mineral water sitting in the bin between the seats. Claire twists off the cap, takes Ryan's left wrist, and pulls it closer, then pours water over it to wash away some of the blood, wishing that she hadn't when she can clearly see most of the damage. It is a messy situation, prying small shards from the lacerated flesh while the blood keeps welling up and obscuring her vision. When she is more or less finished with the left hand, she takes out a small yellow bottle of antiseptic and looks up at Ryan.

"This is definitely going to hurt."

"Go ahead."

The Marine closes her eyes and Claire pours the liquid over the hand. When she looks up again, Ryan is motionless but her face is waxy. Taking out some gauze, Claire packs it on the wounds as best she can, and then wraps it tightly with bandage.

"This isn't going to work for very long. You need stitches."

Ryan meets her gaze and nods mutely. Biting her lip, Claire begins to clean up the right hand, tears falling as she surveys the injuries. She wipes them away angrily, but not before one or two fall onto Ryan's hand. She is hoping that the Marine won't notice the difference what with the warm blood coating her skin, when Ryan speaks.

"Are you crying, Claire?"

"A bit." She busies herself cleaning the lacerated hand.

"A bit like my 'bit of a headache'?"

"No, a *real* bit. Though that would have served you right." Claire sniffles and almost smiles when she hears the soft chuckle. "So. Are you feeling *a bit* sore right now?"

"No." The blonde is about to object when Ryan says, "It hurts like shit."

Smiling to herself at the admission, Claire looks up. "You're actually saying it hurts? Good."

"Sadist."

"No, I didn't mean... Oh, you know exactly what I meant. Stop being a nuisance." She lifts the antiseptic. "I'm sorry. It's that time."

With a nod, Ryan closes her eyes again and Claire pours the stinging liquid over the open wounds. She looks up and catches Ryan unawares for a moment. The woman has tilted her head back against the headrest and her face is furrowed and filled with grief. Biting her lip, Claire shifts her eyes back to the hand and finishes cleaning and wrapping it. When she straightens, Ryan has not shifted her head or opened her eyes.

"Ryan?"

"Yes?" The Marine opens her green eyes languidly. "Are we ready to go?" Lifting her head, she sits up, and it doesn't escape Claire's notice that she isn't very steady.
"I don't think it's a good idea for you to be driving."

"I don't think it's a good idea for me to be walking, either." Ryan lifts a heavily bandaged hand to her face and wipes at her eyes hazily, then shifts her hand away to curl her stiff fingers. When her green eyes meet Claire's, she is serious. "Are you sure I didn't hurt you?"

"No. You haven't. You've never hurt me."

"I have. I hurt your arm at the gas station in Choteau."

"It's a bruise. It goes away." Claire shrugs. "And besides, if you take my hand instead of my arm, it won't happen again."

"I wanted to get to know you first, not just kidnap you and start holding hands. I'm not that kind of girl." There is a grin on Ryan's face, one with a wicked undertone that looks good on her.

"But you take my bra without a problem. So, what kind of a girl are you, exactly?" Claire's tone holds a definite challenge.

Ryan hesitates for a moment and the grin disappears along with the mischievous mood. "You should know. I've told you everything about me."
"No, you haven't."

"Come on, Walsch." Ryan leans her head back tiredly. "You've had me talking since we got into the SUV."

"You've given me all of the facts, that's for sure." Leaning against the vehicle, Claire crosses her arms. "It's what you're good at. I can tell. You mention all of the essentials and leave out the personal stuff, and nobody notices because you're telling them exactly what they want to hear."

"I answered the questions you asked me." Shaking her head, Ryan moves to get out of the passenger seat. "In any case, we need to get going." She frowns in surprise when the blonde firmly pushes her back into the seat.

"No. I was serious. You can't drive like this, Ryan. You're tired, you're losing blood, and God knows what's hammering in that head of yours." She inclines her head and rolls her eyes at the unintentional pun. "Sorry. You know what I mean."

"I was serious too, Walsch. I'm certainly not going to get very far walking right now."

"I'm going to drive."
Surprised out of her torpor, Ryan sits up. "Excuse me?"

"I can drive. I can. I just need … some time." She walks around the SUV and gets into the driver's seat, noticing that Ryan slips off the child lock mechanism before closing her door. When Ryan looks over at her, the green eyes are softer than she's seen them before.

"I don't want you to do this, Claire. If I just rest a little, I'll be fine."

"Hey, I need to do this some time, right?" Though she is trying very hard to keep her tone light, her voice trembles. Grasping the steering wheel tightly, she grits her teeth. Gauze-wrapped fingers cover hers and rub gently.

"Ease up on the grip, Chuck Norris. You're going to break something."

"Okay. Okay." She wills her hands to release some of the pressure.

There's a moment of silence, and then Ryan leans forward to meet her eyes. "You're not breathing, Claire. Take a breath."

When she does, it stutters in her throat. She begins to cry, soft sobs at first and then louder, until tears are streaming down her face and her chest is heaving. She can feel Ryan's fingers in her hair, caressing her head, and as she gasps for air through her suffocating fear she can feel the gaze fixed on her. Leaning forward, she hides her face against her arms on the steering wheel and cries like she hasn't in a long time. When finally her tears diminish and a tired calmness seeps into her, she wipes her face with both hands and sits upright with an awkward laugh.

"I'm sorry."

"What for?" Ryan holds out her heavily bandaged hand. "Want to blow your nose?"

With a snorted laugh, Claire shakes her head. "No. But thanks for being so thoughtful." She looks over at Ryan to find inscrutable green eyes fixed on the horizon.

"So." Ryan's voice is level and light. "Are we going to do this?"

"Yes. Yes, we are." With a careful glance over her shoulder, and hands trembling, Claire steers the car back onto the road, gratified when she feels a hand lightly pat her knee in congratulations.

When Claire sneaks a look at Ryan, her eyes are closed, and her face is colorless and exhausted. Frowning, the blonde reaches out with her right hand and softly touches the other woman's knee.

"Ryan?"

"Hmm?"

"I know I said that you needed to sleep, but I'm a little worried about you. I don't think it'd actually be the best idea right now. Okay?"

Ryan opens her eyes sluggishly. "All right."

"Maybe we can talk a bit."

The Marine chuckles dryly. "It's an excuse. I know it is."

"Maybe. I'm sneaky that way." Claire glances sideways with a smile. "I promise I won't play rough this time."

"Pity. I kind of like that." There is a ghost of a grin around her lips. "That came out wrong. I didn't mean it like that."

"Somehow I think you do." Grinning at the surprised expression, she shrugs. "I tell you what – you can talk about anything; I'll listen." When the Marine begins to protest, she interrupts. "I need the distraction, Ryan. Please. Okay?"

Noting the tight trembling grip, Ryan nods. "Okay. Anything?"

Claire nods. "Anything."

Turning her head, Ryan stares out of the window, her eyes far away. "You said that I hide behind facts, that I tell people the basic truth and don't let them in any further. You're the same, Claire. Except you hide behind other people's truth and pain, so that you don't have to face your own. You like to listen to others because that means you don't have to say anything, and even when you do, it's not about you. You've worked so hard to keep people at arm's length, to not let anybody close enough to hurt you, that you're not used to being looked at. Or looked after. You're in such need of care that you fall apart at the first sign of it, even if it comes from somebody you should be running away from."

She glances over to see tears trailing down the blonde's cheeks, and reaches over to gently brush them away with the back of a finger. "Claire? Am I wrong?"

"No. Of course you're not." There's a touch of exasperation in her thick voice. "You seem to see right through me. I find it a little disconcerting, to be honest. What's inside isn't always pretty."

"What a pair we make." Ryan smiles slightly.

With a chuckle, Claire shakes her head. "Yeah. Next topic. And Ryan?" She looks at the Marine with sadness in her eyes. "Don't talk about me this time, okay? Something else."

"All right." Ryan turns her head to look out of the window again. "Something else." Her voice is soft. "I haven't gone one night without that little boy in his blue shirt visiting me. Not one single night. I close my eyes, and there's that smile. Sometimes he brings the grenade back for me." She stares blindly into the distance. "I can't take this anymore, Claire. I need it to stop one way or another, or it's going to kill me."

They don't speak much after Ryan's surprisingly frank statement. Claire glances over now and then to make sure that Ryan hasn't fallen asleep. The Marine is looking out the window at the passing landscape. The doctor has her panic down to a mild discomfort, and to distract herself she ponders about why she will not let Ryan go to sleep. After all, should her captor fall asleep and stay that way, she could drive into the nearest town and go right to the police station. She also ponders the things Ryan said about her. *The woman doesn't pull any punches*, she thinks wryly, *but she has insight that is more than a little daunting.*

In Neihart Claire pulls into the parking lot of a small shopping center with a pharmacy and a Mom and Pop grocery store. She reaches into the back seat and takes the wallet out of the black bag, ignoring the cold feel of metal as she extracts her hand.

"I'll be right back."

"Claire?"

She turns to face Ryan.

"Please leave the keys. If you walk away, I need to drive."

Claire tosses the keys onto the driver's seat. "Here. I'll be right back. I'm not going anywhere."

Inside the grocery store Claire stands for a moment and seriously contemplates phoning the police. She is debating herself for so long that the rotund clerk in the striped apron stops stocking cereal boxes and approaches her.

"Excuse me, miss. Are you all right?"

"Yes. Yes, fine, thank you. I'm looking for…" she casts around for an item, drawing a blank for a moment, "soda."

"That would be in the fridge at the back." Shooting an odd look at the stationery shelf where she is hovering, and then at her, he turns and goes back to stacking boxes.

Releasing a nervous chuckle, Claire gets the soda, and one or two other things, and then exits. She can feel Ryan watching her as she goes into the pharmacy, though when she comes out Ryan's eyes are closed. Getting into the SUV, Claire puts the grocery bag on the floor at Ryan's feet, and then she scrabbles in the pharmacy-branded brown paper bag.

"Let me see your hands, Ryan."

They are held out to her without protest and she unwraps the bandages, wincing as she realizes that they are already almost soaked through with blood. Taking an anti-bacterial wipe from a small packet, she uses it to clean the hands as well as possible, disheartened by the continuous seepage of fresh blood. As gently as she can, Claire pulls the edges of the larger gashes together and closes them with small butterfly Band-Aids. It doesn't seem to help much, but she at least feels as if she has tried. After covering the battered hands with new gauze pads, she wraps them tightly and tucks the edges in at the wrist.

"Don't move them too much, okay? I don't think the Band-Aids will hold."

"All right. Thanks."

She is aware that Ryan is thanking her for more than the poor attempt at first-aid, and it makes her smile. "Sure. Where are we going?"

"White Sulphur Springs."

"I thought we were headed to Helena. To Grossman."

"Yeah." Ryan looks over her shoulder. "So do they."

To pass the time, Claire chats to Ryan about everything and nothing, trying to keep her awake and alert even though the

Marine assures her more than once that she is fine. Though Claire is doing most of the talking, she does garner some interesting facts from the woman's brief replies: Ryan plays classical guitar, and she used to teach martial arts and self-defense classes at the local gym. Her own conversation touches on her work and her childhood, and though her passenger seems inattentive and dulled, she is sure that Ryan is hearing every word and paying close attention.

As they drive into White Sulphur Springs, Ryan leans forward and pulls a square of paper from her back pocket, unfolding it to read a section with a frown of concentration. At the first telephone booth, she asks Claire to pull over. When Ryan gets out, she doesn't even bother to lock the door. The doctor watches her struggle to get a coin from her pocket with her damaged hands and slip it into the slot. Ryan speaks for barely a minute before she hangs up and gets back into the car. She gives Claire directions and they pass through the downtown area before turning into a street opposite a meadow. There is a large white building on their left, and Ryan instructs Claire to pull into the parking lot, opening her door as the SUV stops and briefly reaching into the bag.

"We're going in here."

"All right."

Claire gets out and locks the door, smothering a smile when she realizes that she's locking the door on a vehicle with broken windows. She joins Ryan and they approach the building. A sign on the gabled roof reads *The White House Center*. It appears to be a long strip of offices for a number of medical specialties. Ryan passes the first and the second, and then approaches the third door. After casting a glance at the bronze plate – A. Chavez / P. D. Margolis – she enters. When Claire steps inside, Ryan is already standing at a small reception area in the empty waiting room, speaking quietly to the receptionist. Claire hears the last part of a statement by the overly made-up blonde woman behind the desk.

"...afraid we do have a policy with regards to walk-ins."

"I understand that." Ryan's voice is calm. "But I do have to see Doctor Chavez immediately. It's an emergency."

"I appreciate that, but I can't just–"

Claire is annoyed that the woman can be looking straight at Ryan's ashen face and not ease up. She steps forward and interrupts smoothly, "Excuse me, and you are?"

The receptionist blinks furiously. "Miss Rhoda van–"

"All right, Rhoda. You have made us aware of your policy." As she speaks, she reaches for Ryan's left hand and begins to unwind the gauze. "But the fact is that we do have a medical emergency." When the lacerated hand is unwrapped, Claire casually drops the bloody bandage on the counter, ignoring Rhoda's sudden recoil as she pulls Ryan closer. Without prompting, the Marine drapes her battered hand over the edge of the desk. "We would *really* appreciate your assistance."

Her eyes fixed on the myriad of ugly cuts across the knuckles, Rhoda gets up so fast that her chair skids backwards. Trying to maintain some dignity, she pulls down the front of her jacket and nods gravely. "All right. I'm certain that I can get Dr. Chavez to see you without an appointment."

When she disappears around the corner, Ryan turns her head and studies Claire with a small grin. "You're wicked, Doctor Walsch. That was first rate."

Claire smiles smugly and shrugs. "I'm used to snotty admin staff. What now?"

"Now we wait."

It is five minutes before Rhoda reappears. To Ryan's skilled observation, it seems as though her lipstick is a slightly different shade. Sitting down at the desk, she fluffs her hair before she sticks a pencil under the soiled bandage and pointedly discards it in her trash bin.

"Doctor Chavez will see you now."

"*Thank you.*"

They follow in the direction of her pointing finger, around the corner and through an open door. When the large swarthy man behind the desk sees Ryan's face, he rises quickly, his eyes wide, but before he can say anything Ryan slides over the desk and smashes her fist into his face. His head snaps backwards and he is forced back into his chair. Even as he raises his hands to his face, his black eyes are wily.

Ryan checks to make sure that the door is closed before she sits down in the chair next to Claire, her tone conversational. "Hello, Doctor *Chavez*. I didn't recognize the name, but I do recognize the face. Were you expecting me?"

"No."
He carefully prods his jaw, rolling it around experimentally before he lowers his hands. Before they can touch his desk, Ryan's right hand is pointing Victor's pistol pointed at Chavez's face.
"Don't."

"I wasn't going to do anything." He sneers at her. "I would be stupid to hide a gun in here."

"I wouldn't presume to guess at the level of your stupidity, but just in case," she gets up to stand behind him, "open the drawers. Let's check together."

He pulls open each drawer and she runs a quick hand through it, assuring herself of the contents before she slips back into her seat.

"So, Chavez, let's have a quick talk."

"You really can't *make* me." He tilts his chin up arrogantly. "What, are you going to shoot me? That'll help."

"I can do worse things than that." Smiling unpleasantly, Ryan cocks her head. "But I forget – you already know that."

"What?" Eyes narrowing, he sits forward and stares at her. "What are you talking about?"

"You know what experience I have with getting information out of people, Chavez. I heard you making comments on that once or twice. It's a subject you seem to like."

"Impossible. You were always unconscious when I came in."

"Sometimes. Not always." Her smile is ferocious. "If I were you, I'd rethink the dosages you use on somebody like me. But let's not argue. To get what I want, you know I'll do whatever I have to. Make it easy on yourself."

The man's deep-set black eyes glare at her viciously. "I hope they kill you slowly when they find you."

"I'll be sure to write and let you know." She glances around the room. "Get your suturing equipment. You may as well be useful while you talk."

"What a set of balls you have, letting me near you with a sharp object right after you threaten to torture me." He doesn't move from his seat.

Getting up, Ryan walks around the desk and perches on the edge of it. "Are you left- or right-handed, Doctor?"

"Right. What's the—" He jerks back as she suddenly reaches forward and grasps his left hand. "No, don't. Wait!"

"Oh. You want to keep it?" Dropping it in his lap, she stands to her full height. "Get your kit, Chavez. I'm waiting."

While he shuffles around like an overgrown sulky child, his lower lip pouting as he gathers what he needs, she takes Claire firmly by the arm and helps her out of her chair. She gestures Chavez into the vacated seat. "Sit here."

When the swarthy doctor sits down, Ryan pulls the other chair closer to him and grasps the pistol in her left hand, pointing it straight at his face. With a resentful glare, he unwraps the bandage around her right hand. Taking off the Band-Aids, he grins at the extent of the damage. When he reaches for the syringe, she shakes her head.

"No. I have no idea what you've put in that. Leave it."

"It's local anesthetic, but suit yourself. I'll enjoy it more this way."

Claire sits in Chavez's desk chair, and, despite Ryan's unflinching face, she can see from his vigorous motions that he is being as rough as he can possibly be with the cleansing process.

Ryan prods his forehead with the barrel of the gun. "Tell me about DEX."

"I don't appreciate that gun in my face."

"I don't appreciate your ugly face near my gun. Tell me about DEX."

He picks up the curved needle. "Who told you about that?"

Losing her temper, Ryan snatches the needle from his hand and drives it into Chavez's thigh. "I don't want to play games with you, asshole. No questions; you just answer what I ask." Smacking away his hand as he yelps and tries to reach for the protruding metal, she glares into his dark eyes. "Okay?"

"Okay! Okay!" He bares his teeth, his eyes filling with tears of pain. "I get it."

"Good. Now get another needle; I don't want your blood near me." She waits until he is back with a clean kit. "DEX."

He drives the hook into her flesh, expecting to see her flinch, but her face is expressionless. With a sneer he begins to suture the first wound.

"DEX05, actually. No idea what it stands for, something electronic and boring."

He scrapes the needle against the open bone on her knuckle. "Sorry. I don't know the whys or whens, all I know is what I was supposed to go in and do–"

"Start by telling me what DEX is."

"In layman's terms, a miniature transmitter and receiver, meant to send electronic signals that are interpretable by a neural system."

If Ryan is startled by his answer, she doesn't show it. The Marine clenches her jaw as the doctor roughly finishes the first wound and starts on the second, jabbing the needle into bone almost immediately. When she speaks, her voice is neutral. "What were you doing at Fairwater?"

"I came in periodically to test your neural responses. We weren't sure where the problem was –"

"What problem?"

He looks up with a sneer "You, mainly. I told them it'd be faster to just eliminate you, but no. They wouldn't sanction that."

"Let's keep the personal comments to a minimum. Your opinion is irrelevant."

"Whatever. There seemed to be a problem with the signal, or your reception of it, resulting in scrambled messages and violent behavior under unacceptable circumstances. And some of the functions seemed to be interfering with your nervous system. Those kinds of things."

"Who was in charge of this?"

"The project?" He gives her a cocky glance. "Yeah, that's what you are – a project. The main guy is Colonel George Turner."

He jabs the needle into her hand too deep, and this time she smacks his jaw with the barrel of the gun. "Don't keep doing that."

"Sorry." Jerking his head away, Chavez continues his stitching.

Shrugging, Ryan prods him again. "Was this a Marine Corps project?"

"Think bigger. Department of Defense." He begins on the third gash. "Not sure how much the Marine Corps had to do with it."

"What was the function of the DEX?"

"I told you that already."

Impatiently she prods him with the gun. "Practical application?"

"In your case, receiving commands in the field – tactical advice, tracking, that kind of thing."

"Tracking?"

For the first time her voice is raised, and Chavez looks up from her hands.

"Yeah, tracking. Following your movements, pinpointing your location. That's the part that seems to be screwing with your nervous system."

"Where is this thing now?"

"What thing?" He finishes suturing the last big cut and clips off the thread. "DEX? You want to know where DEX is now?" He begins to laugh. "That's rich! You–"

Ryan shifts closer to him, right up against him, and though Claire can't see her hands between the two of them, she can see Chavez's face as his laughter stops in mid-burst and his dark eyes widen and begin to bug out.

Ryan's face close to his, she leans in and hisses in his ear. "It took them an electronic current and many *very* long needles to even come *close* to breaking my spirit. It took me one little needle to break your silence, and it would take just one twist of my wrist to break the rest of you. Do you want to do this like civilized people, or would you like some practical experience for your next conversation about torture?"

He nods vigorously, and Ryan shifts against him again, her motion eliciting a moan from him before she sits back and lifts her left hand, the pistol now securely in the other.

"I got blood on your shirt. So sorry. You were telling me about DEX."

Morosely he takes the needle and begins to sew up the wounds in her left hand. "DEX. It's in your head."

"What?"

She jerks upright and he stabs the needle deep into the muscle by accident, but she doesn't seem to notice. Pulling it out, he takes a deep breath and begins again. "It's a miniature electronic disk planted in your head. Behind your ear on the right side."

She lifts her hand slowly as if to touch her head, then, realizing that she still has the gun clasped in it, she lowers it slowly. "Who put it there? When?"

"Turner, at that Kosovo affair."

"Who sends the commands?"

"I don't know that." Chaves starts on the second laceration. "When we were there working on you, Turner was in control of that, too."

"How do the impulses come through?"

He grins. "You know that, Ryan. A signal goes directly into a receiver implanted in your cochlea." At her blank look, he adds, "Your inner ear. Or as you seem to call it, the voice of God."

Her hand is clenching around the hilt of the gun. "How deep is this thing?"

"About half an inch, maybe a little less."

"And the receiver?"

"That would take a much more extensive and delicate operation to remove, but without the disk it's useless anyway."

When Ryan turns her head to look at Claire, the anguish in the green eyes is devastating. Claire gets up and approaches Ryan, her face concerned, but Ryan shakes her head. "Please go and make sure that Rhoda's still as blank as she seemed before." As the blonde walks out, Ryan catches the black glance Chavez shoots her. "Hey. I call it like I see it. I would have said something worse if there hadn't been a lady in the room."

"A lady, huh?" He begins the next suturing with a vicious jab to Ryan's hand.

"Yeah. You probably don't know what a lady looks like. As far as I can see, you prefer the slutty stupid kind."

"Last I heard, you did too." He smirks. "Quite the legend."

Coming in on the last exchange, Claire raises her eyebrows and leans against the table behind Ryan. The Marine doesn't appear to notice her.

"Can you take it out?"

"I'm assuming you mean DEX." He finishes the last of the sutures and takes a critical look at her hand. "That should do. Just don't move the fingers too much; you'll tear the sutures. Or actually, do move them. It'll hurt, and I like the thought of that. Yeah, I could probably take it out, but it would be better if that were done in–"

"Fine. Let's do it." She waves him out of the seat with the gun. "Give me something to wrap my hands with, and then you get together what you need for the extraction."

He tosses a roll of sterile bandage on the table and Claire picks it up. "Sit down." Her voice is soft. When the Marine complies, the doctor begins to expertly roll the white bandage around her hands, tying them off then gently maneuvering the large hands to make sure that the bandages are tight enough. "That should be fine. Be careful with them, please."

"Thanks." Ryan flexes each in turn before she leans closer and speaks, her breath warm against Claire's cheek. "Do you know how to shoot?"

"I do." At the Marine's gaging stare, she nods firmly. "I really do. I took some lessons…"

The rest of the sentence is left unsaid, but Ryan understands what the precipitating factor was. She holds out the gun, grip first. When Claire grasps it unwillingly, Ryan wraps her hands around the blonde's grip, her eyes intense. "If he's going to be cutting into my head, I can't keep an eye on him. I'm giving you the gun, Claire, and I want you to keep him in line until he's taken that thing out of my head. Please." She is almost begging. "If you want to shoot me afterwards, then go ahead, but just let him get that fucking thing out first. Please."

"All right."

With Claire's promise, Ryan gets up and watches Chavez with avid eyes until he pulls his instrument tray closer and gestures toward the bed. Sitting down on it, Ryan wraps her hand in his shirt and pulls him closer.

"I've told her to shoot you if you do anything you shouldn't. Do you understand?"

"Yeah."

"And no injections." Releasing his shirt, she rolls over onto her stomach. "Get going."

Claire moves so that Chavez's body isn't blocking her view, but grimaces as she realizes what he will be doing. He thoroughly disinfects the area just behind the right ear before he grasps the scalpel.

"Don't jerk." When he begins to cut into her, Ryan remains motionless.

Behind him, Claire closes her eyes for a moment against the sight of the blood welling up, and then moves so that his body is once again blocking her view. When he glances back at her, she lifts the barrel and cocks her head.

With a grin, he continues, speaking to her as he makes another incision. "You're probably less of a lady than she thinks."

"Get it over with. I don't want to chat."

"You know, of course," he glances at her again, "that if you keep the gun on me without being under duress, you're an accessory to the crime."

"You're an ass. That's what I call duress."

"He's right." Ryan's voice startles them both. "Walsch, if you don't shoot him if he misbehaves, I'll do very bad things to you. Understood?"

"Perfectly. You heard her. Finish."

Chavez snorts roughly. "If you talk while I'm cutting, I'm going to hit things I shouldn't." Taking a pair of flat-nosed silver tweezers, he presses them into the deep incisions. "Lie still."

To her credit Ryan does, her body rigid but motionless as he probes with the instrument, searching. Pulling out the foreign object, he drops it into the metal kidney basin and begins to clean up the copiously bleeding head wound. There is silence in the room as he puts stitches in the flesh and dabs it with a brown liquid before he sticks on a square Band-Aid.

"There. Done." Turning around, he looks at Claire, his mouth in a half-grin. "You're not going to shoot me. She's not your friend."

"Neither are you. Shut up." She lifts the gun higher, her eyes sharp above it.

"Come on. She's a ruthless killer. You understand that." He moves a step closer to Claire.

Behind him she can see Ryan lifting herself into a sitting position, her eyes closed as she takes a few deep breaths. "Get back. I'm warning you."

"Just give me the gun and we'll call the police. It'll be better for her, too. She needs help. You know she does."

When Claire makes a sudden move to the side, he turns with her, and then goes sprawling as Ryan places her foot in the small of his back and kicks him forward onto the floor. Towering over him, she says, "Thanks for the help, Chavez. Do you run a cash practice?"

When he nods, she prods his side with her foot, motioning him towards his desk. Sitting down in the seat opposite from him, she motions Claire into the chair next to her and takes the gun back, lowering it until it's pointing at him under the lip of the desk.

"You know what I've got in my sights now, Chavez, and that's the one thing you do truly care for, isn't it? Tell Rhoda to bring you the money."

"But…"

The sound of a gun cocking provides motivation. He lifts the intercom phone and speaks into it sullenly, and when Rhoda comes in and discreetly slips an envelope into his hand, he doesn't return her bright smile. After she leaves, he slides the envelope over to Ryan.

"Take it. Just take it and go. I don't ever want to see you again."

"Aw, thanks, Tony. You're a champ." She slips the envelope into her pocket and rises, pulling Claire up with her. "Be a gentleman and see us to the door, will you?"

Scowling, he grudgingly gets up. As he circles the desk, Ryan's foot meets his jaw in a roundhouse kick which snaps his head back. Eyes rolling back comically, he collapses in an unconscious heap.

Shoving the gun back into her waistband under her shirt, Ryan pulls at Claire's sleeve.

"Come on."

She stops and plucks the bloody microchip from the kidney basin and stuffs it in her pocket. When they pass the reception desk where Rhoda is filing her nails, Claire stops.

"Rhoda, Doctor Chavez said to tell you that he's on the phone." She leans forward conspiratorially. "To his wife, I'd have to gather from his mushy tone. He doesn't want to be disturbed for about ten minutes."

The receptionist's face clouds over and she begins to type peevishly as they walk out the door.

"That was mean. I loved it."

Ryan waits at the passenger door, and Claire unlocks the driver's door with an amused smile. She gets in and starts the car before she shifts sideways to look at Ryan. "Where to now?"

"I want to see Turner."

"Not like this, Ryan." Claire shakes her head resolutely. "You're in no condition to do anything, never mind face Doctor Frankenstein. I'm going to find a hotel or something, okay?"

"Okay."

"Which direction do we need to go?"

The Marine winces against the light. "It doesn't matter right now. We'll get back on track tomorrow. Let's just get on 89 and see what comes up."

Ryan rests her head back gingerly as Claire carefully follows road signs to Highway 89. It takes just under an hour before they pull up in front of the Wilsall Grand Hotel. It is not the Ritz, but the old-fashioned lobby is clean and there are few people about. Taking the black bag out of the back seat, Claire slings it over her shoulder and gets out, keeping a careful eye on Ryan's stilted movements.

In the lobby, they approach the check-in desk and the pillbox-hatted short man standing behind it.

"Welcome to the Wilsall Grand. How may I help you?" He seems bored.

Claire decides to do the speaking this time. "I'd like an en-suite room for the night, please."

"Fine." He clicks on his keyboard. "Preference for floor, beds?"

Claire is watching Ryan pulling the envelope out of her pocket, her hand slightly unsteady, and misses his question the first time.

"Miss? Preference for floor, beds?"

"Whatever."

Taking the cash, she notes his eyes straying to the bandage around Ryan's hands and the Band-Aid on the back of her head. Leaning forward she presents him with her best smile and a good view of her cleavage.

"We'll be satisfied either way."

Choking on whatever images his mind has just conjured up, the clerk selects a key and squeaks out the room number before he turns around and slinks into a back room, effectively disappearing. Hearing a muffled chuckle behind her, Claire shrugs nonchalantly.

Their room is on the third floor. When she opens the door they are greeted by a basic, clean room with a large double bed. After closing the door behind them, Claire puts the black bag on the chair and presses Ryan down onto the bed, then kneels to untie her shoes. The Marine watches her in silence. When Claire is finished, she motions for Ryan to stand and then undoes her pants.

Ryan smirks blearily. "Claire, I'm flattered, but I'm a bit tired…"

"Oh, hush, will you." Pulling the pants down, she has Ryan step out of them, then folds them up and places them neatly on the chair. "Get into bed."

Ryan does so without comment. Her face is as white as the pillow case on which it is resting.

In the bathroom, Claire gets a glass of water and shakes four aspirin from the bottle, then passes them to the reclining woman. "Here."

"Thanks." Ryan swallows them and puts the partially full glass on the bedside table, her eyes closing for a moment. When she pries them open, Claire shakes her head.

"Close your eyes. Relax. You'll be fine. Go to sleep." She is unwittingly repeating the Marine's earlier words to her.

Ryan closes her eyes, but keeps her head turned towards Claire. "Claire? In case you're gone when I wake up, I just want to say now that I'm sorry. And thank you."

"Shush." Claire sits down on the edge of the bed. "Go to sleep. I'll see you later."

She waits for the woman's breathing to become deep and rhythmic, then leans forward and places a hand lightly on Ryan's forehead; it is still too warm. Sighing, she stares down at the angular face, the semi-circle of dark lashes above sharp cheekbones, the straight nose with the slight bump halfway down – maybe broken at some stage? - and the lips that, even in sleep, look solemn and serious. Claire does not understand herself. She does not understand her compulsion to stay, when she should be running as fast and far away as she can. And she does not understand why, knowing all of this, she is still sitting here staring at a sleeping woman.

Ryan opens her eyes and rolls over, groaning slightly at the pain the motion elicits in her head. It is dark in the room, the curtains closed; the only source of illumination is her bedside lamp. When her eyes inadvertently fall on the light, the brightness shoots daggers into her skull. Touching her forehead, she frowns at the bandages and the low-grade burning sensation which persistently courses through her body.

"Damn."

Cursing the inevitable aches and pains, she lifts the blanket off her and sits upright, immediately shifting back to a horizontal position when her head begins to pound unbearably. Swallowing down the rising bile, she peers around her. Apart from her, the room is empty.

What did you expect? You told her to run when she had the chance. She had the chance.

The thought comes unbidden, and in spite of its cynicism Ryan actually smiles. For a long time she has desperately tried to avoid such internal dialogue, however impossible a feat. And now, here it is, and she knows they are her *own* thoughts and nothing more. The content is not earth-shattering, but the concept is spectacular. Ryan lies quietly for another few minutes before she moves again. This time the pain is not as bad, and she swings her feet off the bed and sits for a while before she gets up. Her legs are alarmingly shaky, but she braces herself and walks the short distance to the bathroom. She wants to take a shower, but with her hands wrapped and the dressing on her head, she is not sure whether she will manage. Instead, she uses the toilet and returns to sit on the bed, reaching for her pants. Her head pounding, she is bending down to slip her feet into the pant legs when the door opens. Alarmed, she shoots up and almost falls over from the sudden lightheadedness.

Claire Walsch is standing in the doorway with a number of bags in her hands, and her expression is undeniably concerned.

"Are you going somewhere?"

Ryan promptly sits down, abandoning the pants as she props her forearms on her knees and hangs her head to regain her equilibrium. "I thought you'd gone."

"I told you I wouldn't." Not chastising, just a fact. "How are you feeling?"

"I'm fine." Looking up, Ryan catches the raised eyebrows and amends, "I feel like a tank drove over me. And then reversed to drop a grenade on me. But otherwise, perfect." She studies the bags in Claire's hands with interest. "What have you got there?"

"I hope you don't mind. I used some of the money to get you a shirt and a pair of jeans, and the same for me. And some socks. Oh, and," she deadpans, "I replaced my bra."

She tosses the bags on the bed and then takes out the items and shows them to Ryan. The denim pants are plain and seem to be her size, and the shirt is a green V-neck with a white dragon design over the arm. Lastly, there is a green baseball cap. "Since you lost the other one. I hope they're the right size."

"They look fine. Thank you." Ryan eyes the jeans and light-blue polo Claire has bought for herself. "Nice shirt. The color will look great on you." Lifting an eyebrow, she purses her lips. "Hey, where's the bra?" To her satisfaction, a faint blush appears on Claire's cheeks.

"I'm wearing it. It was an emergency."

"I paid for it and I don't get to see it?"
"You didn't pay for it." Claire is smug, and quietly amused by Ryan's rare playfulness. "Anthony Chavez paid for it. Would you like me to go and show *him*?"

"No. I *really* wouldn't."

"I thought as much. Here's something I think you might like." She holds out a toothbrush and toothpaste, which Ryan takes with obvious gratitude.

"Thanks, that's a great idea."

Ryan considers standing, and is surprised when she feels a hand wrap under her arm and pull her up. Shooting the blonde a grateful nod, she then slowly makes her way into the bathroom to brush her teeth, savoring the experience.

While Ryan is busy, Claire steps around her and opens the bathtub's hot tap, waiting for Ryan to finish and go back to bed before she, too, brushes her teeth. Then she retrieves her clean clothes. "I'm going to take a quick bath, if you don't mind. There's some coffee and a bagel in that paper bag on the side table for you, if you're interested."

"Okay. Thanks."

While the doctor splashes around in the bath, Ryan holds the cup carefully in her stiffened and slightly swollen hands and savors the strong brew, ignoring the bagel in spite of the hunger pangs roused by its scent. When the coffee is finished, she discards the cardboard container and attempts a few slow stretches, impatient with the stiffness of her body and the pounding in her head that both impair her steadiness.

Claire emerges from the bathroom, followed by a cloud of steam and a whiff of fresh, clean aroma. In the process of toweling her hair, she stops at the sight of Ryan standing perfectly still, her eyes closed. "Ryan?"

"I'm fine." Straightening up carefully, Ryan sits down on the bed.

Claire bends forward and towels her hair vigorously, and in that moment the Marine cannot help but notice the tempting movements of the curvaceous body. Mentally berating herself, she looks away as the blonde straightens up and flips her shoulder-length hair back, combing through it with her fingers.

"I've run you a bath."

"Oh." Ryan looks down at her hands. "I'm not sure how I'm going to manage that, Claire. I think I'd probably better skip it."

Claire's eyes follow hers to her bandaged hands and she bites her bottom lip. "Oh. Yeah. Would you let me help you?"

Ryan looks away, frowning. "I'm not an invalid."

"Don't start that again. I'm offering my help; it doesn't diminish you in any way to accept it."

The tone is so terse that Ryan stares in astonishment. There is silence for a moment, and then she nods. "I'm sorry. You're right. I'm being ungrateful. I'm just not used to needing help." Getting up, she walks into the bathroom and sits down on the edge of the tub, looking up at Claire. "Would you help me with my shirt, please?"

"Sure." Claire reaches down and carefully pulls the black shirt over her head.

Glancing down at her panties, Ryan arches an eyebrow. "I believe I can handle those." She gets up and hooks her thumbs into the sides, managing to pull them down as Claire tactfully turns around, but when she wants to get into the bath she realizes that she can't support herself on the edge with her hands, and her balance is less than ideal.

"Claire?"

"Yeah?" the blonde replies, her back still turned.

"Can you lend me a hand here?"

Turning, Claire wraps a hand around Ryan's arm and helps her into the bath with the other hand lightly on her side.

"Thanks."

"Not a problem." Picking up the soap, Claire lathers up the sponge. "I'm sorry; it's going to have to be a sponge bath for you today. I don't think you're going to have much luck holding anything yourself."

"With a sponge bath, who needs luck?" Ryan drops her head forward, and with only a moment's hesitation Claire begins to wash her shoulders and back.

The blonde uses long strokes to wash the tapering back, studying the prominent muscles and bones beneath scarred skin. The Marine's build is athletic, her physique probably inclined to leanness even without the recent lack of food. The shoulders are square and strong, and her arms well-defined. When Claire passes the sponge forward over Ryan's chest, she falters for a moment. "Do you want to...?"

"No. Go ahead." Ryan leans back slightly to allow Claire easier access, draping her hands over the sides of the tub as the blonde awkwardly lathers soap over her chest and then washes it off, moving with some relief to her stomach. "Time to get up?"

"Yeah." Claire is about to start lathering Ryan's muscled thigh when the other woman clumsily takes the sponge out of her hands.

"I should probably take it from here."

"Yeah. Probably. I'm going to drink my coffee. Call me when you need me."

After she has finished washing to her best ability, Ryan lies in the bath for a while, relaxing. Though she will say nothing, in order to spare Claire further discomfort, she has actually enjoyed the attention a little too much. Writing it off to the fact that she hasn't been touched kindly in many years, she gets out of the bath under her own steam. The towel, however, proves tricky. When she calls Claire's name, the blond head pops in almost immediately.

"I hate to ask, but..."

Claire looks at the towel grasped awkwardly in one hand and takes it from her.

"Of course." She dries the Marine's body efficiently. When Ryan's nipples stiffen under her hands, she feels herself blush hotly as she quickly moves to dry her shoulders and back. The fading bruise is still blooming at the base of Ryan's spine, and Claire trails a finger over it before she can stop herself.

"How did this happen?"

Ryan arches away from the touch. "One of the orderlies kicked me."

"What?" Claire is outraged. "That's unacceptable!"

"To be fair," Ryan says idly, "I punched him in the head."

"Why?"

"I was tired. The voice told me to. He was rude. Take your pick." She shivers and takes the towel from Claire to wrap herself in it, then walks into the room. "It's a little chilly, isn't it? Can you help me with..." She nods at her clothes. To her surprise, Claire shakes her head.

"No. I think you need to get back into bed for a while."

"What's the time?"

"It's just after seven p.m."

"I slept too long already." Ryan runs a hand over her head. "They'll be coming for me. You realize that?"

Her gaze is direct, and Claire returns it. "I realize that. But if they come for you while you're in this condition, there's nothing you'll be able to do anyway, Ryan. Get a little more sleep. Tomorrow you can go on as usual."

"There hasn't been a 'usual' for me in a very long time, Claire." With a wry grin, Ryan moves to the bed, discards the towel and climbs under the covers.

Peering into the paper bag, Claire takes out the bagel and holds it up, her eyes reproachful. "Hey, you should be eating. All the rest in the world won't help you heal on an empty stomach."

"Not just now. I want to ask you something."

The tone is serious, and Claire walks around to sit on the other side of the bed. She pulls off a piece of the bagel and pops it into her mouth. Ryan rolls around to look at her, waiting until she's finished chewing before she speaks.

"Why didn't you run, Claire?"

The blonde's fingers still, and she stares blindly at the bedcovers. "So you're done with me?"

Ryan sits up, irritably pulling the blanket higher as it shifts down. "Let's not play games, Claire. You of all people should know better."

Heaving a sigh, Claire looks away, a laconic smile on her lips as she absentmindedly plucks another piece off the pastry. She chews pensively and then returns her gaze to Ryan. Her eyes are distant and slightly confused. "You're right. I'm sorry."

"You say that a lot, do you realize? Don't be sorry, Claire, just tell me what's going on."

"I don't know." Claire's expression is open and honest. "I don't know, Ryan. I *know* I should have run when I had the chance. I *know* I should have pointed the gun at you when I had the chance. I know all of those things. Why I didn't? That part I don't know."

"I thought that therapists knew everything about this kind of thing." Ryan smiles slightly to show that she is teasing. "Okay. I'm not going to make you leave if you don't want to, Claire, but in the interest of honesty, I have to tell you that my motives for keeping you around are less than stellar."

"Wow. That certainly *is* honest."

Ryan shrugs. "I'm not much of a liar. As long as I have you with me, whoever is tracking me might be just that little bit more cautious. They probably won't want to risk hurting a civilian." She fixes her fierce eyes on Claire. "I want you to understand that. I enjoy your company, and I think you are a strong and lovely person, but apart from that – you are also a means to an end."

"All right." Claire picks at the pastry; then, realizing what she is doing, she stills the motion. "I accept that you have your reasons for wanting me around, however detrimental to me they may be. I'm not going to blame you for my choices. I just need a little bit of time to work out why I made them in the first place."

Ryan slides down and puts her head on the pillow, studying the ceiling. "Time may be the one thing I can't offer. Things are going to be happening soon."

"I realize that, too." Claire curls up on her side, propping her head in her hand as she looks over at Ryan. "Can I take my chances? Just for this moment?"

"If that's what you want."

"Ryan, if I knew what I wanted I wouldn't be such a mess."

"You're not a ..." Claire unceremoniously interrupts Ryan's words by stuffing a piece of bagel into her open mouth, so she stops speaking and chews with one eyebrow raised until she can swallow. "Hey! What was that for?"

Smiling innocently, the doctor breaks off another piece. "Open your mouth." When Ryan obeys, she eyes her teeth with feigned suspicion. "Don't bite me." She slots the piece into Ryan's waiting mouth, suddenly hyper-conscious of her fingers brushing against the other woman's lips. Pulling her hand away awkwardly she sets the rest of the bagel on the side table so that she can turn her gaze away for a moment.

When she looks back, Ryan is watching her silently. "You need some sleep too."

"I don't think... No, I'm fine."

"I'm the only one allowed to say that, Claire. Come on. Get in." Her eyes soften. "Don't be nervous. I won't touch you, I promise."

"You think I'd worry about that?" Claire shakes her head. "I'm not scared of you, Ryan. This is positive **bliss** compared to..." She pauses and then shakes her head. "I mean, I'm not putting you in the same category as *him*. That came out wrong. I wouldn't... I'm sorry." She breaks off helplessly, and when she looks up, her eyes are glassy with tears.

Ryan sits up and reaches over, pulling the blonde to her with surprising gentleness. At first Claire stiffens, and then her body sags as she presses her face into the hollow at Ryan's shoulder. When she sniffs and tries to pull back, the strong arms tighten around her and a warm hand cups her neck.

"Shhh. Stop fighting now, Claire." Ryan begins to rock her tenderly. "You've been hurting for a very long time. Let it go. You're safe. I promise."

For the second time, Claire really cries, and it should embarrass her, this sobbing on the shoulder of a woman she only met three days ago - under appalling circumstances - but somehow the arms around her and the slow heartbeat under her ear comfort her in a way she can't describe. She sobs like a child until she gradually regains control over her breathing, and then she pulls back, slowly becoming aware of the warm body against hers and the way in which her arms are wrapped around the bare shoulders. When she flushes the other woman lays a finger under her chin and tilts her head up.

"Don't be embarrassed. There's no harm in letting somebody help you once in a while."

Smiling faintly at the repetition of her own words, Claire nods, deciding to ignore Ryan's mistaken assumption about the cause of her blush rather than mortify herself even further by revealing the real reason. "Thanks. That was exhausting. Can we go to sleep now?"

Ryan flashes a ghost of a smile. "Okay." She is caught off-guard when Claire reaches down and removes her blue shirt. "Sorry." Her eyes are twinkling as she turns her head away. "That *is* a nice bra, by the way."

Blowing Ryan a raspberry, Claire slips out of her jeans and slides under the covers. Ryan is on her side, turned towards the bedside table, and somehow Claire thinks that she's lying exactly that way because it leaves a vast amount of space to her side, ensuring that they won't touch. Curling up, she puts her left hand under her pillow and pulls her right arm close to her chest. When Ryan turns off the bedside lamp, she flinches.

"Um..."

"What's wrong?"

She hesitates for a moment, but knows that Ryan will push her for a response if she pulls away now. "Would you mind if I touch you, Ryan?"

"What?" When the blonde reaches out and touches her fingertips to Ryan's shoulder blade, the Marine twitches and then exhales. "Oh. That's okay, Claire."

In the darkness, Claire smiles sadly. "It took two weeks to break you, a needle to break Chavez, and just a few small words to break me."

"Someone like you should never have been broken in the first place." As Ryan settles, her back shifts beneath Claire's touch. "Get some sleep."

Sierra pulls up in Rear Admiral Victor Banks' driveway, then dials a number from memory as Alpha and the other two men slip into the back to suit up.

"Turner."

"We're at Banks' house, about to clean up." He gestures sharply with two fingers and the other men move stealthily around the back of the house. "I'll keep you updated."

"Fine."

The phone clicks. Drawing his own pistol with its long, fitted silencer, he glances around, checking for bystanders before he gets out of the van. The street is empty. When he reaches the back, one of the men has already put his hand though the broken windowpane and opened the kitchen door. They spread out, their backs pressed against the walls as they steal down the corridor. At the first door, Alpha glances in.

"He's in here." His voice is muffled, low.

They carefully secure the rest of the house before they return to the first bedroom where Alpha is waiting. Inside, Victor Banks is lying on his side on the bed, the right side of his face mottled with dried blood. His hands and feet are tightly tied. Sierra approaches, but when he reaches out his hand to the pulse point in the man's neck, Banks opens one gray, blood-encrusted eye and peers up at him warily. Even the typically calm Alpha almost recoils before he composes himself.

After clearing his throat arduously, Banks speaks, his voice gravelly. "Well. You took your time."

"Admiral Banks." Sierra nods before he turns to Alpha and speaks to him in a low voice. Then he takes the phone from his pocket and steps into the hallway, hitting the redial button. When the man on the other end of the line answers, he speaks tersely.

"Banks is still alive. .... No. Just blunt force trauma to the head. ... Done."

He steps up to the tall man in black at the doorway. "Tango. Sweep the study." Then he returns to the bedroom where Banks is lying. The Rear Admiral is repeating his request to be untied when Sierra shoots him in the head.

About two hours later, the team is on its way to Great Falls. Alpha is driving and Sierra takes the moment to slip the small flat device out of the pouch at his waist and switch it on. He studies the movement on the screen without expression before he hits redial on his mobile phone.

"Turner."

"She's off course, on 89, just past Belt, going south."

"Hmm." The colonel ponders for a moment. *Interesting.* Banks gave her something other than what they had anticipated. "Stay on course to Helena. She'll be there soon; you be there first."

"Isn't there one of your guys in Neihart or White Sulphur?"

"Anthony Chavez." Colonel Turner has never liked him much. "It's not important. By the time you get there, she'll be on her way to Helena and then you're behind. Move your ass, Mahoney."

"Fine."

"And Mahoney, *don't* keep flipping that fucking thing on and off. If she's driving it could cause a problem, and I don't want her to go anywhere just yet. Understood?"

"Understood."

Sierra kills the call. In silent disapproval of Turner's attitude, he leaves the signal on for a little longer than necessary, and when he finally flicks it off he is smiling. Well, on the inside.

The drive takes them over three hours. Alpha is a meticulous driver and does not rush, certain that they are already ahead of their prey. In Helena, they fuel up and hang around, keyed up and frustrated by the lack of activity. When the sun begins to set, they book into a seedy motel on the outskirts of the city. Tango, easily bored, suggests that they go to the bar for a game of pool. It is still early and they make their way to the dark, dusky room, perching on the uncomfortable red vinyl seats as Tango checks out cues and then racks the balls.

The barman eyes them sullenly. He had thought that it would be his lucky day, four big men who look like they can each put away a barrel of beer coming in, and then they order soft drinks. *Soft drinks*. For God's sake. He spits on the floor. Damned fairies.

While Alpha breaks forcefully and Tango looks on with interest, Sierra keeps an eye on the device that he has placed on the counter. In the course of two hours, he switches it on seven times, his eyes focused, and just before half past ten, he stands up and beckons the other three men. He does not speak within hearing distance of the barman, who is glaring at them for reason beyond his comprehension or interest, but starts walking towards their rooms, knowing they will all be beside him without prompting.

"We're leaving."

"All right." It's Alpha, the obedient one. "Didn't Turner tell us to stay in Helena?"

"Yes. The target hasn't moved for six hours, maybe more. Looks like she went through White Sulphur Springs and ended up in Wilsall. Either there's a problem, in which case we need to be there now, or she's staying the night, in which case I want to be tight on her tail when she leaves. I'm not sure Turner has as much of a handle on this situation as he thinks he does."

When Bravo speaks, it takes them by surprise. "If she's going to Helena eventually, why don't we just wait for her here?"

"Because I don't lay bets on *eventually*. She's not stupid. Something's happening, and we're not in on it. Yet." Sierra shoots Bravo a sarcastic glance. "What's the problem? Missing your beauty sleep?"

"No."

"Good, because you're driving. Alpha goes like an old lady. Let's pack it up and get on the road."

It is dark when Ryan inexplicably jolts awake. Something has caught her attention and she is not sure what, and that is her least favorite scenario. She lies perfectly still and listens, alert to the sounds around her – from the irritating muffled dripping in the bathroom to the slight hitch in Claire's breath as she shifts in her sleep. There is something just beyond, niggling at her awareness.

She carefully rolls over, annoyed to feel remnants of her headache, and slips from under the blanket to put her feet softly on the carpet. Sitting still, she closes her eyes and holds her breath for a few seconds, and then exhales slowly. She does not sense that the threat is immediate, but she is not about to take any chances. Stretching her back gracefully she rises, then edges around the bed, placing her feet carefully and precisely. At the foot of the bed she stops, turning her head towards the bathroom door. Nothing. She turns her head to her right, towards the window and the chair. Moving to the window, she slides a finger between the curtains and peers out. It is a dark night, pitch black with no moon, and she can barely make out anything in the alley below. No movement there.

She turns back, stops in front of the chair and frowns. Reaching out, she rifles through the clothing by touch alone, singling out her cargo pants and sliding her fingers into the pockets. She scowls as she pulls out the sticky DEX chip, hot to the touch, and lifts it up to her left ear. It is not her imagination – the electronic device is humming at a low frequency.

And then it stops.

Claire is thrashing about, in the throes of an unpleasant dream, when a hand touches her shoulder.

"Claire..."

"No!" She sits bolt upright, her breath catching in her throat, and spots Ryan crouched at the side of the bed.

"Shh. I'm sorry. You wouldn't wake up." The Marine rises. "You have to get dressed."

Claire notes that Ryan is fully clothed. "What?" She yawns and wipes her eyes. "What's the time?"

"About a quarter to one." Ryan tosses her clothes onto the bed. "*Now.*"

Still drowsy, Claire gets out of bed before remembering that she is in her underwear. Flushing hotly, she shoots a quick glance behind her, but Ryan is shoving things into the black bag, her back towards the blonde. Claire begins to dress hastily.

"What's happening, Ryan?"

The Marine surveys the floor for any stray articles as she answers. "The thing... DEX... I think it's been sending out signals throughout the night. We're being tracked. We need to get out of here."

Sitting on the edge of the bed, Claire slips her feet into the trainers and ties the laces. "If you think they've been tracking you all this time, then what's the difference right now?"

"It's the middle of the night, and it's gone off twice in an hour. Something feels wrong."

"Where is it now? DEX, I mean." When Ryan pats her pocket, Claire frowns. "Why don't you just get rid of it?"

"I want them to think I still have it in me." Ryan is impatient. "We have to go."

She opens the door and steps over to the glass window across the hall, glancing down almost cursorily at the parking lot before her posture stiffens. Turning around, she motions Claire, who has just come out of the room, back inside.

The blonde frowns as she stops in the middle of the room and watches Ryan cross the floor. "What—"

Pressing the bag into her hands, Ryan opens the curtains at the window and glances outside before she twists the ancient bronze latch and slides the window open with difficulty, her hands burning with the strain. Striding back to the door, she closes and locks it before she returns to Claire and pulls the pistol out of the black bag.

"Fire escape." Her free hand propels the blonde forward.

Claire feels dread rising in her throat. Grasping the bag tightly, she climbs out of the window onto the metal grid and looks down. It is so dark outside that she has trouble seeing the rungs that lead to the level below. Behind her, the metal creaks in protest as Ryan swivels her legs out and puts her feet down.

"Get to the ground floor, Claire."

The doctor begins to numbly descend, placing her feet carefully on the narrow metal rungs. She is already on the first floor when she realizes that Ryan is not behind her. Glancing upwards, she tries to make out the dark form on the platform above her.

"Don't stop moving. Go."

Claire is about to comply with the hissed command when all hell breaks loose. A gunshot sounds from above and is echoed by another. The crash of breaking glass tinkles into silence, and, after that, the uncanny stillness of the night hangs in the air. Pressing herself against the wall, Claire stares upwards in shock, trying to see anything, and she almost screams when someone suddenly appears in front of her.

Ryan wraps an arm around Claire and pulls her close, shielding the blonde as she extends her right hand and fires upwards. When an answering shot whistles by she holds her breath, waiting until silence settles again before she swings around, propelling Claire towards the steps as she presses her back against the wall.

"Move. Quiet." The hoarse voice is barely more than a hiss.

Inching along the metal surface, Claire approaches the staircase and is about to put her foot on the first step, when many things happen simultaneously. A shot from behind her is immediately answered by a shot from above, and in the same moment that the report rings out and she flinches, Ryan's arm wraps around her waist from behind. The Marine roughly pulls her down onto the steel grate and crouches over her, breath hissing from her throat as she cranes her neck to look upwards.

Apparently satisfied about whatever it is she has been watching for, Ryan quickly gets to her feet, clumsily lifting Claire with her by hooking an arm around her waist. Trying to assist, Claire wraps a hand around Ryan's shoulder, yanking her hand back in recoil when she feels the sticky wet mass on the Marine's shirt. With a sharp gulp, she slides her hand up again, only to have it intercepted and deflected smoothly by Ryan's bandaged hand.

"Ryan? Are you hurt?"

The Marine's head shakes as she hisses, "Fine. Get moving." Pushing her forward firmly, Ryan turns and moves back to the wall, pressing her back against it. "Go!"

With the murmur of their unknown assailants above them, Claire stands at the top of the stairs, glancing down at the street below for a second. Then, without conscious decision, she turns back and throws herself against Ryan's body. This time when her hand makes contact with the angular shoulder, there is a definite shudder from Ryan.

"Damn it, Claire, *go!*"

Shoving her hand into Ryan's pocket, Claire wraps her fingers around the small electronic chip and then takes off silently down the stairs. Ryan is left slamming her fist against the wall behind her in furious frustration.

"Fuck! Claire!"

Glancing upwards, Ryan tries to gauge the movements of the assault team. With gritted teeth, she slides the pistol into her waistband, wraps both hands over the railing behind her, and lifts her legs over the balustrade. When she is standing on the edge of the landing, she turns and steps off, dangling her legs as far down as her blazing hands will allow before she lets go and drops to the ground. The distance is further than she had guessed and the landing jars her. Rolling adroitly, she crouches low and scans the alley to her left and right. On the left side, the faint pool of a streetlight illuminates the empty street sixty feet away; on the right side, the alley ends in a locked service entrance, flanked by large rubbish bins and stacks of empty crates.

Wondering with unease which direction Claire has chosen, Ryan turns to the right and lopes silently towards the crates, stepping between two and pressing her back to the rough, whitewashed wall. She slips out the pistol and aims it towards the staircase where she can now make out the dark figures in silent descent. There are four of them, and they move in a way she knows means nothing good. Perfectly still, she fixes her sight on the first man. He stops at the foot of the stairs and turns his head to murmur to the man behind him, then pulls something off of his belt and studies it for a moment before they all take off in the direction of the street.

Ryan keeps the pistol at the ready, her eyes focused, in case it is a trap. She is still frozen in the same position when a black van, driving way too fast, shoots past the alley in the street below. From the sound of the engine, she can tell that it is quickly moving away from her. Exhaling roughly, Ryan slides down the wall to her haunches, growling in irritation at the pain the movement causes in her shoulder. For a moment she just sits, silent, before she rises to her feet and slips the pistol into the back of her waistband. Still moving soundlessly, placing her feet precisely, she approaches the base of the staircase and glances up.

It is as she looks back down that she spots Claire's golden hair, like a flash under the spot of a streetlight. The doctor comes running from the left side of the street, her eyes darting left and right before she enters the alleyway. When she sees Ryan at the stairs, she stops and bends double, supporting one hand on her knee and the other tightly clasped around the strap of the bag.

Ryan rushes forward, her fingertips swiftly, proficiently checking the woman's back and sides. "Claire? Are you hurt?" She is still speaking in a hiss, but it comes out louder than intended, sounding like a shout after the deep silence.

The doctor quickly shakes her head. "Fine. No breath." She gasps for air a few times before her breathing slows and she can straighten up. "You okay, Ryan?"

"We need to get going before the police get here. C'mon. Gunshots will draw a response from the local authorities." Wrapping a hand around Claire's elbow, she leads her back into the street.

They turn right and corner the building, entering the dark parking area where they left the Trailblazer. Claire scrabbles around in the bag and pulls out the keys. "Who's driving?"

"You are."

Ryan waits patiently for Claire to get in and unlock the passenger door. Before she settles in the passenger seat, she slips the pistol from her waistband and puts it into the glovebox. Out on the street, Claire turns left, driving past the alley. The very next street has a gas station on the corner, and Ryan instructs Claire to pull in. They fill up the SUV and then leave Wilsall, Claire driving cautiously until she is on the highway moving south-west towards Bozeman.

When Ryan is sure that they are not being followed, she plops back against the seat, her breath leaving her in a loud whoosh. "So. What happened?"

Claire's smile is shaky, and barely visible in the darkness. "Luck was on my side. You wouldn't believe it."

"Give it a shot." The doctor groans at the unintended pun, and Ryan chuckles softly. "Sorry."

Claire's voice contains traces of both amusement and nervousness as she recounts her actions. "Well, I went into the street, and from there I ran to the gas station. It was the only place with its lights still on. There were two guys in a Taurus filling up, so I knocked on the window and asked one of them for directions to Helena. While he was talking, I dropped the... DEX into his car."
Incredulous, Ryan shifts sideways in her seat. "And then?"

"And then he made an inappropriate comment, and I told him that if he saw my husband coming up on his tailgate tonight, he'd better be sure to step on the gas." She shrugs. "And then I hid around the corner until the guys left and the van went by."

In the darkness, Ryan shakes her head as she opens the glove box and begins to root through it. "You've got a quick mind, Doctor. And phenomenal luck. What if there hadn't been anybody at the station?"

"I don't know. I hadn't thought that far ahead. Actually, up until the actual moment of opportunity, I hadn't thought at all. What are you looking for?" Claire turns her head and peers at Ryan in the darkness. "Are you okay?"

The candid "no" catches the blonde off-guard, and she has no time to respond before Ryan continues.

"You were brave, Claire, but if you ever do anything like that again, I'll shoot you myself." When there is no answer, Ryan puts a hand on the tense arm. "Don't think that I don't appreciate it, but I can look after myself, and if something happens to you because you're trying to help me, I wouldn't deal well with that. Okay?"

"Okay," Claire responds tightly.

"That's not good enough, Claire. I don't want you to protect me - we could both get hurt that way. Do you understand? And say 'yes' as if you mean it."

"*Yes!*" The doctor's voice is irritable, but when she continues her tone is softer. "Yes. I'm sorry. I was trying to help because you were hurt."

"Thank you." Ryan shifts her focus. "Are you wearing a belt?"

"I hate questions that start like that coming from you. No. Why?"

Ryan lifts the black bag onto her lap and searches through the contents. Not finding what she's looking for, she puts the bag back on the floor at her feet. "Claire, pull over for a moment."

The doctor complies and is surprised when Ryan asks for the keys and gets out, opening the hatch at the back of the SUV. When she gets back into the vehicle and passes back the keys, she's holding something bundled in her hand.

"What's that?"

In answer, Ryan switches on the inside light. In her hand is a short length of nylon towing rope, which she hands to Claire. Without comprehending why, the doctor takes the rope. When her eyes fall on Ryan's blood-streaked left arm, she inhales sharply.

Shifting, Ryan lifts the arm towards her without expression. "I need a tourniquet." When Claire raises wide, worried eyes to her, Ryan cocks her chin impatiently. "Come on."

Following Ryan's instructions, the blonde ties the rope around the arm, looping it under the armpit and over the shoulder several times. It is a poor wrap and looks extremely uncomfortable. Where the shirt is shredded and most sodden, at the juncture of her deltoid and pectoral right under her collarbone, the material is bunched up awkwardly, and Claire is sure that there must be incredible pain where the rope unavoidably crosses the wound.

When she is finished, Claire studies Ryan's face anxiously. "Is it going to help?"

"Tough place to stop blood flow." The Marine reaches up to switch off the inside light. "I need you to find a hospital in Bozeman."

Gooseflesh runs down Claire's back at this atypical acknowledgment of pain. She can't control the quaver in her voice when she speaks. "Wilsall is closer. I'm going to turn around."

"No. When they realize they've been duped, that'll be the starting point for their search."

"I *understand* that, but I'd rather you didn't bleed to death!"

Hearing the fright in Claire's voice, Ryan stiffly reaches out to pat her leg. "Claire. Don't panic. Just keep driving. I'm fine."

"You keep saying that, but I doubt you've ever *been* fine! You wouldn't know 'fine' if it bit you in the ass!"

Gritting her teeth - both against the pain and the makings of an unwelcome smile - Ryan shifts her left hand over to touch the vehement blonde's thigh. "Hey. Let's go, Walsch."

Silently the doctor puts the vehicle in gear and pulls onto the road again. Ryan puts on the radio and then pulls the bag closer, rifling through it clumsily until she finds her other shirt. Wadding it up, she wedges it under the tourniquet. The painful added pressure makes her swallow convulsively before she pulls the side lever and pushes her seat backwards so that she is reclining somewhat.

"Claire?" she ventures. The doctor doesn't answer. "Claire?"

"Are you going to die?"

"No, Claire. I'm not the type. After the Apocalypse it'll be just me and the cockroaches, building things from polystyrene. Okay?"

The blonde doesn't respond to her joking. Sighing, she tries again. "Look, I'm strong–"

"I hate to break it to you, Ryan, but I don't even know how you're still standing. In the last three days, when you haven't been throwing up and popping pain pills, you've been bleeding."

"Sure. And I can tell you I'm getting damned tired of that," she retorts mock-indignantly, which finally coaxes a small laugh from Claire. Encouraged, Ryan continues. "Okay, so physically I'm not at my best, Doc, but mentally I'm way up there. Trust me."

"I do." Claire sighs and shakes her head. "I really don't know why."

"I don't either, Claire. I don't know why you didn't just run away. Those guys weren't there for you." Ryan is quiet for a moment. "What's going on in your head right now?"

"Million dollar question, that. Can I phone a friend?" Claire bites her bottom lip uncertainly. "You abducted me against my will, used me as a hostage to escape from a shady private hospital, and dragged me around the countryside against my will. And then you pushed me down a fire escape. What's not to stay for?"

Ryan emits a husky chuckle. "I really do not get you, Doc."

"Join the crowd." Claire taps her finger against the steering wheel for a minute before she speaks again. "Ryan? There's something I don't understand. Why did Victor Banks say DEX was a gas?"

"He really didn't know. He was telling the truth."

"So you hit him in the head for nothing? He won't be very happy with you, I'm sure."

"He'll be fine. He'll understand. Besides, it was a twofold gesture. If they found him intact after I left with the information, they'd know he gave it to me of his own free will. His dignity's important to him. I tried to let him keep some."

"Nice of you."

"That's me. Nice to the core."

They drive in silence for more than half an hour, and it is Ryan who speaks just after they pass the sign letting them know that Bozeman is twenty miles ahead. "Claire? You need to start talking to me again." Her voice is weaker than usual.

Anxiously Claire reaches out and touches Ryan's leg in the darkness. "What's going on?"

"I'm fading a little. Don't worry – just give me something to pay attention to."

"Okay." Trying to push down the rising panic, Claire casts around for something to talk about. "I don't have much to tell you in the way of a personal life. Honestly, I'm the most boring person I know." The slight chuckle from the darkness to her right gratifies her. "I work fourteen-hour days at the office, go home, eat a pre-packaged dinner, and go to bed. No pets, no parties, no wild, wicked habits."

"Pity."

"Hah. You sound fine to me." She pats the thigh, more to assure herself that Ryan is still with her than for the Marine's benefit. "On weekends, I go to the movies, museums, that sort of thing."

"You weren't joking - you *are* boring." Ryan's voice is light. "Family?"

"My parents are divorced. My mother is a therapist too. She lives with an absolute asshole in Washington. Dad runs a bait shop in Florida and has a girlfriend a little older than I am. He's made a career of his midlife crisis."

"Sounds lovely."

"All-American. I have a sister in Sacramento. Andy's an archeologist. She's just finished her doctorate."

"Impressive. Do you get along?"

"Like a house on fire. We're very close. She's older by two years, but we're so alike that people always think we're twins."

"So she's beautiful." There is a second of silence. "Ignore me. I'm not well. Hallucinating. Rambling."

"And again with the negating of the compliment? Thanks a lot." Her smile can be heard in her voice. "I spoke to her when you were sleeping, back at the hotel."

"She must be scared for you."

"I told her I was okay, and she knows I wouldn't lie to her." Claire dismisses the topic. "How are you feeling?"

"Pale."

The blonde brushes her fingers against Ryan's left hand and immediately wishes she hadn't. The skin is icy cold, the fingers crusted with dry blood. "Ryan? It's not too far now. Hold on, okay?" She pushes the speedometer up a little higher. "Don't go anywhere. Ryan?"

"Yeah?"

"I *did* judge you, and I'm sorry. I should have been more open-minded, but I couldn't see past what I thought was right."

"Come on, Walsch." The Marine's muscles twitch under Claire's hand. "Who would have believed the voice in my head was real? Nobody could have predicted that."

"I know. But I should have done a better job of listening to you. A lot of what you needed was for somebody to *not* treat you like a freak. I should have been that person. I should have known better."

"Are you staying out of *guilt*, Claire?"

"No. I just..." She shakes her head at herself. "I wonder what keeps you going. You're such an incredibly strong person. You've been beaten and hurt and broken down. On the outside, you're busted, but on the inside you're still fighting like none of it holds you back."

"That sounds more like you, Claire."

"No, it sounds like the exact opposite of me. I'm busted on the inside and working on the surface."

"Not true. You're a fighter too. You just need to take your life back."

"How do I do that, Ryan?" Even in the blackness of night, her hopelessness is palpable. "Where do I begin? I've spent a long time telling myself that I don't need any more than I have."

"It's not about what we need, Claire. If we settled for what we need, we could probably survive on the minimum, yes, but then what? If you don't want anything you'll never push yourself harder to get it, and if you never push yourself you'll stay in the same place forever. You have to want more than just getting by. You have to think you deserve better."

"Do I?"

"Yes. You do."

"How can you be sure?" Claire withdraws her hand from Ryan's arm. "You don't know me."

"I'm a good judge of character, and you haven't proven me wrong yet. You're a strong person, and you're worthy of more."

"I don't feel that way." Claire adeptly changes the focus away from herself. "What is it, Ryan? That pushes you on, I mean."

The Marine shifts a little in her seat. "I *have* to move forward. Back isn't an option. Stopping isn't an option. Forward is the only way."

They enter the outskirts of Bozeman and Claire looks around for street signs, breathing a sigh of relief when she spots the universal white "H" on a blue background. Following the signs, she glances over at Ryan, who is half-illuminated by the streetlights.

"Hey, I found it." There is no reply. Frowning, her heart beating a little faster, Claire repeats herself. Still the Marine remains quiet, and when she peers at the woman's face, it is slack. Putting out a hand, she shakes Ryan's knee. "Ryan?"

Never has Claire known silence to be so frightening. She can hear her heart thundering in her ears. At the hospital, she veers into the parking lot and stops right in front of the sliding doors. She jumps out and rushes into the reception area, right up to the large, handsome woman behind the desk.

"Help me! She's been shot!"

Almost immediately, two orderlies appear with a gurney and rush outside, opening the passenger door. A tall, blonde, coolly beautiful doctor in a white coat strides out of a side room and joins them at the desk. "What is her name?"

"Ryan." Claire is so afraid that she's struggling to get the words out, and the nurse puts a comforting hand on her wrist.

"Calm down, honey. We've got her. Is that a first name?"

"No. Surname. But that's what she goes by."

"Where is the wound?"

"Her shoulder, it's... she made a tourniquet..." She indicates the area on her own body with a trembling hand and takes a shuddering breath.

The doctor leaves her with the reassuring nurse and joins the orderlies outside. They are expertly moving Ryan from the car to the gurney. Her lean body is limp and under the fluorescent lights her face is a stark white. As they wheel her in, the doctor is walking next to Ryan, her fingers clamped around the limp wrist as she speaks to her commandingly. "Ryan? Can you hear me? Come on, open your eyes."

Claire wants to follow them down the corridor, but the nurse gently blocks her way. "Hold on, honey. The doctor will be able to do her job better if you stay here with me until she calls you in. Okay?"

"Okay." Tears well in her blue eyes, and she wipes at them with irritation. The large woman steps around the desk and grasps her upper arm softly, urging her towards the scruffy brown sofa against the wall. The pressure around her arm absurdly reminds her of Ryan, and a sob escapes before she can swallow it.

Leaving Claire on the sofa, the nurse goes to the coffee machine and gets her a dark, sweet cup of coffee. When Claire doesn't immediately take it, the nurse puts the cup in her hands and wraps her own large warm hands around Claire's.

"Here you are. Drink, honey."

And so Claire does. The liquid is hot, and much too sweet for her taste, but it gives her a moment to gather her thoughts.

Watching her carefully, the nurse – Danni Delaney, according to her name tag – goes to fetches a clipboard and a pen, returning to sit down kitty-corner to Claire on the edge of the sofa.

"What's your name, honey?"

"Claire. Claire Walsch."

"Okay, Claire, can I ask you some questions?"

"Yeah." Her voice sounds shaky, even to her own ears.

Danni notices and pats her leg maternally. "Hold on, honey. When I'm finished with the questions, I'll go and check on your…"

Catching the meaningful pause, Claire looks up at Danni blankly before she realizes the implications. "Sister," she mumbles tiredly.

"Of course." Danni's face is carefully impassive. "Your sister. Can you give me her full name?"

"Ryan." Claire realizes that she has said that part already and casts around for a memory of the first name written on the file that Art gave her what feels like months ago. "Leah. Leah Ryan."

"All right." Danni scribbles on her form. "Social security number?"

Tired, Claire wipes at her face. "I don't know that."

"Don't worry, honey; that's fine. Do you have another contact for her? Someone else we can call?"

"No. No, I don't." Claire's jaw muscles clench. "There's just me. I don't know who else to call…"

Sensing her distress, Danni puts down the clipboard and takes the coffee cup from Claire, setting it on the carpet before she takes Claire's smaller hand between hers.

"Hey, Claire, you're doing fine. All right? Right now she's in with Doctor Jensen, and I promise you there's nobody better. Your sister will be just fine." Danni is surprised when her reassurance bring an unexpected smile to the blonde's face.

"Yeah. She's always fine."

"That's the spirit." Picking up her clipboard, Danni poises her pen above the paper. "Can you tell me about the shooting?"

"I wasn't there when it happened."

The pause before she says it, and her quick delivery, give it away as a lie. The nurse looks at her curiously before she moves on to the next point. Claire gives her as much information as she can, reverting to using her own personal details for lack of any other option, before Danni returns to the desk.

"Claire, I'm calling the local police first thing in the morning to report the shooting. They'll want to come in and talk to your sister. Okay?"

Claire's eyes are exhausted. "I suppose you have to."

"Yes. Just so you know." Danni's face is painstakingly blank.

"Okay. I understand."

Claire gets up and walks around restlessly, picking up magazines and discarding them without even a glance. She puts her hands in her pocket and shifts them around, then pulls them out and pats them against her thighs. When Danni offers her a tablet to help calm her down, she refuses at first, and then accepts in pure frustration. As it kicks in, she can finally sit down and breathe, her jangled nerves dulled by the medication. She is still sitting quietly on the couch, her insides knotted and churning, when Doctor Jensen comes down the hallway and stops at the desk, talking in a low tone to Danni before she approaches Claire.

"Miss Walsch?"

Claire shoots up from the sofa. "Yes."

"Miss Ryan has been moved to the ICU. The gunshot wound caused a fair amount of muscle and tissue damage, but she's lucky – if it had been an inch higher, it would have shattered the collarbone. Blood loss was also a concern." She elegantly pushes a lock of blonde hair behind one ear. "It is a fairly straightforward injury as they go, Miss Walsch, and your...sister?... is in no immediate danger. We're going to keep her in the ICU for observation overnight and if she's stable tomorrow, we'll move her to a ward. After two or three days we re-assess her progress and take it from there."

There is a moment of contemplative silence before she speaks again. "I've also re-stitched her right hand and cleaned the sutured wound on her head. Can you tell me what caused those injuries?"

"She took on a window, knuckles first." Claire shrugs tiredly. "As I told Nurse Delaney, I wasn't there when the shooting happened."

"All right." Doctor Jensen nods, unconvinced. "I'll be keeping an eye on Miss Ryan today, and I'll be sure to let you know if anything changes. Do you have somewhere to go?"

"No. I'm not...we're not from here."

"Okay. I think you need to get some rest. I'm going to ask Danni to take you to one of the residents' rooms. Try to get some sleep. Everything's under control."

The doctor returns to the desk and speaks to the nurse again, and when she disappears around the corner, Danni leads Claire to a small bare room with a narrow bed against the wall. Claire does not imagine that she will ever be able to sleep, knowing that Ryan is alone and in pain somewhere in the hospital, but she has barely put her head down on the pillow when she drifts off into a solid, nightmare-filled sleep.

Four hours later, when a hand tentatively touches her shoulder, she jerks awake and shoots up. "Ryan?"

It's Danni Delaney with another cup of sweet coffee. "Here. I'm sorry to wake you, but Miss Ryan's awake. Doctor Jensen thought you'd want to see her."

"Yes, please."

She swings her legs off the bed and sips at the dark beverage, almost wincing at the tang of the sugar in her throat, then stands up and follows the tall nurse down the corridor. They pass a few open wards and then enter the ICU, where Danni indicates the beds to Claire and then leaves her to her visit.

Ryan is the only occupant, her relaxed face pale against the pillows. Her eyes are closed, and Claire takes a moment to glance at her heavily bandaged upper arm and shoulder, visible under the sleeveless white hospital gown. When her gaze shifts away from the injury, Ryan's green eyes are open and focused on her.

"Hello, Walsch." A ghost of a smile twists around her lips.

With an answering smile, Claire steps closer. "Hello, Marine." She reaches out and almost touches the bandage before she pulls her hand back. "How does your shoulder feel?"

"It's okay."

Claire bites her lip, but she doesn't quite manage to repress the tears that well up in her eyes.

Looking up at her, Ryan frowns. "Hey. Don't. What's the matter? I'm fine!"

"I know." The blonde turns away to hide her embarrassment. "I know. You scared me, that's all."

"Claire." When the blonde's back remains turned, she tries again. "Claire? Please come here. Or at least have the decency to stand on my good side so I can pull you closer."

A slight chuckle escapes Claire as she sniffles and walks around the bed to stand at Ryan's right. Reaching out, the Marine irritably shifts her arm to settle the IV before she grasps Claire's wrist and pulls her towards the bed, slipping her hand into the other woman's. "I'm all right. Okay? Practically indestructible. Did you get some sleep?"

"Yeah. Divine Danni Delaney put me up in one of the resident's rooms."

"Who?"

"Danni. The lovely nurse at reception."

"Oh. I missed her somehow." Ryan squeezes Claire's hand before she lets it go. "Are you okay?"

"I thought you were dead, Ryan." Claire's bottom lip trembles. "Other than that? Peachy." The small muscle at the edge of her jaw jumps, and she leaps desperately at the first words that tumble out. "Nurse Delaney's calling the police this morning, to report the shooting."

Ryan nods to herself. "Okay. She has to."

"Yeah." Claire's eyes are big and anxious. "What now? What's next?"

"Nothing. Nothing's next."

"But what are we...you have to...if you wait for them, you'll..." The smaller woman exhales unevenly and wipes a trembling hand over her face.

Without any outward sign of discomfort Ryan sits up, the ugly hospital gown crinkling as she shifts. With a frown, she peels off the white sticking plaster and pulls the IV needle out of her arm. She takes Claire by the hand and pulls her into an awkward, one-armed hug.

Even as Claire's arms wrap cautiously around Ryan's waist and the blonde head rests against the side of her face, Claire weakly protests, "No. You shouldn't have done that. I'm going to hurt you."

"Shhh." Ryan's hand rubs comfortingly over Claire's back and then slips up to cup the back of her neck gently. "I'm sorry that I did this to you, Claire."

"What?" As Claire's mouth moves, her lips brush against Ryan's neck.

"That I caused all this upset in your life. It was a very selfish choice I made."

"I don't care about that right now, Ryan. I just care that you're all right, and here, and with me." Claire unconsciously rubs Ryan's back, stopping to caress the skin where her fingers inadvertently slip into the opening at the back of the gown.

Ryan shivers at the gentle touch and draws back slightly. "Claire..."

When Claire turns her head, their eyes are inches apart, their faces so close that the warmth of her breath washes against Ryan's cheek. The Marine opens her mouth to speak and without forethought, Claire leans closer and captures Ryan's lips with her own. The kiss is gentle, lingering and hesitant.

Groaning softly against Claire's mouth, Ryan sinks into the sensation, closing her eyes as the blonde's soft lips brush over hers. Only when Claire's hand slips up to cup her cheek, do her senses return. Pulling back from the warm, inviting mouth, she ends the kiss. Claire moves forward to recapture her lips, but Ryan turns away slightly.

"Wait, Claire."

It is almost her undoing when the blonde woman pulls back. Her blue eyes are wide, and her pupils dilated. A faint blush covers her cheeks, and heavy breaths escape her slightly open mouth. Ryan has to stop herself from sliding her fingers back into the mussed blonde hair and pulling Claire down for another kiss. Clearing her suddenly scratchy throat, Ryan takes a shaky breath. "We shouldn't be..."

"I shouldn't have..."

Having begun speaking at the same time, they both stop speaking at the same time. The silence hangs in the air before Ryan starts again. "Highly stressful or emotionally draining situations drive people to do things they wouldn't normally do."

The blue eyes search her face and dart towards her lips. "Is this something you wouldn't normally do, Ryan?"

"Maybe. No, not lately." Claire's hungry eyes and parted moist lips are wreaking havoc on her already battered senses. "But I was talking about you. You're in a state of shock..."

There is just the faintest pressure of fingers beginning to caress the bare skin at the edge of the hospital gown again, and when nails drag gently over the surface of her back, Ryan jolts and arches away, biting her lower lip against the dull pain in her shoulder. "Claire…"

"I'm feeling a lot of confusing things right now, Ryan, but I don't think shock is one of them. At least not the way you meant it." Claire pulls back a little and rests a hand on the other woman's hollow cheek. "Tell me you don't want me right now, or shut up and let me kiss you."

At a loss for words, Ryan takes in the beautiful face with a quiet intensity before she abruptly wraps her bandaged hand in the blonde hair and pulls Claire towards her. Their mouths meet in an impatient clash, and this time it is electric rather than soothing.

Claire feels her stomach drop as if she is on a rollercoaster ride as Ryan's lips impatiently cover hers, and when the Marine demands entrance to her mouth, she complies with a groan. Ryan's hand splays against the back of her head, her fingers tangled in the blonde hair as she urgently pulls Claire to her. When their tongues meet, Claire has to move her hand from Ryan's back to the bed to support herself as her knees threaten to buckle under her.

Ryan's torso trembles slightly at the physical strain, but she does not notice. It feels as if the breath is being drawn from her, inch by inch, as if her heart is clenching with every demanding stroke of the blonde's tongue. Finally her body's limitations become so pronounced that she cannot ignore them any longer. Gasping, both at the unexpected passion and the fire spreading in her arm and shoulder, she pulls away and slumps back on the bed.

Left in mid-kiss, Claire keeps her eyes shut and concentrates on getting her erratic breathing back to normal. When she has regained some sense of control, she glances down at Ryan, her eyes drawn to the kiss-bruised lips, dark in the pale face. "Are you all right?" Her voice is thick and liquid with desire.

Ryan nods. "I'm fine." She closes her eyes and furrows her brow. "Actually... I don't know."

Chuckling at the unusual indecisiveness, Claire lays a warm hand on the Marine's arm. "Is your shoulder hurting?"

"That too."

The blue eyes fix intensely on her mouth. "What else?"

"I think I'm drowning."

A muscle jumps in Ryan's neck, and Claire lowers her head and presses her lips against it softly. With a muffled groan, Ryan pushes against Claire's shoulder until she lifts her head and glances up.

"You need to stop, Claire." Ryan's voice is husky and rough. "I can't take much more of this right now."

"I…" Claire swallows and looks around blindly. "I probably need to get Danni or Doctor Jensen to put that IV line back in." Without a backwards glance, she walks away.

One night ago

Sierra perches at the bottom of the staircase, studying the blip on the small monitor; Alpha, Bravo, and Tango flank him with their assault rifles poised, eyes cautious and alert. His monitor indicates that the target is running down the street when she should be almost incapacitated by having had the tracking device turned on for such a long time.

But then, right from the very beginning of the mission, she's been doing things she shouldn't have been able to do.

Lifting his hand, Sierra motions to the team and they take off soundlessly towards the street, ignoring the dark black alley behind them. Taking care to avoid the pools of light created by the high street lamps, they slink along the side of the next building towards the signal. Suddenly Sierra freezes and lifts the device to his eyes, studying the movement with incredulity.

"Fuck!"

He turns on his heel and begins to run back in the direction of the alley. Without question, the other men sling their rifles on their backs and follow him. They run past the alley and round the hotel, hurtling past the small unmanned security booth and coming to a halt at the black van. Bravo clambers into the front seat; Tango joins him in front and the others pile into the back and slam the sliding door. As he's grating the gears in rare frustration, he snaps over his shoulder, "She's in a moving vehicle."

The tires squeal as he pulls away. They tear down the street, past the dark alley, and Sierra barely glances to the right as they pass a gas station on the next corner.

"Probably left from there."

Their quarry is moving at quite a clip, and Sierra presses down on the gas pedal. His first mistake was in coming to White Sulphur Springs when he should have stayed put in Helena, and if he loses her now, it will be his second - and most likely his last. Colonel Turner isn't partial to personal failure.

Beside him, Tango sits quietly, sharp eyes watching the road. It is he who is first to spot the red taillights in front of them.

The car is black, low slung and semi-sporty. It doesn't look like it's going to slow down any time soon. As they draw closer, the taillights of the car ahead pull away. With a gritted curse, Sierra increases his speed and closes in again. When he pulls up alongside the car, Tango leans over and tries to peer into the window, but the darkness of the night and the tinting of the black car's windows make it impossible.

Without preamble, Sierra swings the van to the right and straight into the path of the black car. The driver of the car slams on his brakes, but has to twist the steering wheel wildly to avoid hitting the van. The car ends up careening into the bushes at the edge of the road with a horrible crunching sound.

Sierra brings the van to a halt a couple of hundred feet down the road and reverses sharply to stop at the site of the accident. The car's front end is crumpled beyond repair, and a dazed man with a gash across his forehead is climbing out of the shattered driver's window. When he sees the van stop and the four men climb out, he recoils, but his legs are still inside the car, so he falls out onto his face. As he is lying on the ground looking up, the silhouette of a man bends over him, blocking out the sky.

"Where is she?"

"I swear, man! I didn't know she was married! She wasn't wearing a wedding ring or nothing!"

Sierra frowns at what appears to be guilty ranting from the injured man. He peers back at Tango, who has pulled out the passenger, another male – unconscious – and is searching the wrecked car, as are the other two men. Finally Sierra directs his attention back to the man lying at his feet. "Who?"

"The girl! She asked for directions. Never said she was married. I thought she was hot, but I didn't mean anything by it, man!"

"Shut up." Ignoring the whimpering, Sierra turns to watch as Tango, Bravo, and Alpha efficiently check the interior of the vehicle. When Bravo lifts his head and murmurs something, Sierra is there immediately.

"What?"

In answer, Bravo holds up the small tracking device that is supposed to be lodged inside Ryan's head. Sierra takes it between two fingers, almost trembling as he considers crushing it in rage. The other men watch him, waiting for a command, unprepared when he loses his temper.

"Fuck!" The barked profanity sounds out sharply in the quietness of the night.

Even as Danni Delaney slips the needle back in, causing minimal discomfort, she is glancing at the pale patient with a measure of concern. Ryan's eyes are closed and her breathing is hitching slightly. When Danni has finished sticking down the new strip of plaster, she touches Ryan's right shoulder sympathetically. "You look like you're struggling. Do you need something?"

Desperately.

"No thank you. I'm fine." Ryan half-smiles her thanks, and as Danni leaves the room, she closes her eyes, falling straight into a delicious memory of Claire Walsch's lips, which at some point changes into a delicious dream.

At Danni's suggestion, Claire takes a shower in the residents' bathroom, standing under the spray of water in a daze for a long time before she shakes herself awake and begins to scrub her body vigorously, trying not to linger too long on certain sensitive parts. She has no idea what has just happened to her. That heady intoxicating rush and loss of control have not woken in her since...before the incident. She cannot even remember when last there was the slickness between her legs that she is now gingerly washing away. Resisting the urge to slip her fingers down and ease the throbbing – this is neither the time nor the place - she takes a few deep breaths and shuts off the hot water tap, almost yelping as the shower suddenly becomes cold.

Lust cooled sufficiently, she lathers herself up and finishes her ablutions, stepping out to dry her body. When she walks out into the hall, Doctor Jensen is just passing by and stops to talk.

"Was that good?"

It is a completely innocent question, but it brings a flush to Claire's cheeks. "Yes, it was. Thank you."

"It's a pleasure." Doctor Jensen turns to answer the quick question of a nurse and makes a note on the man's clipboard before she turns back. "We have some extra space where you can sleep tonight, and tomorrow Nurse Delaney will help you with a list of hotels and inns in the area where you may be able to get a room."

"Thank you very much, Doctor. I really appreciate the thoughtfulness of everyone at this hospital. And I must say that Nurse Delaney is a definite asset."

"That she is." Doctor Jensen smiles and brushes her hair back with one hand. "If you need dinner tonight... she'll be able to suggest a few options."

For a moment Claire thinks that the doctor with the ridiculously attractive cover-girl smile is about to ask her to dinner, and when it doesn't materialize, she is absurdly relieved. "Thank you very much. I'll be sure to check with her."

It is still early in the afternoon and Claire makes a quick call to Andy, assuring her that she's fine. She wants to call Art and let him know where she is, but she understands him well enough to know that he will be too concerned not to take action, and right now the last thing she needs – *they* need – is the extra attention. Instead she hangs around the waiting room for an hour and pretends to read the magazines, while inside she is wondering why she has to physically hold herself back from visiting Ryan.

And why she wants to hold herself back at all.

Danni Delaney's suggestion is pizza from a small place called Quattro, which gets the nod because apparently their crust is fantastic. Phoning through an order for a "Four Seasons", Claire retrieves the wallet from the black bag in the Trailblazer and picks through it, giving the delivery boy with the roving eyes a generous tip and a gracious smile. The smell wafting from the box is divine, and as Claire approaches Ryan's bed, her stomach is twisting for more than one reason.

Doctor Jensen is at the patient's side, her slender hands quick as she examines the stitched wound on Ryan's shoulder. Apparently she is satisfied with the progress, and as she is rewrapping the arm, Ryan looks past her at Claire.

"What have you got there?"

"Four Seasons pizza. Can I tempt you with a slice?" She holds up the box a little awkwardly.

Ryan swallows conspicuously. "Uh. No. Thanks."

With a frown, Claire addresses Doctor Jensen. "Shouldn't she be eating something?"

"Yes." The doctor fixes the bandage and then straightens up. "She should. But the meds may be making her a tad nauseous. By tomorrow, definitely. You're much too thin. You need to watch yourself or you'll end up in here again. Or somewhere else you don't want to be. Okay?" The admonition is aimed at her patient, who nods. "Good. Take it easy." She leaves the ICU, and Claire, who is standing a good ten feet away from Ryan's bed.

When the doctor turns the corner, Ryan gazes at Claire with tired eyes. "Is there a reason why you're standing in the next county, Walsch?" One eyebrow lifts slightly. "Do you regret what happened earlier?"

"No." Claire holds her gaze hotly. "I don't."

"Then come a little closer, please."

"I...." She looks down at the box in her hand, and when she lifts her head again, her cheeks are flushed but her expression is candid. "I'm afraid that if I do...they might have to pry me off you with the Jaws of Life."

Ryan laughs, a real, actual, low husky laugh. The rare sound surprises Claire, and its timbre sends a shiver down her spine.

"You asked."

"I did."

The vivid green eyes close. Pushing down her primal response to Ryan, Claire steps closer concernedly. "You look exhausted."

"I'm so tired, suddenly." Ryan peers at her, eyes crinkling at the sudden proximity. "Eat your pizza; it's going to get cold."

Pulling a chair closer, Claire sits down and pulls out a slice. The crust is as good as Danni Delaney said it would be, and she chews with satisfaction, licking her lips before taking the next bite.

"That good?" The sight of Claire licking her lips causes a sharp twist in Ryan's gut, a response she tries to ignore as casually as she can.

"Mmm."

The throaty response causes another reaction, this time slightly lower, and Ryan doesn't speak again, aware that her voice will betray her. She watches as the blonde demolishes four slices in what must surely be record time, and when Claire puts her fingers in her mouth one by one, and sucks off the greasy film, Ryan closes her eyes and wills the surge of desire to go away. When she opens them again, Claire's cornflower-blue eyes are examining her face.

"You okay? Relatively speaking, I mean?"

"Yeah." There's a rough edge to her voice, and she clears her throat. "I think I'm on my way out."

"I'm keeping you up." Gathering the pizza box, Claire stands. "I'll let you get some sleep."

"No goodnight kiss?"

Incredulously Claire stares at Ryan, but the Marine's face is inscrutable. Frowning slightly, Claire places the pizza box on the chair and approaches the bed, the desire to call the dark woman's bluff rising in her. She intends for it to be a light, uncomplicated kiss, but as she leans closer and their lips touch, the frisson between them flares and her breath leaves her chest in an audible sigh. Straightening, Claire attempts to ignore the flush that is spreading across her cheeks.

"I hope you sleep well tonight."

"Oh, I'm sure I will." Ryan closes her eyes and a small smile curves around her lips. "Good night, Walsch."

Claire is sleeping soundly when a commotion outside wakes her. Groggy, she turns over in the small cot and stretches, starting when the door bursts open and Danni Delaney steps into the room, her tall frame filling the doorway. Behind her Claire can see a uniformed officer hovering at the door and Doctor Jensen rushing down the hall, twisting to avoid colliding with an orderly moving quickly in the opposite direction.

"Miss Walsch…"

Claire shoots up, anxiety unfurling across her face. "What's happening, Danni?"

The statuesque nurse puts her hands on her hips exasperatedly. "Actually, we were hoping you could tell us that. Your sister…"

Wide-eyed, the blonde quickly gets to her feet. "Ryan? What…"

Danni shrugs. "Miss Ryan appears to have discharged herself some time during the night."

"Are you sure she left of her own will?" As soon as the question leaves her mouth, Claire curses her carelessness, but after a brief speculative look at her, Danni answers tactfully.

"Very much so." The nurse reaches into her pocket and pulls out a folded piece of paper. "She left you a note." Holding it out, she presses it into Claire's uncertain fingers. "You have any idea where she went? She should still be in hospital. The officer wanted to talk to her about the shooting."

"I don't know. She could be anywhere." Claire unfolds the piece of paper, not noticing when Danni leaves the room. The handwriting is sprawling and elegant.

Claire

I don't want you in the middle of this. My reasons for keeping you around aren't enough anymore. I'm so sorry that I hurt you.
Phone your sister. Go home. Buy a car. Drive it! Get a great life.
You deserve it. You deserve so much more.
It's not about surviving.
It's about thriving.

Ryan

"Damn it." Claire crumples the paper and clenches it in her fist in frustration. "That rat kissed me goodbye."

She does phone Andy. Her sister is at first alarmed when she hears her voice; then, elated when Claire asks her to help with an airline ticket home. In fact, she is ready to come and fetch Claire herself, and the doctor has to refuse four times before she capitulates sulkily.

Next, Claire considers whether she should phone the police to report that she is not a hostage any longer. She does not want to get Ryan into any trouble, but she is not sure what the consequences could be. She is also not sure of the jurisdiction of the situation, and so, after a moment's deliberation, she phones Doctor Tilley-Clapham at Fairwater Private Hospital. His secretary puts her through and when he answers, his tone is curt.

"Tilley-Clapham."

"Doctor Tilley-Clapham, this is Doctor Claire Walsch."

There is a stunned silence at the other end before he speaks again. "Doctor Walsch? Where are you calling from? Are you all right?" The concern is polite and cursory at best.

"I'm fine, thank you. Captain Ryan...discarded me early this morning in Bozeman."

"Oh. Good. That's good to know. Can Fairwater arrange a flight back here for you?"

"No, thank you. My sister has already arranged something for me. I would, however, appreciate it if you could have my handbag and coat sent to my house."

"Not a problem at all." His acquiescence is hearty, and very fake. "Do you have any idea where Ryan may have gone?"

"No."

"Well, all right. It is good to hear that you're safe, and if Fairwater can do anything at all to make up for the inconvenience, we will gladly do so. Of course, the NCIS will be in touch with you regarding Captain Ryan, sooner rather than later."

"You have my contact information." How like him to describe a kidnapping as an 'inconvenience'. "Actually, there's one thing you can do, Doctor. Can you arrange for a vehicle to take me to the airport in Wilsall?"

"Sure thing." He takes down the details of her location, also jotting down the description of the stolen SUV at her insistence, and then rings off with another hearty insincerity.

When the taxi stops in front of the hospital, Claire says a heartfelt thank you and goodbye to nurse Danni Delaney and Doctor Jensen, whose beautiful face is lined with exhaustion. The drive back to Wilsall is without incident – the driver is a quiet man who has no need for conversation, a fact she registers with gratitude – and she picks up her ticket from American Airlines, boarding immediately.

It does not escape Claire's notice that, wherever she goes, she is looking out for a familiar lean shape. When she is finally sitting in her aisle seat, she is glad to close her eyes for a while and try to block out the myriad of thoughts rushing through her head. The airhostess hovers, concerned about her obvious exhaustion, and offers her extra cups of coffee that she accepts without protest.

By the time the airplane lands in Seattle, Claire's practically empty stomach is unsettled from the overdose of caffeine. She stands at the baggage carousel for a full minute before recalling that she has no luggage, and when she steps out of the arrival area, it is another long moment before she comprehends that the mirror image approaching her is not, in fact, a mirror.

Andy opens her arms and wraps them around Claire, pulling her close.

"Shit, Claire, I'm so happy to see you!" She twists her head to plant a firm kiss on her sister's cheek. "I was so worried. Are you all right?"

Holding onto Claire's hands, she steps back and looks her up and down.

"Poor sis. You look worn out."

"It's been quite a ride." Claire shoots a reproaching glance at her sister. "Andy, didn't I tell you not to come?"

"Probably. I wasn't listening." Andy fondly places a warm palm on Claire's cheek. "I wouldn't let you get home all alone, C. I've been worried sick. By the way," she says dryly, "I figured you wouldn't have let Mom and Dad know, so I called them. They've been frantic, sis. They send their love."

"I would've called them. Later." Claire grudgingly smiles when Andy rolls her eyes. "Yeah yeah. Thanks for doing that."

"Not a problem." Andy pulls her closer and wraps an arm around her waist, shepherding her to the central terminal. Her hand pats at Claire's waist experimentally. "Have you lost weight, C?"

When Claire shrugs, Andy rubs her side fondly. "You haven't got the weight to lose, sis. I'll have to fatten you up while I'm here."

"How long are you staying for, And?"

"For however long you need me. As long as it's not more than two weeks." Andy grins, and Claire can't help but smile back. They are on their way out towards the parking garage when two men in neat black suits appear from a side door and approach them with intent.

"Hmm. Sexy." Andy nudges Claire, but the doctor simply watches them without comment. They stop in front of the sisters; one man so tall that they have to tilt their heads back to look up at him, the other of average height and benignly handsome.
"Doctor Claire Walsch?"

It amuses Claire that the two men look between her and her sister, obviously unsure of the sudden duality of their quarry. She stubbornly considers the option of staying quiet and letting them figure it out for themselves before exhaustion kicks in and quashes her sense of humor.

"Yes. Can I help you?"

They both fix their eyes on her. The taller one flips open a badge case as he speaks. "NCIS. We need to speak with you regarding the recent incident involving Leah Ryan."

Andy protectively steps closer to her, and she reaches out a hand to pat her sister's arm in reassurance. "That would be fine, officer. Lead the way."

The shorter man flashes a smooth smile at Andy. "We would like to speak with Miss Walsch alone, Ma'am, if you wouldn't mind."

"It's *Doctor* Walsch, and yes, I do mind. My sister's not going anywhere without me."

The two officers glance at Claire, but she stares at them blankly until the taller man capitulates with grace.

"All right. Please step this way."

They lead the two women through a side door and into a corridor with a maze of doors. Opening one reveals a small conference room. Courteously, the men pull out chairs and seat the sisters before they take places on the opposite side of the table.

"I'm Agent Justin Leary, and this is my colleague, Agent Francis Mitchell." The shorter man is taking the lead. "We are here to conduct an inquiry with regards to the Ryan situation."

Claire is surprised that she manages to keep the flicker of distaste from her face. "What can I help you with, Mr. Leary?"

"We would like to ask you a few questions regarding Ryan."

"*Captain* Ryan." She ignores his slight twitch at her correction. "Go ahead."

The taller man interjects smoothly at this point. "Would you mind if we tape this conversation?"

He slides a small recorder out of his pocket and places it in the centre of the table, raising his eyes at her enquiringly. When she shakes her head, he presses the record button and states all of their names – as well as the date, time, and location – before he nods to Leary to continue. The shorter man shoots a handsome smile at Claire.

"Doctor Walsch, please state for the record that you have given your consent for this conversation to be recorded."

"I have."

"Can you tell us on which day you were abducted from Fairwater Private Hospital by Captain Leah Ryan?"

"It was the..." She hesitates. "Excuse me, I'm a little tired. It was the morning of the 13th of June. 2005."

"Can you please give us a recap of the subsequent events?"

Claire recounts the happenings as factually as she can, her voice even and calm and her manner detached. Even while she is pondering the wisdom of her actions, she omits the fact that she knows about DEX, choosing instead to say that she was excluded from certain conversations, such as the one at Rear Admiral Victor Banks' house. When she reaches the part about the White Springs Hotel and the shooting, she deliberately minimizes her role in the escape. The two men listen without comment until she is finished, and then Agent Mitchell speaks.

"Why didn't you escape at the hotel, Doctor Walsch? You must have had ample opportunity."

"I was being shot at by what I assume to be your men, Mr. Mitchell." Irritated beyond all reason by his tone, she shoots him a fixed glance. "Come to think of it...why *was* I being shot at, Mr. Mitchell? Was my safety not a priority?"

"I'm afraid I cannot comment, Doctor Walsch." Mitchell briefly glances at Leary before he continues, his expression blank. "Had they been NCIS, your safety would have been paramount, but we were not attending to any...situation in White Sulphur Springs at that time."

Claire's brow furrows, as much in frustrated exhaustion as in confusion. Catching Andy's perplexed expression she shrugs minutely before turning her attention back to Mitchell. "If not NCIS, then who?"

"I'm afraid I can't speculate, Doctor."

She shakes her head tiredly. "There seems to be quite a lot you can't do, Mr. Mitchell."

He bridles at the not-so-veiled insult. "We are only aware of the situation as it relates to us at this time, Ma'am."

"Then one of us has obviously misjudged *the situation*, Mr. Mitchell." She is clasping Andy's hand so tightly that her sister has to tap her to loosen her grip. "Be that as it may... Any other questions?"

"Why did you not abandon Captain Ryan at the hospital, Doctor Walsch?"

"Because at that point in time Captain Ryan no longer presented a threat to me, and I was concerned about her welfare."

Agent Leary sits forward and cocks his head. "Why?"

"Why not?" She looks at him quizzically. "She had been injured, Mr. Leary. It would have been heartless not to be concerned. And at least *she* wasn't shooting at me."

"Okay." Agent Mitchell knits his big fingers together with badly concealed frustration. "Did Captain Ryan at any point discuss any military matters with you?"

"She'd been locked up for a very long time, Mr. Mitchell." Claire allows a measure of amusement to creep onto her face. "How much exactly did she know?"

"Just a yes or no will do, Doctor."

"No. Unless you consider copious vomiting a matter of national security."

The tall man ignores her jibe. "Do you know where she went, Doctor Walsch?"

"No." When both Agent Mitchell and Agent Leary stare at her, she shrugs her shoulders impatiently. "What? Oh, do you want to see the map she left me with her current location circled in red?"

Agent Justin Leary raises his eyebrows stoically. "Doctor Walsch, we are not the enemy. There is no need to be sarcastic."

"Excuse me." Andy slips into the conversation gracefully. "Mr. Leary, my sister has been through an awful ordeal, which, may I remind you, was brought on due to negligence on the part of the government. She is tired and needs a lot of rest, and quite honestly you are treating her as if she is the criminal here. If you have any further pressing questions to ask, I suggest that you ask them now so that I may take her home." Standing, she puts a hand on Claire's shoulder. "And may I suggest that you work some sort of sincere apology into it."

An unreadable look passes between Leary and Mitchell before Justin Leary stands up, his face expressionless. "Doctor Walsch, I would like to apologize on behalf of the US Navy for the trial that you have been through. Rest assured that we will do everything in our power to have the perpetrator brought to justice and the situation rectified."

Claire nods. "Thank you. Is that all?"

When Francis Mitchell rises too, Claire stands and leans back against Andy for a moment. "Thank you, gentlemen. Goodbye."

They are led towards the central terminal and can almost feel the men's eyes on them as they make their way to the National Car Rentals counter. Leaning on the hardboard surface, Claire bumps Andy lightly with her hip.

"Thanks, And. I don't know why you didn't become a lawyer."

"I like dusting off dead things. Don't think law would have inspired much interest for me." Andy passes over her credit card and scribbles her elaborate signature at the bottom of the form before she turns abruptly and pulls Claire in for another tight hug.

When she speaks, there are tears in her voice. "I'm so glad you're okay, Claire. I don't know what I would have done if..."

Claire stays in the comforting embrace until Andy sniffs once and steps back, taking the car keys from the smiling attendant. Her eyes don't meet Claire's. "Let's go."

In the parking garage they find the National sign and get into the green Chevrolet Aveo waiting for them. Andy is an assertive driver, and she steers them safely through Seattle on the I-5 Express Lane, veering off towards the left just before Lake Union. Maintaining a one-sided conversation, she occasionally glances towards Claire, who is sitting quietly, staring out of the window. When Andy touches her sister's leg tentatively, Claire glances over with distant eyes.

They stop in front of a pretty brownstone building on 31st Avenue West and inside, Claire knocks on the caretaker's door. After intensive questioning about first her health and then her mental state, he unlocks her door and gives her the spare set of keys to use until hers are returned to her.

It is a surreal experience for her to be standing on her own doorstep, looking in at the small dining room and kitchen as if she hasn't seen them in years. It has only been a week, and her life has been irrevocably changed. Waving Andy forward into the spare room, she makes coffee, not realizing that she is crying until her sister's arms wrap around her from behind and Andy's body is solidly pressed against hers. Claire stands quietly and lets the tears run down her cheeks, and when control returns, she inhales tentatively a few times before giving Andy's arms a loving pat and stepping out of them.

Andy's eyes are concerned as she takes her cup of coffee from Claire. "C? Let's talk about it."

It is with a sense of amazement that Claire realizes exactly how long it has been since Andy last saw her cry. After that night she has never opened herself to anybody, including her sister. Smiling a small but genuine smile Claire picks up her cup and nods.

"I'd like that."

They move into the living room with its gorgeous view of the park, and Claire sinks down into one of the brown distressed leather sofas and pulls her legs in under her, sipping from her cup absentmindedly. There is a moment of silence before she notes Andy's blue eyes on her, and the worry hidden in them. Smiling, she cocks her head.

"I'm okay, And."

"Is it true?"

Resisting the urge to answer immediately, Claire pauses and ponders. It is a set routine between them, this slow, honest asking and answering, and she knows better than to reply without thinking it through. Andy would know.

An image of Ryan's fierce green eyes flashes into her mind.

"Yes. It's true."

Andy knows not to push. She keeps quiet, watching the play of emotions on Claire's face, until her sister speaks again.

"You know, Andy, she was different than I'd expected."

"Did she do anything to you?"

"Yes." Claire can see the anger suddenly washing through her sister, and waves it down. "Whoa, Andrea. Hold your horses. It's not what you think."

"Don't make me have to grill you, Claire! Come on. *Talk.*"

In spite of the frustration in her sister's voice, or perhaps slightly because of it, Claire grins a little, and even though Andy's still angry, her lips twitch slightly.

"Everyone's wondering whether she hurt me, And. Whether she touched me or anything." She smiles at her sister. "Well, she did touch me, but ..." Words fail her and she puts a hand on her chest, a motion that her sister's sharp eyes don't miss.

"*Is* she crazy?" Coming from Andy it is a straightforward question, no sensationalism or opinion.

"Not even close."

Claire begins to tell her, about the abduction and the flight and the events that ensued. The differences, though, between the story that she told at the airport in the conference room and the one that she is telling her sister now cannot be more pronounced. Claire is not taking care to keep the emotions from her face or her voice, is not omitting the facts which she withheld from the NCIS. She relays the information about DEX with a breathless intensity that draws her sister into the story and keeps her listening perched at the edge of her seat with a stunned expression.

At the end, she considers leaving off the part where she kissed Ryan, but she understands that Andy will know there's more, and Claire cannot keep it from her. When she finally finishes speaking, her sister sits back and scowls, an expression born more of compassion than confusion.

"The moment I saw you at the airport, I could tell that something had opened up in you again." Andy's voice is quiet. "You've been pulling back for such a long time. I hated not being able to reach you."

Claire smiles ruefully. "You would like her. You really would. She has this way of looking right through you, past the barriers you put up, without judging what she sees. I was so vulnerable and emotionally exposed, Andy, and she was so very gentle."

She puts down the cup. "Now, looking back, I don't know why I did what I did. Ryan graciously wrote it off to my charged emotional condition, but that wasn't it. She has a strength inside her that goes beyond anything I've ever experienced. Being with her ... I felt safe. Which is absurd, considering that I was in physical danger most of the time, mostly caused by her!"

She chuckles at herself, causing Andy to laugh softly.

"I don't know if it makes any sense, but she has some sort of ... peace inside her, and I wanted a part of that."

Andy nods thoughtfully and turns her next words over in her mouth before she speaks them. "I don't understand all of it, C, but seeing you like this, so animated... I don't think I need to. I do think it's a pity that it was *her* who brought that out in you."

Claire considers protesting, but brushes the thought aside almost immediately, trusting Andy not to disappoint her. And, of course, her sister doesn't.

"Not because she's dangerous, or a fugitive, or even a woman, Claire. Simply because she won't be around to build on that with you. You've found a sensation worth holding on to, and you can't."

Smiling at her sister over the rim of the cup, Andy takes a sip of her cooling coffee, and Claire waits silently until she speaks again. "I'm sorry, sis. That's the only thing I can say. I've always wanted the best for you."

"Aw, Andy." Claire gets up and crawls onto the couch next to her sister, laying her head in Andy's lap and looking up at the ceiling. "Weirdly, I think that *was* the best thing for me. She woke something in me that I thought I'd lost forever, and even if she can't be around to see it, I can't go back to where I was before."

"The gift that keeps on giving?"

Claire smiles at Andy's dry quip. "Yeah. Something like that." Rolling over, she wraps her arms around herself. "Shit. I feel like I've run a thousand miles. I'm so tired."

"Then sleep, baby sister." Andy strokes her hands soothingly over her sister's disheveled hair. "I'll be here when you wake up."

In a quiet corner away from the now-open boarding gate at Sea-Tac, Claire and Andy stand close together, loath to say goodbye.

"Are you sure you're going to be okay?"

"Absolutely. Don't I look okay?"

Andy looks her sister up and down, and then grins. "You look so much better than you did two weeks ago, C. Seriously. I thought my heart would break when you came back so tired and skinny and sad. But I'm not even going to think about that – you've got your spark back. Just relax a bit and enjoy the leave you've got."

"The leave I've been forced to take."

"Yes, Claire. Don't pout. Most of us would jump at the chance of a month's paid leave, *offered* to us, no less. Don't even think about going back earlier, you hear me? Now I'm sure I don't even have to say it, but if–"

"–I need you, I'll call," Claire finishes, and they laugh in unison before she continues, "Promise you'll visit again soon?"

"What's stopping you from coming to Arizona?" Andy demands.

"Dust, heat, work…"

"Hey, I work too!"

"Yes," Claire says, feigning a placating tone, "but you set your own schedule, And. Also, your fossils don't complain if you leave them for a bit. Don't be difficult. I know you quietly adore Seattle."

"*Very* quietly. So quietly, it's almost non-existent." Andy opens her arms. "Come here."

They share a long, tight hug, and then Andy starts towards the gate. "I'll see you soon, sis. You look after yourself. I love you."

"I love you, Andy."

Claire reads through the third question of the document on the table in front of her, and then reads it again, still without any comprehension. Since she's come back to Seattle, she sometimes feels as if she's being watched, and right now the prickles on the back of her neck are giving her the creeps. Taking a steadying breath, she puts down her pen and sits back, scanning the interior of the cafeteria. She is unreasonably irritated when she catches sight of Art Clarke, hovering by the sandwich stand. When he realizes that she has noticed him and strolls over awkwardly, she has to firmly tell herself to be nice. It is not his fault that she finds his nervous and overly protective attitude stifling. He's just being a good friend.

"Hey, Art." She greets him with an only slightly forced smile when he sinks into the chair opposite her. "How are you?"

"Great, thanks." He reaches for the sugar sachets in the container at the center of the table, and then seems to realize that he has nothing to put sugar in. "How's your day been so far?"

"Same old." She glances down at the paperwork, and when she looks back up, she catches a glimpse of sadness in Art's face before he manages to rearrange his expression.

"Art. I'm fine. I really am. I wish everybody would stop treating me as if I'm made of glass."

"I care about you. *We* care about you." He leans closer, his eyes earnest. "This sort of trauma doesn't just go away in a few weeks, Claire. I know you know that."

"You don't even know what happened!" she bursts out. "I'm sorry, Art, but everyone's expecting me to be … I don't know… weepy and traumatized, and nobody really knows what happened except for me, so you have to take my word for it when I tell you I'm coping just fine!"

Art catches one of her gesturing hands mid-air, and she has to restrain herself from pulling away. "I'd know what happened if you told me. I want to talk to you about this, Claire, but–"

"I'm seeing Gillian Beckwith over at Arcadia Centre, Art. You know she's fantastic."

"I want to talk to you, Claire. As a friend."

Finally succumbing to the desire to pull her hand out of his grip, she leans back in her chair and shakes her head. "It's easier with a stranger. You know that."

"Yeah." Art runs his hand through his floppy hair. "It's just that since you've come back, you seem different, and there's this gap…" He falters, seemingly searching for words. "It's just *different*, and I don't know how to help you."

"Different isn't always worse, Art, and thank you for the thought, but I don't need any help from you. I'm better than I've been in a long time. I'm absolutely *fine*." She falters at the word, and then chuckles to herself. It almost turns into a full guffaw when she realizes that Art is looking at her with the sort of solicitous gentleness one reserves for the pitifully demented. "Art. I'm fine. Really. I just need to get this form filled in."

"Is it something I can help you with?"

"No." She could actually use some help on this, but doesn't want to encourage him. "Thank you for asking, though."

"It's a pleasure." He rises from the table, and then pauses. "Claire... erm... you wouldn't perhaps want to go to the opening of that new art gallery down on Sheridan Street with me tomorrow night, would you?"

Once she would have enjoyed that; now she knows she won't. Art seems to be hovering somewhere between wanting to save her, and simply wanting her, and she of all people understands how those lines can blur. She also knows that every time she goes out, she still searches incessantly for any glimpse of a familiar figure. Art might be frustrating her, but he is too good a friend to deserve the half-measure of attention she will inevitably give him. Neither half-measures of attention, nor false hope.

"Thanks, Art, but I think I'll pass." *And I hope this will pass, too.*

Andy doesn't even have to ask who is calling. "It's late. You should be sleeping. How are you, sis?"

"Good. Really good. How's Arizona and how are you?"

"Dusty, warm, busy... You can decide which works for what. So, are you phoning to invite me to your wedding? Has Arthur finally worn you down?"

"Ha, but no. You won't believe what happened today! This morning I get into the elevator at work, and who do I run into but that worm Nesbitt..."

"Claire," Andy interrupts urgently, "if that sorry piece of excrement put a hand on you I'm flying down there right now and killing him. Seriously."

"Hold on a second, And." If Claire's casual demeanor doesn't quite convince her sister that she's okay, then the laugh that follows certainly does. "So of course he barely waits for the door to close before he's offering fake good wishes and getting right into my space. I politely asked him to back off; he ignored me. I asked him again, he crowded me into a corner..."

"Claire..."

"And then I kicked him squarely in the balls."

"Claire! You're my hero!" Andy starts to laugh and then quickly reins it in. "What did he do? What's going to happen?"

"Well, initially he collapsed and shrieked like a five-year old. I'm not shy to admit that I enjoyed that part very much. Then he went to Mr. Glenn with some story about how I'm a bitch who doesn't know what I want, and that I was leading him on, and so forth, and so on."

"The bastard! I'll kill him. Give me his address, Claire. I'm bringing a pickaxe."

Claire chuckles. "Rein it in, Sharon Stone. So, as I was saying, one hour into my working day, I'm on the red carpet upstairs with Lou from HR and some VIP from HQ, being threatened with a disciplinary by Glenn for inappropriate behavior, so I just let him have it."

There is a pause before Andy responds. "You what?"

"I told him everything, Andy. Everything. I just couldn't have it hanging over me anymore."

"Oh, C." Claire can hear the tears in her sister's voice. "I am so proud of you. Whatever happens, you stood up for yourself. You are so brave, sis."

"Thank you, And. It would have been nice had they believed me, but of course that slime Nesbitt was so convincing that I thought it was pretty much the end of my career. So the panel sent me out while they deliberated, which I knew full well was just going to be a discussion about how best to handle me... And then Nesbitt's assistant got wind of the story somehow and asked for a meeting, and it turns out he's been giving her hell for months!"

Andy starts to laugh and doesn't stop for quite a while. When she does, she's almost breathless with glee. "And then? Can you possibly stretch this story out any longer than you already have, Claire? Spill, damn it!"

"As if that wasn't enough to get the committee thinking, three other women stepped forward to say the same thing. And then Glenn decided to request the video footage from the elevator–"

"There's a camera in the elevator? Didn't Nesbitt know, or didn't he care?"

"I don't think he cared, quite frankly. He considered himself above any sort of repercussion. He probably thought his story would be bought completely, and likely it would have, had June not come forward and set the ball rolling. Bottom line, he's in a lot of trouble, and I'm feeling better than I have in years."

"Oh, I wish I could be there to celebrate with you, Claire. I'm so proud of you."

"Me too. I mean, I wish you could be here, and I'm so proud of me." Claire sighs. "I wish Ryan could have been here tonight. She was the one who said there was no back, only forward and onward. She was the one who convinced me of how strong I am."

Her voice breaks slightly. "I miss her, And. I really miss her."

"Little sis, I can't credit her with much, but for what she's given you today, I'll be forever thankful to her."

At half past six on a Thursday evening, two months after she's returned from Bozeman, Claire's doorbell rings. Busy in the kitchen, she tosses the dishcloth over her shoulder and approaches the door, standing on her tiptoes to peer through the peephole. Her eyes widen. Through the slightly distorted lens, she sees Leah Ryan standing in her hallway.

Clearing her throat in astonishment, she runs a hand through her recently cut blonde hair before she grasps the door handle and opens the door. Ryan is looking at something down the hall, and when her head turns at the sound of the door, their eyes meet and the sight of the vividly green gaze almost immediately has Claire trembling.

"Walsch. You look good." The voice is as gritty and hoarse as she remembers it.

"You too." It is the truth. Ryan's dark short hair is sleek, with a sharp widow's peak. Though her skin is still pale, it is now the natural shade of a fair-skinned person rather than the pallor of illness, and beneath the tight black t-shirt Claire can see that her frame is still lean, but a bit more solid. She is wearing a pair of well-fitting jeans, the denim faded over her thighs, and a pair of black boots, and to Claire's eyes she is gorgeous.

They look at each other quietly for a moment, the silence sitting quite easily between them, and then Claire smiles.

"Well, come in, Marine."

Ryan walks past to stand just inside the dining room. She looks around, taking in the kitchen and the part of the living room that she can see, the lovely view of the park. "I imagined your place would look like this."

"Would you like some coffee?"

"Yes, please." Ryan moves to the kitchen counter and watches Claire as she bustles around, her hands shaking almost imperceptibly as she pours the coffee. When the blonde glances up, the green eyes meet hers inscrutably.

Accepting the coffee cup, Ryan is achingly aware of their fingers brushing together.

"Thanks." She remains standing as she takes a sip of the hot beverage. "That's good."

"Why don't we sit down?" Claire moves to the doorway of the living room, and when Ryan approaches, she suddenly finds herself unwilling to move.

Ryan stops next to her and studies her face thoroughly before she raises a hand and slowly brushes her palm over Claire's cheek, her fingertips caressing the skin briefly before she pulls away. "You had flour on your face."

"Oh." One breathless word forced out of her suddenly straining chest is all Claire can manage. Their eyes lock, and Claire parts her lips in an effort to catch her breath.

Ryan's eyes fall to Claire's mouth and she rapidly steps back, interrupting the moment.

"Ryan, why are you here?"

It sounds terse, but the Marine sees beyond the brevity, almost smiles, and shrugs.

"I'm not entirely sure."

Those curved lips that Claire sometimes sees in her dreams are just a step away. Claire shakes her head. "I don't believe you. You always know what you want."

"Tough rep to maintain." Ryan stays just inside the door, even when Claire moves back to sink into her favorite chair. "To start with, I want to know how you are."

"And then?"

"First things first." Ryan arches her black eyebrows. "How are you, Claire?"

She cannot help but smile at the exaggeratedly solicitous tone. "I'm fine, Ryan. In fact, I'm better than fine; I'm great." She notes the Marine's eyes flickering around the room. "You're perfectly safe here. Sit down."

Ryan remains standing. "How's your sister?"

"Andy's good. She came to fetch me from the airport and stayed with me for a while. It was really nice to have her around for two whole weeks. Made me realize that I don't see enough of her."

"She must be upset about what happened to you."

"Yes. Some of it." Claire smiles. "She knows me better than anybody else. She can see I'm okay, though."

"You've gone back to work?"

"Yep."

Claire gives Ryan a quick synopsis about the Nesbitt affair. She realizes as she is doing so that she's telling Ryan more from a desire to see her smile than to impart the information. Ryan's response is as close to a smile as it ever gets, though the enjoyment in her eyes is real.

"Good. You stood up for yourself." She drains her cup and glances around for a place to put it, settling on the small table next to the couch. "Have you been driving?"

"I have, yes. Haven't bought a car yet - I haven't decided on what I'd like - but I will soon. In the meantime, I'm driving Art's car when he lets me."

"Art? Oh, Arthur Clarke?"

"Yes. He's a good friend." She doesn't understand why she feels the need to clarify that.

Ryan nods thoughtfully. "Right. You should get yourself a red car, low on the road. That would suit you."

"Why?" If she were in complete control she wouldn't ask. It's the type of statement that you don't pick a fight with unless you're ready to take the consequences.

Ryan raises an eyebrow. "Because it's charming, and sexy, and slightly dangerous. And..." Brushing off whatever else it is she is tempted to say, she shrugs. "You look very good, Claire. Healthy. Happy."

"I am." Claire sits forward. "So, what's happening with the DEX thing, Ryan?"

"I can't tell you that, Claire. It's not something you should know."

"Okay."

Though she attempts to be nonchalant, the upset shows, and Ryan steps closer, almost extending a hand before she thinks better of it. "It's dangerous. I don't want you involved any longer."

"I understand. How are you getting around without being caught? Did you drive all the way here?"

Ryan smiles and slips a passport out of her back pocket. She only flips it open long enough so that Claire can identify her picture - showing long lustrous hair - and the first name Isabella, before she closes it and slips it back into her pocket. "I know people I really shouldn't."

Claire grins. "Of course you do. Isabella... Do you speak Spanish?"

"Yes. My mother was Hispanic. I grew up in Mexico."

"When did your mother pass away?"

"A long time ago." Ryan leans against the doorframe.

"Sit down, please?" For emphasis, Claire pats the couch next to her chair. With amused eyes, Ryan pushes herself away from the door and sits down on the edge of the couch, but even then her bearing is erect and stiff-backed. *She sits as if she is at attention*, Claire muses.

"How is your shoulder?"

"It's fine." Catching the grin, Ryan cocks her head. "All right, a bit stiff now and then, but mostly fine." As if to demonstrate, she rolls it around, though it doesn't escape Claire's notice that the movement isn't quite as loose as it should be.

"And your hands?"

"All fixed."

Ryan lifts a square hand towards Claire, and without thinking the blonde grasps it in her own and draws it nearer to inspect it. There are faint white scars visible in places, but the skin is neatly healed. It is when the hand in her own twitches slightly that she begins to note the heat of Ryan's hand seeping into her flesh. Studying it wordlessly, she examines every inch of skin, from the long tapered fingers to the narrow bony wrist, memorizing all of the scars and marks, and when she looks up, it is to find the green eyes fixed on her with a muted hunger burning in them.

Taking a slow settling breath, Claire raises the hand to her lips and places a lingering kiss on the pale skin, feeling the fingers shift slightly as she does so. She lowers the hand but does not let it go.

"What else?" Claire's voice is low and throaty, and she does not care.

Ryan stares at her greedily, so much hunger evident in those green eyes that it makes her shiver. "What?"

"What else did you come here for, Ryan?"

The green eyes don't shift from hers. "For you."

Claire swallows convulsively. She wants to be levelheaded, she wants to be strong, but the energy from this woman is washing over her mercilessly and the memory of their one kiss is setting her on fire.

Has been doing so night after night.

Ryan moves forward, kneeling in front of Claire as she cups her cheek with hot fingers.

"You can tell me to go right now, and I will."

"Don't." Claire does not remember formulating the word, but even as she imagines she's only thinking it, Ryan's green eyes flash.

"Claire." The Marine's voice is ragged. "I can't promise you anything. I don't have anything. All I want is to see if this...thing I remember between us is real."

"I don't want promises. I want you." Claire closes her eyes as fingertips stroke her face ever so softly. "Just for tonight. I don't care about tomorrow. Please, I want *you*."

When Ryan's lips brush against hers, Claire opens her mouth in a silent sigh. Ryan nips at her bottom lip and then draws it languidly it into her own mouth. Her tongue passes over it lightly and Claire moans against her, returning her kiss with rising passion. Their mouths clash and withdraw. Claire wraps a hand around Ryan's neck and pulls her closer, forcing their lips together fiercely, and with a groan, the Marine wraps her hands in Claire's hair. Their tongues collide and stroke, thrust and tease, and when Ryan lowers her head and drops burning kisses on Claire's neck, the blonde gasps, trying desperately to recover her breath.

Her attempt is thwarted by the intensity of sensations flooding through her as Ryan briefly sinks her teeth into the juncture of her neck and shoulder before she fiercely kisses the abused spot. Her hands slip from Claire's hair to her knees and she parts them firmly, moving forward between them to press her body against Claire's. Her hands slide up the blonde's thighs to cup her hips as she moves her mouth to the other side and begins to caress the sensitive skin just under Claire's ear. When Ryan's hands pull her forward and her throbbing center presses against the flat stomach, Claire wraps her arms around the strong shoulders and arches helplessly.

"Ryan..."

It's breathless and soft, but Ryan is listening. Her mouth stills its amazing motion. "What?"

"I..."

Sitting back immediately, Ryan slips her hands from Claire's hips to her knees. "If you want me to stop, I will. Right now."

The flush on Ryan's face and the breathy quality of her voice challenge the ease of the statement, but Claire doesn't doubt her. Shifting her hands from the solid back, Claire caresses her shoulders and neck with feather light touches.

"No. I don't want to stop. It's just... I'm not good at this."

"You seem to be doing fine to me." Taking a deep breath, Ryan sits back on her haunches. "What can I do?"

"I don't know. This is silly. I'm being silly. I'm just worried that I might not be able to..." Claire drops her gaze.

A hand under her chin lifts Claire's head, and Ryan looks into her eyes frankly. "Hey. You're not being silly. You're in control, Claire. Set the pace. Take the lead. I'll do whatever you ask me to. Or not."

Claire's smile is shaky. "Okay." She licks her bottom lip. "Can you just kiss me?"

"Absolutely."

The kiss begins again, slowly. Soft lips brush against Claire's in rhythmic strokes, and it is she who eventually deepens the contact. Splaying one hand against the back of Ryan's head, she pulls the Marine as close as she can, while the other hand slips over the lean shoulder and down her back. Claire parts her legs and drags Ryan closer, then stills as her groin presses against Ryan's stomach again.

Ryan's mouth slows its movement to allow Claire to make a decision. When Claire's hips tilt forward and press against her, Ryan groans and slides her hands up Claire's legs, skimming over her thighs and buttocks to rest her fingers loosely on the curves of Claire's hips.

The blonde is kissing her ferociously now, the initial hesitation lost to a sudden wild intensity, and Ryan can feel the muscles in her straining thighs flutter as she struggles not to press forward into Claire's thrusting hips. The feeling of the blonde's rocking motions against her body, combined with the overwhelming force of the kiss and the fingernails trailing over her shoulders, is sending shivers down her spine and rendering her light-headed.

So much so, in fact, that it takes her a moment to realize when Claire abruptly shifts her mouth away and leans in to kiss a hot trail down Ryan's neck. Arching towards the blazing mouth, the dark woman wants to gasp, but she doesn't seem to have the air in her lungs. Her hands tighten convulsively around Claire's hips, and it is with real effort that she loosens her grip. The searching lips trail down her neck, alternating between gentleness and fierce passion, and the throbbing of her skin – and other parts of her body – leaves Ryan weak.

Claire pulls at the V-neck of Ryan's shirt, seeking access to the ridge of her collarbone. She marvels at the feeling of the Marine's smooth skin beneath her hands. Her hips are still rocking rhythmically against Ryan's torso; she has given up trying to control them. Her wet, aching warmth drives her forward pitilessly.

A part of her mind is telling her to slow down, to see this for what it is – lust, pure and definite – and to pull back, not succumb. This is the part of her mind that she is pushing away to make way for the breathtakingly raw passion she craves, as she slips a hand under Ryan's shirt and drags her nails over the muscled torso. Ryan moans and the vibrations purr against Claire's mouth. She pulls back to stare hungrily into the feverish green eyes.

Without warning, Claire stands, hoisting Ryan up with her by grasping her shirt. Ryan stumbles to her feet, her breath short and jagged, and when Claire starts to pull the black shirt up she silently lifts her arms to let the material be peeled from her body. Flinging the shirt carelessly into a corner, Claire places both hands on Ryan's tight stomach. She relishes the feeling of trembling muscles beneath her touch for a moment before she firmly glides upwards, her fingers kneading gently as they cover Ryan's high, small breasts.

Claire seems not to notice Ryan's hands slipping up under her own shirt; she is focused on running her ardent hands over the body she has incessantly been dreaming about, her fingers and palms and nails everywhere at once. She brushes over Ryan's belt buckle, and when her fingers return to fumble at it, Ryan takes a deep breath. Claire undoes the belt impatiently, unsnaps the top button, and then pulls Ryan close again. One hand slips upward to draw teasing nails over a tight, rigid nipple as the other caresses Ryan's stomach, slowly slipping beneath the waistband of her underwear to comb through the silky hair there.

Ryan's back arches and she leans against Claire for support as the blonde runs trembling yet urgent fingers between the warm, soaking folds, her breath straining against Ryan's neck as she strokes wet skin. Ryan's shoulders twitch when Claire's fingers tentatively explore the entrance of her sex, and when they flick over the swollen bundle of nerves at the apex, she emits a guttural groan.

"Damn, Claire."

A feral smile crosses Claire's lips. Leaning forward, she tilts her head and captures Ryan's earlobe between her teeth, nipping at it sharply before she draws the skin into her mouth. The rhythm of her fingers is relentless, torturously dragging through the slick folds, culminating every stroke with a firm upwards flick. When Claire finally slips her fingers inside, Ryan almost falls. She tries to spread her thighs, but her motion is constricted by the jeans still around her waist.

Claire is marveling at the softness, the heat around her fingers. When she captures the sensitive bud between two fingers and gently squeezes it, something unintelligible escapes Ryan's throat and gooseflesh rises on her torso. Desire spreading through her, Claire thrusts her fingers into Ryan, the heel of her hand dragging roughly over the swollen flesh with every stroke. Her motion is constrained by the taut fabric of the underwear, and she growls and withdraws her hand, forcing a sharp exhalation from Ryan. Claire impatiently pushes the jeans and underwear to Ryan's feet, not bothering to undo the boots before she moves them forward in a few awkward steps to press Ryan against the wall.

Her hand finds its way back between the slick thighs, and Ryan leans back against the cool plaster and tilts her hips forward as Claire enters her and begins to thrust again. As Ryan's body arches and her muscles spasm, Claire continues to thrust, desperate to maintain the connection between them. Ryan's hand on her wrist finally prompts Claire to withdraw. Leaning forward, she rests her palms against Ryan's heaving ribs and her forehead in the hollow of her neck, smiling as she feels hands caressing her back.

"God." Ryan's voice is husky.

"No need for formality. 'Claire' is still fine."

Resting her head back against the wall, Ryan shoots the blonde a smoldering look. "Is Claire?"

Blood rushes to Claire's cheeks... and other parts of her anatomy. Studying the flush with suppressed amusement, Ryan reaches down to pull up her jeans, leaving the belt unbuckled. When she reaches out and runs a slow hand across Claire's side, the blonde exhales raggedly.

"Can we go to the bedroom, Claire?"

Claire nods, and leads Ryan to the main bedroom and the soft bed standing against the far wall. Leaning down, Ryan unties her boots adeptly and discards them along with her socks and jeans, leaving her in only her black panties. When she stands, Claire's eyes are roaming over the sensual expanse of pale skin and the long lean legs. Now, after the blinding haze of hunger for the Marine has settled, she notices the star-shaped scar that decorates Ryan's shoulder. When Ryan approaches the bed, Claire reaches out and carefully touches the raised skin.

"It still hurts?"

Humming a low, vague answer, Ryan grasps the hand trailing along her shoulder and pulls Claire closer, until there is barely a foot of space between them. Placing her other hand lightly on the narrow waist, Ryan looks down into Claire's eyes.
"I simply have to kiss you again. May I?"

The words are so simple. Nodding, Claire closes her eyes and tilts her head, slipping her arms around the strong shoulders as Ryan's warm mouth descends on hers. The kiss is less raw this time, more sensual, and as she feels the rough hands slip under her shirt to brush over her lower back, Claire twines her fingers in the short, shaggy black hair. Ryan's mouth is firm yet gentle, her tongue asking for entrance before it explores her lips with a feather light stroke. Sinking into the sensation, Claire slips her hands lower to journey across the bare back, tracing the still slightly protruding bones and scars that feel like velvet under her fingertips. Ryan's hands begin to mimic her trail, caressing Claire's back in sure swirls and touches, slipping up over the bra strap and under it. When Ryan pulls her mouth away, Claire almost mewls in protest.

The Marine's green eyes are heavy-lidded. "Will you take off your shirt?"

Claire's hands are trembling as she begins to undo the buttons, and once or twice she fumbles and has to try again, but Ryan's hands do not move from their resting place on Claire's lower back. It is only when Claire shyly opens the shirt and slips it from her shoulders that Ryan steps back a little. Her expression filled with desire, she studies Claire's chest, her firm round breasts barely covered by the neat white lace bra. Reaching out, Ryan trails a forefinger over Claire's lips, down the side of her neck, into the dip at the base of her throat, over the clear line of the collarbone, down the swell of her chest... Where the bra strap joins the cup, she pauses for a moment before she traces the outline of the bra, dipping in ever so slightly, so that her finger passes barely half an inch above the hardening nipple. When Claire's back arches, the ghost of a smile creeps around Ryan's mouth.

"And this comes off, too. Please."

Claire reaches back with both hands to undo the clasp and the motion pushes her breasts forward sharply. Ryan's finger trails down into Claire's cleavage and up the other breast, but when the blonde lifts her hands and slips the straps from her shoulder to let the bra fall to the ground, the Marine lowers her hand to Claire's hip and pulls her closer. She gazes at the blonde's breasts in clear appreciation before she closes the gap between them, pressing her bare torso against Claire's as she runs her hands over the naked back offered to her. Claire's rigid nipples press against the underside of Ryan's breasts as the blonde arches into her.

Kissing Claire's face and neck teasingly, Ryan begins to run her fingertips down Claire's side, each time brushing closer to the sides of her breasts. When the blonde exhales shakily and lifts her arms to wrap them around Ryan's neck, the Marine smiles a little and brushes her thumbs lightly over the side of the pale, full breasts so readily accessible, repeating the motion when it elicits a soft gasp. As she repeats the stroke a third time, Claire moves out of her arms, her breathing strained. Reaching down, she takes Ryan's hands in hers and places them on her breasts.

"Please. You're killing me. Touch me."

Ryan's hands are tender and sensual as they stroke, and teasing as they nip and knead at the pale flesh. She runs her thumbs lightly around the hard pink nipples until Claire is writhing, her body aching, and then Ryan abruptly bends forward and wraps her lips around the nub, teasing it with her hot tongue. The blonde's lips part and she gasps, straining forward into the contact. When

Ryan's lips move to the other breast, Claire moans softly. Leaning back, the Marine watches her wanting expression before she slips a finger into the waistband of Claire's pants and pulls slightly.

"Off?"

Without hesitation the blonde unsnaps the waistband and pulls down the pants, stepping out of them and immediately into Ryan's arms again. The soldier runs her hands down Claire's side, over her ribs, and fleetingly against the sides of her breasts, then strokes downwards again, back over her sides and down to her soft hips. Hooking her thumbs in the sides of the white lace panties, Ryan leans in for another kiss, this one searing and breathless, her hands splayed across the blonde's hips, and when Claire presses herself against the lean body, the Marine pulls her in closer, continually caressing the flesh beneath the filmy material.

Wrapping her hands around Ryan's shoulders, Claire pulls her backwards to the bed, stumbling a little in her hurry and sighing in relief when she feels the edge of the mattress pressing at the backs of her knees. She moves out of Ryan's grasp to sit on the edge of the bed, and Ryan follows, propping one knee on the bed. Leaning forward, she supports herself on her hands either side of Claire's hips and tilts her head for a kiss, surprised when the blonde slips both hands into her hair and sharply pulls her closer. Claire's mouth is insistent and demanding, and it is finally she who pulls Ryan down on top of her, sliding a hand down to hold the woman's hips against hers. Growling, Ryan runs a hand down Claire's side, dragging her fingertips over the smooth skin of her thigh before she slips her leg between Claire's. Her hard thigh shifts against the blonde's wetness, and the curvaceous body jerks and arches with a low groan. Supporting herself on her hands, Ryan leans down and captures her lips relentlessly, her hips undulating rhythmically and her thigh brushing insistently against Claire's hot center.

This time it is Claire's hands that shift helplessly along the bare heat of Ryan's spine, her back arching and her thighs clenching with every thrust of those hips. Yearning is building inside her, tumbling low inside her stomach and throbbing between her legs. The slow, skilled movement of the body stretched out on top of her, and the thigh between hers, is heightening the inexplicable desire Ryan awakens in her. She spreads her thighs and lifts her hips in an attempt to increase the pressure, and Ryan stops the delicious motion.

"Is this all right?"

The low voice sends a chill down her spine and her body shudders. Licking her lips, Claire closes her eyes against the sudden lightheadedness and when she opens them, her words are concise and unambiguous. "Please. Take me."

It has stopped raining outside. The moon is bright and insistent, its beam focused through the window on the glistening bare bodies stretched out on the bed with an idle lack of restraint. The taller woman has one hand propped behind her dark head. Her other hand is tangled in the blonde hair of the head resting on her torso just below her small breasts. The other woman is lying on her back, her right arm stretched out along the lean leg so that her hand is curled around the knee; her own leg is casually draped off the side of the mattress. Occasionally she turns her head to kiss the breast closest to her mouth, a motion that causes a half-smile on the dark woman's face every time.

"That was fantastic."

Claire grins at the purred words. "It was better than that; it was phenomenal."

"Phenomenon: something exceptional; a singularity." Ryan nods. "Yes."

Turning her head, Claire shoots her lover a look of feigned surprise before she lightly nips at the underside of the firm breast. "Huh. Sex turns you into a dictionary, does it?"

Ryan moves the blonde head away from her breast with a stifled grumble. "Stop that. You'll kill me. I need to catch my breath." She rubs absently at the stiffening nipple, causing Claire to catch her own bottom lip between her teeth hungrily as Ryan continues, "I'm just pondering the aptness of the word. You do something quite...strange... to me."

"Should I patent it?" Rolling over, Claire eyes the flat stomach pensively before she begins to plant kisses along the defined valley in the center of it.

Ryan groans and closes her eyes, slipping her fingers back through the blonde hair. "No. Definitely not. People with less stamina than me would just explode."

"That's everybody." The kisses stop and Claire rests her chin on the hard stomach beneath her, raising her eyebrows impishly. "It's lust, Ryan. Welcome to pure, unfettered, raw lust. I hope you have a lovely stay." She runs her hand teasingly up Ryan's leg. "Combined with a strong dose of emotional connection brought on by a forcibly vulnerable situation. It's a classic reaction to extraordinary stress – simple adrenaline, amongst other things."

"You're sexy when you're talking shop." Ryan reaches out to caress the smooth shoulder blade. "So that's what this electricity is – adrenaline and lust?"

"If you have to put words to it. But it's just my opinion, of course."

"I can live with that."

"Sounds like you have your breath back. Good." Pushing herself up, the blonde straddles the dark woman and leans forward, her shoulder-length hair brushing over the pale skin as she plants a hot kiss on a corner of the square jaw. Ryan's hands splay over Claire's thighs and then shift upwards to caress the curves of her small hips and smooth back.

"You're gorgeous."

Claire begins to move her hips and her hands in a rhythmic action, and after that there are only the sounds of adrenaline and lust, the movement of naked body on naked body, and the beam of moonlight that is gradually diffused by the rain.

When Claire wakes up, it is raining lightly and she is alone. Everything is saturated with memories of Ryan. Her muscles ache, her white sheets are disheveled and crumpled, her pillows are perfumed with the dark woman's scent. There is a Ryan-shaped indentation in the flat sheet beside her. When she stretches her naked body drowsily, for a moment she imagines that she can still feel the woman's fingers deep inside her. Ryan is everywhere, and Ryan is nowhere. Ryan is gone.

Again.

The next time she wakes, Claire rolls over lazily – an appreciative grin on her face at the slightly uncomfortable sensations in certain areas – and pulls open the bedside table drawer to take out a remote. The pressing of one button slides open a rectangular panel in the wall to reveal a small LCD television, and another button switches on the streamlined gadget. Tousling her already mussed blonde hair with one hand, she switches from a cooking channel to a nature show, yawning as she flips through a few more. The Cartoon Channel earns a skewed, amused grin, but she passes that by too, opting for the serious face of the CNN anchorman as he grimly intones something about Iraq. Even the grainy, unsteady film footage flashing across the screen doesn't dampen her mood. She is reveling in the languid state of her body when her eye is caught by something familiar on the screen. It is the face of Rear Admiral Victor Banks. With a start, she scrambles for the remote, almost knocking it off the bed before she manages to turn up the volume.

"...two months ago in Fort Benton. The assailant was a personal friend of Admiral Banks. Local police believe that there was a scuffle, after which Banks was shot at close range with his own pistol."

The picture behind the anchorman changes, and now it is Ryan looking out from the screen, her green eyes menacing and cold in the exceptionally bad grainy photo.

"Captain Leah Ryan is extremely dangerous and believed armed. She was last seen in the vicinity of Bozeman, Montana. Authorities caution the public not to approach or attempt to apprehend her. If you see this fugitive, contact your local police department, or Colonel George Turner's office at the number shown on the screen."

"Colonel Turner's office. This is Lance Corporal Mathews speaking. How may I direct your call, Ma'am?"

"Good afternoon, Lance Corporal Mathews. Is there any chance that I could speak with Colonel Turner?"

After a pause, he replies, "I'm afraid not, Ma'am. Colonel Turner is not in at the moment. What is this in reference to?"

"This is Doctor Claire Walsch. I urgently need to speak to Colonel Turner with regards to the Ryan incident."

"Doctor Walsch." His modulated tone tells her that he recognizes her name. "If you wish to leave your number, I will make sure that Colonel Turned is informed of your call immediately upon his arrival."

She recites her number, twice for safety's sake, even though Mathews sounds more than competent, and rings off with a sigh.

Ten minutes later, her phone rings.

"Claire Walsch."

"Doctor Walsch, this is Colonel Turner. You wish to speak to me about Captain Ryan?"

"I do. Thank you for returning my call so promptly."

"Not at all." His voice is gruff, brusque and to the point, even though he is clearly making an effort to be civil. "What is it you have to tell me?"

"Colonel, I would like to talk to you about the death of Admiral Banks."

"I see." He is silent for a moment. "Doctor Walsch, have you seen Captain Ryan recently?"

"Yes."

"All right."

There is no trace of surprise in his voice, and for the briefest moment, Claire wonders if stoicism is something that these military types are taught, or whether it is those types that are attracted to the military.

"I'll be at Naval Station Everett in three days, Doctor Walsch. Please speak to Mathews for directions."

Traffic is heavy on Monday morning, and though Claire has the radio turned to her favorite station, her thoughts are a million miles away. She is anxious, and somehow she is embarrassed that she feels that way.

Early this morning she called Art Clarke to let him know in as casual a manner as possible where she is going. Even so, the call created confused questions which she could not answer. Art is not sure how to behave around her lately. It is fairly obvious that almost losing her has awoken him to new realizations. Claire tries to be understanding, but his suddenly tentative behavior and interminable fussing drives her insane. She misses her funny, relaxed friend, and yet - beyond being kind - there is nothing she can do to bring him back.

The DEX situation hovers in the back of her mind. She has tried to imagine what Ryan will be doing next, what her next course of action might be, but no feasible plan or idea occurs to Claire. It does not help that when her thoughts move in that direction, they linger on the Marine.

On the one hand, Ryan has influenced her – more by example than instruction – by the manner in which she leads her life so fearlessly. On the other, she is supremely aware of how little she knows about Ryan, of how the sudden emotional turmoil has thrown her together with somebody whose life is shrouded in ambiguity.

Nevertheless, now when she thinks about Ryan, Claire's doubts are consistently being nudged aside by the smoldering memory of the naked Marine with her head thrown back. It is a deliciously illicit thought; one she intends to hold on to as long as she can.

Colonel George Turner is a squat, wide man, not fat so much as solid. His heavy brow and bushy gray scowl give him the air of an aggressive bull, an image that is enhanced by the manner in which he holds his elbows away from his body. He is lacking in people skills, which is immediately clear when he ushers Claire into his temporary office.

"I've appropriated an office for our meeting. Sit."

He indicates an old stiff-backed chair in front of the basic desk and Claire complies, churlishly wanting to resist because of his tone but having no actual reason to do so. Instead of sitting down on the other chair, he perches on the edge of the table, simultaneously looming over her and invading her personal space. She has no real doubt that this is his precise intent.

"So…Ryan. You have something to tell me."

"I do." Claire has been in the company of far worse, and she is not flustered by this man. "Last night on the news, I saw mention of Admiral Banks' death. The report says that Ryan is the suspected killer."

"Yes."

"It can't be. I was with her at that time. She implicitly told me that he was still alive after we left his house."

Turner folds his beefy forearms. "Doctor Walsch. Did you, in fact, see for yourself that Banks was alive when you left?"

Claire's first impulse is outrage, but as she attempts to temper her anger she is already acknowledging the truth of Turner's question. Taking a deep, settling breath, she bites down hard before she replies, "No. I did not."

"So, all you have is the word of a dangerous woman notorious for her unstable temper?"

It's a complex question with unfair implications, but now is not the time to start a pointless argument.

"Yes." Claire frowns. "Why is this item only now in the news, Colonel?"

A tight smile crosses his wide lips and slightly lifts the incongruously beautiful dip of his Cupid's bow. "That, Doctor, is the right question." He unfolds his arms and rests his hands on the edge of the table top. "Your announcement of Ryan's innocence, though noble, is completely useless, because Victor Banks died *this* week."

"What?" Claire blinks up at him in confusion, her mind addled even though she understands somewhere deep down that this must be the simplest explanation. "*This* week?"

"Yes. Otherwise the news item would have been broadcast previously, as you yourself indicated."

Her forehead is furrowed. "And you think that Ryan had something to do with it?"

"Not *some*thing, everything. We found the weapon; her fingerprints are on it."

"For God's sake! He was a *friend* of hers!" She shakes her head. "You can't possibly believe this."

"I can, and I do." Pushing himself up from the wooden surface, he struts around to the other side of the desk and sinks into the old leather chair. "What you believe is *your* business. Now, tell me about when you last saw Ryan."

"I…" Claire struggles to get her thoughts organized. She does not want to share any part of Ryan with this man. "Captain Ryan came to see me last night. She wanted to make sure that I was all right."

"And?"

"And nothing. It was purely a social call. She was concerned about my wellbeing."

The lifting of his heavy eyebrows tells her that he thinks she is lying. "Your hostage taker arrived at your door to ask how you were. Is that what you're telling me?"

"Yes." Claire can't help the defiant note that creeps into her tone.

"And you expect me to believe that?"

"It's the truth. What you believe is *your* business."

For a moment it looks as if he is considering inflicting bodily harm. His jaws grind together and his eyes narrow as he visibly makes an attempt to rein in his temper. "And *that* is what you came all this way to tell me, Doctor Walsch?"

"No. I didn't come all this way to tell you that. I never, in fact, declared any enthusiasm to discuss this with you. What I came all this way to do, Colonel," she shifts forward and fixes him with a straight stare, "is to tell you that I do not believe Captain Leah Ryan was capable of killing Admiral Banks. I know she did not kill him when she had the chance. I think you're hanging her out to dry for reasons of your own."

"And what would those be?"

"I haven't the faintest idea, Colonel, but I can tell you that you've picked the wrong victim."

He sits back and glares at her. "You are welcome to your opinion. In the grand scheme of things, it changes nothing. I do have one more question for you." Reaching down, he pulls open a drawer and withdraws a large manila envelope. Opening the flap, he slides out several large photos and deftly spreads them out on the table, facing Claire. "Do you know this woman?"

His thick finger is pointing at a woman present in all of the photos. Judging by the shade of her skin and the mass of black hair cascading down her back in beautiful loose curls, she appears to be Latina. Warm brown eyes shine out of an exceptionally attractive face as the woman laughs at something being said by her attentive companion. Ryan. Considering the length of the Marine's hair, the photos are recent.

A sudden silence wells up in Claire as she looks from each photo to the next. Two dark heads, equally attractive, together in intimate, relaxed conspiracy. The woman laughing at something Ryan is saying, her head thrown back in abandon. Ryan reaching forward to touch her hand, green eyes serious as she leans closer. Ryan looking to the left and seeming to spot the photographer, her eyebrows drawing together. And then, finally, Ryan, turning her back on the photographer, shielding her companion from the lens with what seems to be a kiss. Claire's stomach clenches. They are entirely too close, too comfortable together.

The blonde shuffles the photos around before she responds. "No. I don't know her."

"Are you sure?"

Claire takes a last look at the gorgeous face laughing up at Ryan. "Yes. That's not a face you forget. Who is she? Where were the photos taken?"

"I don't know who she is, which is why I asked you." He reaches forward and gathers the photos, slides them back into the envelope, not bothering to put it back in the drawer. When he stands and offers his hand, the motion is almost offensive in its dismissal. "Thank you for coming in, Doctor Walsch."

Left with no option, Claire rises and shakes his hot, large hand with distaste. Before she leaves the office, she turns. "Colonel, you may not care, but I'm telling you for the last time that the woman I know is not capable of the thing you're saying she's done."

"Then perhaps you don't know her, Doctor. Good day."

She is angry as she leaves. Angry at Colonel Turner for what he's about to do, for the truth of the blow he's just struck; angry at the rest of the world for not doing anything to help; angry at Ryan for kissing a gorgeous woman, and angry at herself for being angry about that. After all, Ryan does not belong to her.

But the ease Ryan shares with the other woman rankles, the companionship in their eyes, the casual touches. Though Claire knows she has asked for no more than the heat and the fire and the intensity between them, she still feels betrayed.

She is berating herself so severely and deeply that she does not notice the tall man until he has walked several steps with her. Slowing down, she glances up at his handsome face.

"Yes?"

"Are you Doctor Claire Walsch?"

He is polite, but his voice holds a hint of something she can't place. "Yes." Irritation makes her edgy. "What is it now?"

"I need to speak with you."

"What about? Who are you?"

He looks down at her bleakly. "I'm Leah Ryan's husband."

He is over six feet tall, broad-shouldered, blonde, and square-jawed, and he is married to Ryan. Shaking her head, Claire reaches up to rub a suddenly aching temple.

"Excuse me?"

"Christopher Melville." He extends a hand which she shakes blindly. "You look a little pale, Doctor Walsch. Shall we sit down somewhere?"

When she nods, he takes her arm in an old-fashioned, courtly manner and leads her across the road to a bench flanking the beautiful old fountain in the middle of the paved plaza. When she sits, he perches next to her, his body twitching with nervous energy.

"Do you have any idea where Ryan is?"

"No." She runs her hand through her hair and studies him from under lowered lashes. "I didn't... Ryan never said she was married. She doesn't have your name."

"She preferred her own. And she's not exactly free with information, that woman." He shrugs. "You wouldn't have had any cause to know." When he suddenly shifts forward and grasps her hand, she almost recoils. "Please, Doctor Walsch. If you know *anything*, you need to tell me. Ryan needs my help. She's in very deep trouble this time."

"*This* time?" Claire pulls her hand from his, watches him warily.

"She's always been a time bomb, my wife." A wry smile crosses his lips. "It's usually just a question of scale."

"Why would you say that?" Her tone is purely professional, and yet the crinkling of his eyes as he glances at her, and then away, makes her think that he is aware of exactly why she would ask. He fiddles with the gold ring on his thumb before he replies.

"She has been experiencing psychotic episodes for the last five or six years. It is not public knowledge, but…"

"I know this." Claire's abrupt answer startles him, but she can't tell whether it's the brevity or the content that has surprised him.

Biting the inside of his lip, he looks at her warily. "You know? Oh. Of course you do. You consulted in her case. I'm sorry. I'm not thinking clearly right now –the situation is so stressful…"

"Naturally." It's what she says, but his demeanor strikes her as more primed than anxious. It's in his taut limbs, the alertness of his eyes, and the apologetic smile that slips through too often. She doesn't call him on it, but she knows that if she watches closely enough, she will see the moment when he slips. It's a game she plays every day. "You think there's something wrong with her?"

"Don't you?"

"No. I think that her behavior has been completely out of her control. It's not something for which she should be held personally accountable."

He picks up on the vague therapeutic direction of her words, as she has intended him to, and he cocks his head with a half-smile. "Of course you'd say that. You think there's good in every person, right? If you just dig deep enough." Raising his eyebrows, he folds his arms. "When I met her, she was already like that, Doctor. She's *always* been like that. Volatile. It's a word every single person who knows her would use. Be careful."

His last words are a gauntlet thrown at her feet. She would like to stay cool and collected, but the day is not even halfway gone yet and her thoughts are a frantic mess. "What do you mean?"

"Exactly what I'm saying. Her fire can be enthralling, but it's also completely unrestrained. Take my advice, Doctor. Don't get burnt."

The man is playing some game with her, one that she cannot even begin to understand yet. She takes a calming breath to center herself. "Mr Melville, what exactly is it you need from me?"

He smiles grimly, a tacit understanding of the dynamic between them. "I want to know if you can tell me my wife's present whereabouts."

"No, I can't. I'm sorry. However, were she to contact me, I would inform her of your concern."

"I'm sure you would." With a nod he stands, towering over her and blocking out the sun. His head is just a silhouette as he stares down at her. "Call me, Doctor Walsch." The card appears out of nowhere. "It's in your – and her – best interests."

Claire watches him until he rounds the corner before she scowls down at the card in her hand.

Christopher Melville, Consultant

The phone numbers follow, but nothing else. Turning the card over, she glances at the blank back and then slips it into a pocket. "Can this day just end right now?"

When Claire gets up and walks to her car, her stride is much heavier than it had been earlier that morning. This time she is perversely pleased with the traffic. It gives her time - and a reason - to be sorry for herself, and time to think about Ryan and the morning's bizarre events.

She does not trust Colonel Turner, not one iota, but he is saying things she cannot summarily write off. She trusts Christopher Melville even less, and yet she can't discount his words either, not until she knows what the truth is.

Or if one truth even exists.

Facts seem to shift every minute, reassembling every time she speaks to somebody new, and she can't turn anywhere for a definitive version. Ryan is the one constant she wants to believe in, for selfish reasons, and yet the Marine is the only one who's being persistently brought into question. And the only one she can't reach.

Claire argues with herself all the way home. She knows what she should do. She should step away and disengage. Remove herself from the situation for the sake of her safety and sanity. She also knows herself well enough to know that this is the last thing she's going to do. If Ryan were to walk back into her life tomorrow, she'd still find her breath catching and her chest burning with the primal response Ryan draws out of her. It's the one place where her control seems to have no sway – and no place.

Claire walks into her apartment, throws the car keys on the small table to the right, and immediately picks up the phone. She dials a number from memory and twirls the cord around her finger as she waits.

"Andrea Walsch speaking."

"Andy, it's Claire."

"Claire? Is something wrong?"

"No. Yes. Can I come and visit you for a bit?"

"Sure. What's the matter, sis?"

She tries to muffle her sigh so as not to alarm her sister further. "Nothing, and everything. I need a break. The world is wearing me down." She can almost hear her sister's smile at the weighty last sentence.

"Okay, C, tell me when you're getting here."

"I haven't made plans yet. I'll phone the airlines now and get back to you."

"All right." Andy's voice is gentle. "Take care of yourself, C. I'll speak to you later."

"'Kay." Claire puts the receiver down and then almost knocks the phone over when it suddenly begins to ring under her hand. Shaking her head at her own nerviness, she lifts the headset to her ear.

"Hello?"

"Claire." There's only one voice as throaty as that. "Are you all right?"

She means to say *I'm fine, thank you,* or *coping, thank you,* but exasperation makes it impossible. "What the hell is going on?"

"What did Turner want?"

"How did you know I went to see him?"

"I wouldn't allow him to hurt you, Claire. What did he want from you?"

"To know why you were here. And to ask what I know about the woman you were talking to in the photos he has." She has to fight the wholly human desire to be snippy about it, make some sort of sarcastic comment, and though she succeeds, Ryan clearly catches a hint of it in the change in her tone.

"Claire, she's a friend."

"I could see that." On the verge of losing her temper, Claire decides to steer the conversation into a different direction. "And I met your husband."

The moment when you're waiting for someone to speak, hoping fervently that they'll say exactly what you want them to, can feel as if it's stretching out over a million years. Torturous years, because even that supreme willing of the truth to be what you want it to be doesn't drown out the volume of the disturbing possibilities you're facing.

"Chris?" Ryan definitely isn't saying what Claire would like her to. "What's he doing there?"

"Trying to find you and keep you out of trouble, according to him." Claire closes her eyes and drops her head back against the wall in weariness. "I would have loved for you to tell me that wasn't the truth, Ryan."

"I don't lie, Claire."

The blonde's already frayed temper snaps. "Don't give me that shit about omission, Ryan. Don't. It's as bad as lying, okay?"

"I'm sorry. We're estranged. Have been for years. I don't think about him much." It's so infuriatingly matter-of-fact. "Don't let him close to you, Claire. He's not a good guy. He's dangerous."

She's so tired. "He says that about you. Turner says that about you. Is it true?"

"I said that about myself, too, Claire. Remember? It's not a lie. But I wouldn't hurt you. They don't have the same reservations. And I can't stay near enough to protect you, because my presence will put you in greater danger." Her frustration is well masked, but still perceptible. "I need you to look after yourself."

"Ryan, why did you call?"

"To make sure you're all right. Are you?"

"No. There are too many things..." She clears her throat. "I'm thinking about going away for a little while."

"That's a good idea, Claire. You should do that. I don't want you involved in any of this."

"It's too late for that *now*, don't you think?" Shaking off her anger, Claire tries to soften her voice. "What's next?"

"There is no 'next' for you. I'm sorry that I mixed you up in this." Ryan's voice is warm. "But there are things I'm not sorry for, and I hope that you're not either, Claire."

The doctor softens in spite of herself. "Ryan, are you kissing me goodbye *again*?"

The chuckle is low and vibrant, and sends a shiver down her spine. "Probably. I'm sorry. Claire – take care of yourself."

"You too."

When she hears the phone disconnect on the other end, she replaces the receiver with exaggerated care and slides down against the wall. She ponders whether she wants to cry or scream, and when she's ascertained that it's a good measure of both, she sobs out a laugh at herself.

There are many warring emotions – anger, frustration, uncertainty, melancholy – and she stays on the floor for a while, breathing deeply to settle her thoughts. Then, rising, she lifts the telephone and calls Andy again.

"Andrea Walsch spea— Claire?"

"Yeah, Andy; it's me again." Her voice is dispirited, but steady. "I don't think I'm going to come down there."

"Why not? What's going on? What's the matter?"

Her sister sounds as if she's on the verge of having a breakdown herself, and with a wry grin Claire tries to calm her. "Whoa, Andrea. Nothing's wrong. I'm just tired of running away."

"If there's something to run away *from*, you'd damn well better start running, sis." Decisively, she adds, "If you're not going to come here, then I'll come to you."

"No. No, Andy, it's not necessary. Really. Everything's fine. I've just had a bad day."

"You sure?" Her sister's voice, so similar to hers, sounds faintly suspicious. Imagining the wary look that goes with it, Claire feels the tiniest bit of cheer flowing through her.

"Yeah, I'm sure. Don't send the Coast Guard. Okay?"

There's a small silence on the other end before Andy speaks. "Okay. Claire? Phone me tonight."

"I will." With a smile, Claire rings off. Her mood is always improved by talking to Andy, who's so like her, inside as well as out, that she rarely needs to explain herself.

The blonde is determinedly on her way to the car when a stranger approaches her from behind.

"Excuse me. Doctor Walsch?"

Turning around, she glances at him, her gaze darkening when she sees the white military uniform. In the shadows of the setting sun, all that she can see is that he is a swarthy, heavily built but smallish man, and that he is smiling pleasantly.

"Can I help you?"

She is already beyond irritated and it's more of a verbal assault than a question, but his expression doesn't change.

"I'm from Colonel Turner's office." His voice is striking; a low, deep rumble. The polite smile is getting on her nerves for no discernible reason.

"Can I see some identification?"

He pulls out his credentials and passes them over, watching with curiously tranquil hooded eyes as she checks them thoroughly. They identify him as Corporal Seth Eric Mahoney.

Everything seems to be in order, and she passes back his identification with an irritated sigh. "Hasn't the military hassled me enough?"

"I'm sorry, Ma'am, I wouldn't know. Colonel Turner's asked me to show you some photographs for possible identification."

He's already approaching her, quickly, with something in his hand, and she begins to speak.

"I don't think that's–"

His calloused hand shoots out and clamps something firmly over her face.

As she struggles to push his solid body away, she's terrifyingly aware of the sickly sweet fog of chloroform strangling her and dragging her into the darkness.

When next she comes to her senses, her head is throbbing. The blindfold around her eyes is adding to the sensation of dizziness, and the gag is doing the same for the nausea rising in her throat. As far as she can tell, she's sitting on a hard chair, her arms tied behind her and her feet somehow fixed to the legs. Trying not to alert anyone who might be watching that she is conscious, she shifts her hands ever so slightly, testing the bonds. A tentative shift of her legs leads to the same conclusion: She is completely incapacitated.

Breathing as slowly as her rapidly escalating panic will allow, she rushes through her options, trying to think of any course of action that will release her from her predicament. If there is any way out, she is not able to come up with it; fear is scattering her thoughts. The bonds around her wrists are uncomfortably tight. When she shifts again to ease the numbness, whoever is in the room with her takes notice.

"Back with us?" When she does not respond, there is a gritty chuckle. "How could you think that we wouldn't find out it was *you* who dropped the transmitter into that car, Claire? Did you really think we wouldn't know?"

She tries to ease her disorientation by turning her head in his direction. When next he speaks, he has moved, as if he considers it a game.

"If you took the bug, you obviously knew what was going on. Ryan didn't force you to do what you did. Am I right?"

She again turns her head in his direction. This time he stands still.

"Of course I'm right. She's apparently a mighty persuasive woman, though I don't personally comprehend why. I don't get that. I also don't understand why you thought you'd walk away after that. You're too smart to have made such a stupid mistake, Claire. I'm an important man. I have ears *everywhere*. I hear *everything*."

Suddenly his voice is much closer... much too close, and much too intimate. "Unlike you. You apparently don't hear anything. Everybody's told you to stay away, and still you can't. I don't know whether it's stubbornness or determination. Either way, you fucked up royally, and you're about to pay the price."

His breath is warm on her cheek. "How much do you know, Claire?" A short laugh. "I suppose I should remove the gag. There was one 'guest' who vomited from the chloroform and choked. Unlike you, I learn from my mistakes." His finger probes the material and then pauses. "You'd better be quiet. Do you hear me? No funny stuff."

The blonde shakes her head desperately, and he pulls down the gag. Taking a quick, sharp breath, she lets out a piercing scream, which is muffled almost instantly by his large hand clamping down over her mouth. He waits until she is straining against his hand for breath before he pulls back his hand and hits her, hard. The blow rocks her back in the chair and the shock drives the air from her lungs in a painful contraction. For a moment she lets her head hang to one side, wincing against the unfamiliar spreading pain in her skull. When she looks up again, she can already feel her eye swelling, and the warmth of blood on her upper and lower lip.

Turner watches with mild satisfaction as a line of crimson snakes from the blonde's nostril and joins the blood welling up from the split on her lower lip. The set of her head is amusing him; her arrogant posture makes it clear that she may be down, but she's not beaten. He doesn't appreciate the attitude, and he waits until she's cocked her head directly in his direction before he hits her again. This time when her head snaps back, it takes significantly longer before she lifts it to focus in his direction again.

"Bastard."

It's a little muffled through the blood, but he hears it nonetheless. With a gruff laugh, he steps back. "I wouldn't insult me, Doctor. I have a very short temper."

"So do I. What do you want?" Her voice is thick.

"From you? Nothing. You just sit here and look good until Ryan turns up. After that, I'm afraid your future gets bleak."

"You're trying to use *me* to lure her in? She's smarter than that. Won't work."

"Well, I wouldn't be so sure." There is a palpable smugness in his voice. "I don't know the details – and I'm not much interested in them, either – but I hear that the two of you had a nice visit."

At the blank look on her face, he snorts. "Hey, you fuck whoever you want; I don't really care. I hope it was good, though, because it'll probably be your last." He pauses. "Though not hers, I'd have to assume, judging by those photos I showed you."

Though her face doesn't change expression, he can see a swift flinch traveling over the bloodied features. It makes him chuckle. "Such a fickle woman, that Ryan. I think you're quite pretty."

She licks her lip tentatively against the sudden burn of the open wound, and clears her throat before she speaks. "What happened with DEX?"

"Hm." He grunts. "Is this the part where I tell you everything and then you're rescued by your hero so that you can clear her name by repeating the sordid tale? It's not going to be one of those, Doctor, so don't get your hopes up."

"What happened with DEX?" she repeats. "What went wrong?"

"You think something needs to have gone wrong for Leah Ryan to go off her head? Oh dear." He barks out a laugh. "Maybe you know something I don't. Or maybe I know something you don't want to hear."

He's silent for a moment before he speaks again.

"She is the biggest mistake I ever made. It was in Kosovo, '97, when she got captured. The soldiers they eventually found her with weren't Serbian. We took them all out, so there was no one left to ask. We still don't know why they didn't just kill her. They tortured her for two weeks in ways she wouldn't even tell us about when we got her out, but one of the things she did mention was regularly being subjected to high voltage shock. We checked the implant when we brought her back, but with all of the physical damage and her brittle state of mind, it was very difficult to be completely sure that the unit was functioning properly."

He sounds as if he's trying to convince himself.

"She seemed fine when she asked to be sent back into the field. We did extensive psychological tests, ran the transmitter and couldn't find any problems. We even checked again, after she started to disintegrate. The only thing we can assume now is that whoever...worked on Ryan had patched into her implant somehow, and after laying low for a while, had started to interfere with our commands and transmit their own. The parties involved in Yugoslavia didn't have that kind of technology then, so the 'who' part's still a mystery, and will probably remain that way."

"Couldn't you backtrack to the source of the commands?"

"We tried. Whoever was on the other end was well hidden. We were circumvented more than once." He strides away, amused by the way her blindfolded head follows him, as if she is somehow keeping an eye on his movements. "Anyway, it's over now. We couldn't reverse the threat, so we're removing it."

"Why didn't you just remove it to start with? That would have been the easiest solution, wouldn't it?"

"Sure," Turner shrugs, "but do you honestly think we were going to miss the opportunity to see what we could track back? Miss the chance to do further research on the vulnerabilities of DEX that she'd uncovered? If she wasn't going to be useful to us in the field, she was sure as hell going to be useful elsewhere. We didn't spend millions of dollars on this project just to back off because some little thing went wrong."

"Why did you say Ryan was your biggest mistake?"

He looks at her calculatingly. "If we hadn't checked you ourselves, I would be wondering whether you are wearing a wire right now."

"I'm not. I just want to know."

"I know you're not. I was thorough." He enjoys the disgusted twitch of her lips. "She was a mistake. We wanted Banks, who was effective, focused... and pliable. And there was some leverage with him. When he suggested Leah Ryan, I thought that her endurance and determination would be positive assets. They weren't. At first she went along with everything, but then she began to resist, fighting for control. You can make the suggestions subliminally, but there's nothing that can force her to follow them, and that's where we went wrong. She's so damned obstinate. When she decided to check herself into Fairwater, we tried to talk her out of it, but she had a mind of her own. So to speak."

"Why *exactly* would you want to keep her out of the hospital if she was beginning to show signs of mental instability?"

"So she bombed a couple of civilians, felt like she wanted to do things she shouldn't... Whatever. As long as my team kept quiet and the Navy didn't look too closely, what Ryan did wasn't any different from a whole bunch of soldiers out there, Doctor. She would have been invaluable to the project if she hadn't been so hardheaded."

"Did you help her escape from Fairwater?"

He turns his back on her impatiently. "We're finished talking."

"**Did** you help her escape?"

She hears the stomp of the footsteps as they approach, but can do nothing to avoid the hand that connects with her face yet again. Agony blooms behind her eyes and it is all that she can do not to just let her head drop forward onto her chest, helpless in the onslaught of pain. Another gush of warm liquid over her lips, and this time she wonders whether her nose might be broken, judging by the blinding pain radiating from it. She keeps her mouth shut as the footsteps recede, only letting a small muffled groan escape once he sounds as if he is far enough away. Her head is pounding, and the copper taste in her mouth is making her gag. He moves about at the edges of her fuzzy periphery, and she is only vaguely aware of his position until a phone rings somewhere to his left.

Turner picks up the mobile phone. "Hello?"

"I've got something you want. I'll trade you." It's a man's voice, with an almost teasing note to it.

Turner frowns. "How did you get this number?"

"That's not important."

"I'll have you traced. You know that."

"By the time you find this location, I'll be gone. Just give me what I want, Colonel. It's not much. And the reward for you will be worth it."

Turner pauses and cocks his head to one side. "Melville?" The amused exhalation on the other end of the line confirms his suspicion, and he sniffs disdainfully. "What could you possibly have that I want?"

"It's not what, but rather who." Melville chuckles smugly. "Let me give you my terms. The Marine Corps treated me appallingly, especially considering that it was *my* signature that kept Ryan there for as long as you needed her. If I tell anyone what I know, Turner, you'll be in for a shitload of pain."

Turner laughs, genuinely unfluster. "Your reputation and your record would precede you, you idiotic moron. What's the point of this little chitchat you're wasting my time with?"

There is a moment of silence, and when Melville speaks again, his voice is tight. "What I want is reinstatement and my record cleared. Easy enough, right? No skin off your nose. You can do that with one phone call."

"I can do that, yes, but why in the world would I want to?"

"Because I have the one person who'll help you hook the elusive Captain Leah Ryan."

Turner rolls his eyes at what he considers to be ridiculous theatrics. "Oh for fuck's sake, don't make a soap opera out of it; just get it off your fucking chest!"

"Tut. Impatience." Melville sighs. "Okay." When next he speaks, the handset is slightly away from his mouth. "Say something, honey." There's a small moment of silence before he speaks again. "Come on, now. Don't be like that." There is a muffled and unidentifiable sound before he speaks again. "Fine, then. A little encouragement never hurt anybody."

There are sounds of a struggle, the sharp curse of a man, a woman's exhalation of pain... and then, finally, she shouts. "Stop it! Don't touch me!"

Startled, Turner yanks the phone away from his ear and stares at it, stunned.

The voice on the other end of the line belongs to Claire Walsch.

In the ensuing silence from Turner's end, Melville speaks again. "I trust that you understand the importance of this deal to you now?" He sounds smug.

For a speechless moment, Turner stares at the blindfolded blonde woman tied to the chair. His jaw muscles clench before he lifts up the phone, his eyes never leaving his captive. "You're trying to trick me, and I'm not falling for it."

Now the silence is on the other end of the line. Perhaps Melville expected the confrontation to be unambiguous and quickly concluded, but when he speaks again, he sounds just a little uncertain. "She's sitting right here. How can it be a trick?"

"The problem with your story," Turner has to remind himself to be calm, "is that I have Doctor Claire Walsch sitting right here in front of me."

"Oh, come *on!*" Melville's voice has risen another few decibels. "You can't bluff when I'm holding all the cards, Turner! I'm looking right *at* her! Stop fucking with me!"

Despite the evidence of his own eyes, Turner can't ignore the stark honesty in the man's voice. If he isn't an exceptional conman, then he must think he's telling the truth. Lowering the handset with a hand that's suddenly developed a minor tremor, Turner strides over to the blonde and roughly rips off the blindfold. She blinks against the sudden light, one eye already swollen almost shut. It is a second before she focuses on him. There is a measure of defiance in her eyes. With a growl, Turner lifts his hand to strike and then thinks better of it. If he hits her now, she'll be out; no good to him.

"What the fuck is going on? Who are you?"

She licks the split side of her mouth carefully before she grins. "You know me. I'm Claire Walsh."

"Fuck!" Things feel like they are rapidly spinning out of control, and it's a sensation he abhors. He hits her then, and watches in fury as her head drops limply to her chest before he lifts the phone to his ear again.

"Did you hear that?"

"*Are you fucking with me?*" Melville's voice is shrill now.

George Turner barks out a rough laugh. "Whatever's going on, we've just both been screwed over. So take your deal and shove it, asshole." With a snarl he disconnects, and then howls towards the door, "Mahoney!"
Sierra appears almost immediately, his eyes flickering to the limp figure of the woman in the chair before he inclines his head at Turner. The colonel's face is red and he's grinding his teeth.

"Sir?"

"Go to Walsch's apartment. Now. If the woman is there, bring her to me. Eliminate any threats. If there's nobody, check the place over. I want to know what happened there."

Sierra's blank eyes flicker over to the doctor again. "There a problem?"

"I've just had a call from Christopher Melville claiming he's got Doctor Walsch, and he wants a trade." He notices Sierra's eyes slipping to the woman again. "I know. Doesn't make sense. But I heard what I heard, Mahoney. Something's fucked up, and I want to know what it is. **Now**."

Sierra's face doesn't shift from its impassive mask. "Done. I'll have to take Alpha with me, Sir."

"Take the whole fucking alphabet with you, Mahoney." Turner's voice is curt with impatience. "I don't care. Right now it helps fuck-all to have this woman here. If she's not who I think she is, then I don't know where Ryan's going to turn up. Be on your guard."

"Sir." Sierra turns and leaves as swiftly as he entered.

With a grunt Turner approaches the unconscious woman and wraps his fingers in her hair, lifting the bloodied face to peer at it furiously. *Impossible! This* is *Claire Walsch!* He waits for her to open her eyes, itching to do more damage out of pure frustration, but her face remains slack, the blood running freely over the right side of her face from the widened split over her eyebrow. With a curse he releases her head and turns, kicking out at the table. Overbalanced, he staggers forward and knocks his hand painfully against the desk.

"Fuck! Fuck! Fuck!"

Christopher Melville drops the phone from his suddenly boneless hand, and turns to stare at the woman trussed up on his sofa. Her face is still red from where he had gripped it, and there is a bleeding gash just under the right eye where he'd accidentally scratched her with his ring. Even so, her blue eyes are glaring at him with the same intensity they had when he'd first turned up at her door.

"What's going on?" he growls.

His question brings a slight smirk to his hostage's face. "Why, whatever do you mean?"

At the sarcastic reply, he bites his lip in fury as he slams a fist against the wall. "What the *hell* is going on? Who **are** you?"

Her unfriendly grin widens. "I'm Claire Walsch. Isn't that who you think I am?"

"Shut the fuck up!" When the flat of his hand meets her face, she turns with the impact and then looks back at him impassively.

The lack of response only angers him further. "Tell me!"

"I have nothing to tell you."
"Who are you?"

"Claire Walsch."

This time he uses his fist. It connects with her jaw and sends her backwards onto the couch. A fine trickle of blood runs down her mouth where she's bitten her lip, and he doesn't even notice when it begins to drip onto the dull blue fabric of his couch, leaving a small but spreading dark stain. He eyes the unconscious woman balefully, flexing his hand as he paces up and down in the small room.

Turner is still grinding his teeth in fury when the phone rings. The ID shows *Caller Unknown*. "Mahoney?"

"Hi. I hear you're looking for me." The hoarse voice shows clear amusement.

"Ryan." And now his plan has to go ahead, regardless of the bizarre hitch. "Did you also hear that I have something you want?"

"Actually, the way I heard it... you're not sure whether what you have is what I want at all." The low laugh that follows the statement enrages him. "What do you have, Turner?"

"Doctor Claire Walsch." His hatred for Leah Ryan is palpable.

"But are you *sure*?"

She's deliberately sugary, and it's driving him up the wall. "I have no idea what you're talking about, Ryan. Get here or I hurt her."

"If she's not Claire, then I wouldn't care much, Colonel."

He feels as if he's going to die of a heart attack at any moment. "Fuck you!"

"No thanks." She's maddeningly conversational. "Hey, let me talk to her, George. Maybe it'll help your case if I can hear that it's Claire."

"You don't get requests, Ryan!"

"Suit yourself. I won't cooperate otherwise."

"You're a fucking bitch. I regret ever getting involved with you."

"I feel the same. It's your own fault though, George. You started this crap. Don't get righteous on my ass now. Put her on."

Turner wrathfully eyes the figure collapsed in the chair. "She's not up to talking to you." Even as he says it, the blonde begins to stir, a low moan slipping from her throat.

Whether or not Ryan hears the sound, his remark doesn't please her.

"You'd better not have hurt her, Turner." A smile begins to twitch at the corner of his mouth at this statement of apparent concern, but the rest of the words wipe it from his face. "You think I care because I fucked her? C'mon, Turner. Don't you *know* what I'm like by now? I wouldn't give a shit. I'd just move on. Unless you piss me off and make it personal, which you now have. I'd be really careful if I were you."

With a snarl, Turner stalks towards the blonde, noting with satisfaction that she cringes away from him. He pushes the phone roughly against her ear. "Tell your friend Ryan that you're Claire Walsch."

Dazed, she stares up at him as she speaks into the receiver. "Ryan?"

The voice is slurred, strained, and it breaks Ryan's heart. She speaks quickly. "Shh. It doesn't matter–"

"Ryan, I–"

"Stop." Ryan interrupts immediately. "Don't say anything. Turner knowing which one you are makes one of you worthless in his game. Be brave, Walsch; I'm coming for you." She barely finishes the sentence before Turner's back on the phone.

"So? It's Claire Walsch, Ryan."

"I wouldn't be so sure if I were you."

"It's her. I'm looking straight at her."

"So is Christopher Melville."

"He's bluffing."

"He's not a good liar, George. I know him." She chuckles. "It seems you've got a problem."

Turner takes a few deep breaths before he speaks again. "Here's the fucking thing, Ryan. If you don't pitch up in an hour, I'll shoot this bitch regardless of whether she's Walsch or not. Okay? That'll be on your conscience. Got space?"

"Sure." The Marine sounds unflustered. "Do whatever you feel like, George. I might be further than an hour away. Just remember that whether she's Claire or not, she's the only chance you have. Blow it, and the next time you see me, it'll be at my discretion, by my rules. Oh, how much *fun* we'll have! You know how I like to have fun. See you, pal."

The click in his ear mobilizes the squat, bullish man. With a roar, he begins to pound the wooden desk, not stopping until he is out of breath and his fists are bruised and bleeding. Then, with a curse, he dials another number.

"Sir."

"Mahoney, tell me you found them."

"No, Sir. We did find signs of a struggle. Smith at ComCor managed to track Melville. Idiot's actually using his own mobile. He's not far from here; we're on our way. Location should be coming up on your handheld about now."

After pulling open the top drawer of the desk, Turner clamps the phone between shoulder and ear to free his hands to check his encoded mail. The very first from the top is from Alistair Smith at ComCor – a detailed address in a suburb not far from Walsch's.

"Okay. Mahoney, don't hurt the woman."

"Sir. And Melville?"
"I don't give a shit what you do with him."

He slams down the phone and glares into space for a while before he stalks to the window and slides it up, resting his hands on the sill while he takes in deep, calming breaths.

When the fresh air hits her, the blonde opens her eyes blearily and takes stock of her surroundings for the first time. She is in a small room that looks like a government office – all faded white walls and starkness. Beyond a square heating system in the corner to her right and the desk in front of her, there is no other furniture. Based on the simple fact that she cannot see the door, she assumes that it is behind her. The colonel is standing at the window, his broad back to her as he takes in greedy gulps of air. There are half-moon sweat marks under his armpits, dark against his olive-green shirt.

Her right eye is swelling shut, and there is an insistent throbbing at the back of her head. When she tries to move her mouth, she starts at the sting of her split lower lip as the wound breaks open again. A salty drop of blood makes its way onto her tongue. Groggy, she watches Turner for a while as he leans against the window frame, and then she blinks a few times to try and focus her awareness.

There's no point! her mind is telling her. *You're hurt and weak and possibly drugged, and there's no way you're going to escape this bastard by sheer willpower.*

Nevertheless, she pushes her alertness to its furthest – which is not that far at all – and studies her surroundings with exaggerated concentration, committing to memory every small detail for the negligible possibility that it might mean something at some stage. She pushes away the sound of the voice in her head screaming *You're going to die here*, wondering abstractedly whether this is anything like the voice Ryan experienced. It might be from whatever is floating about in her bloodstream, or it might be the surreal situation in which she finds herself, but it almost feels as if time is slowing down and the air is turning static.

As she blinks to rid herself of the awkward feeling, she hears something crackle roughly. At first she imagines it to be another of what are apparently auditory hallucinations, but then the big man at the window turns and reaches to take a two-way radio off the desk.

"Marshall?"

The man known as Tango is barely audible over the crackle of static. "Colonel Turner... problem with...Bravo's ... not sure what...over."

"Marshall? Marshall!" Turner barks into the radio.

"Can't... gunshots... have to stand down..."

"Marshall!" Turner slams down the radio, producing a loud squeal of feedback. Glaring at the electronic device, the big man rattles off a string of curses. "Fucking Ryan! It's a fucking trap! So obvious!" With another few choice expletives, he unclips his holster and slides out his pistol to check the clip. "Thinks I'm just going to march in there? I know better, you bitch. I'm coming for you." He stalks towards the blonde, but this time passes her with only a cursory glance.

There is a moment of silence before she hears the door latch open and then close. Silence. Gritting her teeth, she tries to shift her burning arms to test the strength of the knot. She expects his threatening voice or swinging hand to accost her at any moment, but beyond the thundering of the blood rushing through her head, there is nothing. When she tries to separate her hands, her shoulders start to burn, and when she persists with dogged stubbornness, her head begins to pound and nausea flashes through her in retaliation for the physical strain.

Frustration makes her push too hard, and a sharp pain explodes through her stressed right shoulder. Smothering an involuntary moan, she tries again to force her bonds, abandoning the effort with a sob when her limb protests violently. Dropping her head forward onto her chest, she tries to keep back the hot tears of frustration that are threatening to spill over. It is in that moment of stern self-control that she notices a muted sound that is completely out of place.

Click.

Lifting her head, she looks around as far as her restraints and injuries will allow. Everything seems as it should be, and she is just about to start questioning her own sanity when the window slides open in front of her, seemingly of its own volition. Her breath escapes in a stutter as she gawks at it, unwilling to believe her tired eyes, and when a head suddenly pops up on the outside, the blonde jerks back in dread.

Captain Leah Ryan's vivid green eyes meet hers for a shocked moment, the dark woman silently taking in her battered condition before throwing an arm over the window sill and hoisting herself into the room. When Ryan hits the floor, she rolls behind the desk, out of the blonde's sight for a moment, and rapidly assesses the situation before she rises to her full height. Her expression is concerned as she quietly approaches the other woman.

"Walsch."

Kneeling behind the woman, Ryan begins to undo the knots with great care, sliding a knife out of a sheath on her thigh to saw through the rope where she cannot make headway. When finally she can release the captive's hands, she touches the bruised wrists gently before she helps the woman to her feet. The sudden change of position causes a wave of vertigo in the blonde and she tips backwards, thankful to feel the solid frame of the Marine supporting her. Wrapping one arm around Walsch's shoulders, Ryan leads her towards the door – and then suddenly stops.

"Wait."

Her head cocks to one side, and she listens carefully for a moment before she scowls.

"Damn it." Her voice is a whisper. She leads the blonde around the desk, peering at the kneehole below it before she helps Walsch onto the floor and motions her into the space. "I'm sorry. Keep in there; at least you'll be hidden. If anything happens, someone will come for you very soon."

Ryan's green eyes take in the bloody smears on the bruised face with a flash of melancholy before she touches the woman's cheek lightly. "I'm sorry you're in the middle of this, but you're safe with me. All right? Stay down."

Leaning back against the wooden surface, relieved that Ryan is there and anxious about what is about to happen next, the blonde closes her eyes wearily.

Muttering to himself, Colonel Turner returns to the office. Knowing he would be able to peer down at the front gate from a window in one of the empty offices without being seen, he had gone to the south wing instead of the front doors. Both posts had been abandoned, with no sign of either Marshall or Pitt, and he'd watched for a quiet moment, mistrusting the silence, before he suddenly comprehended that the threat might have been to a completely different area. He creeps back up the corridor, his pistol raised threateningly as he listens carefully for any sound out of the ordinary.

It is a building still considered under construction, bought and paid for by the consortium that does not use his name anywhere in its documentation. The mass of open pipes and exposed wiring makes it tricky to maneuver, unless one is well versed with the layout, but Turner is. If the consortium knows why he insists on being a silent partner and what he uses the premises for in exchange for his notable influence, they do not say.

Stepping over a gap in the floor, he gazes down for a moment, and that is enough time for Ryan to catapult down from the break in the air-conditioning vent and careen into him. Impacting the solid concrete floor winds them both, but the out of shape Turner more so, and while he is still scrambling to his feet, Ryan leaps forward, driving her shoulder into his midriff. The air leaves his chest with an audible "whoof", but with years of assault training under his belt, he manages to hold on to his weapon even as he folds double and catapults backwards.

Ryan's lean body lands heavily on top of his. Using his temporarily winded state to her advantage, she reaches forward for the pistol, wrapping her hands around his and pushing the weapon away from them, but Turner is a big, strong man. With an out-of-breath grunt, he yanks his hands up, pulling her off-balance and forward. When she feels herself being pulled closer, Ryan suddenly releases his hands, leaving the natural impetus of his own motion to pull the pistol away from her as she propels herself forward and slams her head squarely into his nose.

"Argh! *Mother*fucker!" Bringing one hand down to cup his excruciatingly painful broken nose, the colonel jerks the other hand over his body, using the impetus to roll over and shove her off of him.

Wanting to take advantage of his condition, she leaps forward to grab the pistol and almost finds herself the recipient of the butt-end. Ducking his clumsy blow, she grips his thick wrist with both of her hands and snaps it down, intending to loosen the weapon from his increasingly weak grasp, but with both hands occupied, she is unable to stop the bloody hand that shifts from his nose and morphs into a fist heading directly for her jaw. Pulling her head back as fast as she can, Ryan avoids some of the power of the blow by rolling with it, but nevertheless his strength is startling, and the bulk behind it adds force that has her seeing stars.

Blinking quickly to clear her head, Ryan steps to the side and lets go of his hands. Once again using his own momentum against him, wrapping her hand around his upper arm, she tugs him forward as he stumbles, tangling her leg with his to bring him heavily to the ground. Twisting as he falls, he wraps his feet around her ankle and pulls her feet from under her.

Both Marines go sprawling on the concrete. When Ryan hits the ground, she is already catapulting forward for the gun, but this time Turner is prepared. Reaching out, he grabs her by the front of her hooded sweatshirt and drags her closer. As she puts out both hands to keep from collapsing on top of him, the butt of the pistol strikes her with a dull thud, directly above her left ear. Her eyes roll upwards and her body goes limp, a problematic circumstance for him as her body is surprisingly heavy and is now pinning him down. With a grunt, he wipes at the bloody trail under his nose before he pushes at her roughly, the gun clasped in his hand making it slightly difficult. Finally he manages to roll her off to one side, and he is wholly unprepared when the roll simply continues into a smooth rise to her feet. Turner is still lifting the pistol when she leaps into the air and hoists herself into a gap in the ceiling – and promptly disappears.

"Fuck!" With a howl, he starts to shoot into the sheeting, but beyond his own litany of cursing, there is no sound. Moving surprisingly lightly for his bulk, Turner moves around with his gun drawn, listening for any signs of action above. Nothing. The sharp, overwhelming throbbing in his broken nose is making concentration difficult. Pressing at his forehead tentatively with his left hand, he creeps towards the office door, taking care not to make any sound himself. When he opens the door and sees the empty chair with the loosened ropes strewn around it, he bites back the urge to let loose another curse and closes the door softly again.

The blonde has served her purpose. Afterwards he will have her tracked down and eliminated.

He is wondering whether the sheeting will be strong enough to hold him when Ryan's voice drifts down from somewhere above him.

"So, Colonel, can I ask you something?"

In pure reflex, he squeezes off a shot into the ceiling, gritting his teeth in impotent fury when the sound only produces a low chuckle from Ryan. "Come out here, Ryan! Fight like a man!"

"Which man? You? Because in that case can you wait until I can find a civilian to tie up and kick the shit out of? No thanks."

Turner finds the edge of amusement in her voice intolerable. He forces out a laugh and deliberately softens his voice. "Ryan, if you don't attack me, I'll return the favor. I just want to talk to you."

This time it's an actual laugh, one filled with genuine mirth. "You don't say. Okay. Just let me get down from here..."

He's still waiting like an idiot, looking towards the scuffling noise, when a heap of sawdust falls from the partially finished roof and drifts down onto him, settling on his shoulders like a massive load of dandruff. A portion of the fine particles gets into his eyes, and he has to stop himself from rubbing furiously.

"Bitch!"

She laughs again, more softly this time, and he cannot tell where she is, whether she's moved, or if she's about to jump down onto him again.

"I'm not coming down from here to let you shoot me, Colonel. If you want me, you'll have to catch me."

"I could. I could also phone Mahoney and tell him to kill the other woman."

"And then the only leverage you have left will be dead."

"What the *fuck* do you want from me?" He notices his right hand trembling and impatiently steadies it with the left.

As if she can see him, the woman sniggers. "From you? *I'm* the one who's been messed with, chased around the country, shot at... I think the question is: What the fuck do you want from *me*, Colonel?"

"I wanted you to take care of the situation! I wanted you to ki–" He bites back the next words and glares at the roof, defying her to give away her position.

"You wanted me to kill... who?"

"Come down here!"

"Kill who, Turner?"

Roaring in anger, he fires another shot into the roof at random. This time, silence persists, until he thinks that he may have hit her, and then, in the quietness, she clicks her tongue at him.

"Tut. You're wasting bullets. How many left in that magazine?"

He feels as if he is about to explode in fury when footsteps sound on the steps further down the hall. He is aware that nobody is supposed to be in this structure, and he is not harboring any illusions that this will be either Marshall or Pitt coming to assist him. Things have gone horribly wrong for Colonel Turner today, and he is not about to tempt Fate. After a quick glance upwards, he lopes back towards the office door, yanks it open and barges in.

George Turner is not a coward. He has faced threats, weathered dangerous situations, and is still alive to tell the tale. However, he is also not stupid, and the DEX situation is a festering boil that has been threatening to burst open for many years. If he could have eliminated Ryan as he had wanted to, and the blonde doctor to boot, things would have been easy for a man of his rank to cover up, but now that godforsaken Marine's running amok in his hiding place, and the doctor's gone who knows where. It is inevitable that eventually facts about the unauthorized project will leak, and then it is only a matter of time before he is charged and his associates tracked down. And if the government doesn't crucify him, the few associates who are bound to escape exposure will.

There are only a few outs left to him, and at this moment, the one that Colonel Turner takes is the open window. He rushes towards it, slides it up, and is about to take his next action when the slightest of movements attracts his attention. With a frown he turns, slowly, and when his eyes fall on the doctor curled into a fearful ball beneath the desk, his mouth stretches into a harsh grin. As the door erupts inward, filling his field of vision, he lifts his firearm and aims it in the blonde's direction. Something catapults over the desk and then Ryan is between them, her chest blocking his view as she plants herself squarely, point blank between Turner and the desk.

"No!" Walsch screams, terrified, and then the gunshot rings out.

To her eyes, everything slows down – from the sound of her own heartbeat stretching into one dull, booming thud inside her chest to the agonizingly slow movement as Ryan's back arches and she buckles forward towards the broad form of the colonel in front of her.

The blonde wants to scream, can feel the thick pressure building up in her lungs as she opens her mouth, and whilst even the dust particles seem to be hanging by threads in the air around her, her mind is spinning at an impossible speed, howling *NO!* as she tries to get to the falling woman.

Turner's hands appear at the sides of Ryan's body, reaching out at the same time as the Marine extends her arms towards him for a grim embrace. For a long moment the disembodied limbs seem to protrude from her sides, causing an absurd Kali-like image for Walsch, watching from behind them in abject horror. The two figures meld into one as Ryan folds up like a burning paper doll, gradually collapsing onto the ground, her arms wrapped around Turner.

When finally she can move her numb body, Walsch reaches forward to close her trembling fingers convulsively over the hood of Ryan's sweatshirt. She starts in shock and fear when a pair of warm hands wraps over hers from behind and gently pull her into a warm embrace. Trying to pull away, the blonde stares up blindly at the face of the beautiful Spanish woman who is holding her ever so tenderly.

"Ryan?" she asks dumbly.

"It's okay, chica. She's okay."

"But he... Sophia... He shot her..."

Suddenly Ryan's arms unwrap from the burly body under her and she pushes herself up, her green eyes gentle as she looks at the blonde. "Sophie shot *him*, Walsch. He didn't shoot me. Look. I'm fine. Look."

A sob erupts from the blonde's throat and she bites it back, swallowing until her voice is under her control again.

"Okay."

She continues to watch with wide eyes as Ryan turns back to Turner and begins first aid. Ryan applies pressure to the copiously bleeding wound, her focus not leaving the wounded colonel, not even as Sophia Ruiz moves away to check the damage to Ryan's face.

Turner is groaning softly, his hands clenching convulsively, and when Ryan's hands press down on his chest he opens his eyes. His voice is low and breathy. "Ryan..."

Looking over her shoulder, Ryan meets the other woman's dark eyes. "¿Ya viene la ambulancia?" *Is the ambulance coming?*

"Yeah - is he going to make it?"

"I don't know. Depends on how quickly they arrive."

"You should leave the bastard to die."

"I'm better than him, Sophie." Leaning closer to Turner's paling face, Ryan speaks loudly. "Hey. Turner. Talk to me."

"...have *nothing* to say to you..." He closes his eyes petulantly.

With an irritated sigh, Ryan lifts a bloody hand from his body. "Turner, if I lift the other one, you bleed to death like a pig. I'm *so* tempted. Do *not* mess with me right now, okay?"

The smile that flickers over his bullish features is almost admiring. "So stubborn all the time. That's your problem."

"No, my problem is *you*. Asshole." She places her other hand back on his chest and applies pressure. "Tell me. Tell me how I was going to take care of the 'situation'."

"We set it up so you could escape..." He groans at a wave of pain, and takes a few shallow breaths before he continues. "Wanted you to eliminate the people who knew about DEX... Set up a thread for you from Banks' house. Didn't count on him cracking. We were watching his daughter, you know. And you – so fucking stubborn – you just *had* to go a different way..." He closes his eyes. "You were just one big fucking mistake from start to finish."

Fighting the temptation to let him bleed to death, Ryan watches him darkly. "How did you know I'd escape?"

"We pushed." Two brutally simple words. Gathering his strength, he shoots her a crooked smile. "We provoked you, we *hurt* you, we *tormented* you until you snapped. You've been thinking it was all Kosovo, haven't you? The *bad guys*? It wasn't, Ryan. Not all of it. A lot of the time that voice was your own people. We made you, Ryan... to be what you are."

Ryan's face contorts and she clenches her jaw as she glowers at him. "You failed."

"Do you really think so? You're lying to yourself. DEX or no DEX, you are what you are. You'll *never* be free of it."

Gritting her teeth, Ryan glares down at him. "Sophie, can you take over here?"

As she moves away, he grins weakly at her. "I'm not the only involved in this, Ryan. Don't think it ends here."

She freezes, her face unmoving. "Who else?"

"I'm done talking. You'll find out eventually."

Ryan's mouth sets itself into a thin straight line. "Sophie…"

"I'm here."

When Ruiz has her hands securely over the wound, Ryan turns her back on Turner and crouches at Walsch's side, avoiding touching the blonde with her bloody hands.

"Hey." The blonde shifts forward with a moan, and Ryan carefully wraps her arms around her shuddering body. "How badly did the bastard hurt you?"

"He knocked me around a bit." She chokes back a sob. "Ryan…"

"Hi, Andy."

Andy Walsch looks up at Ryan with tearful big blue eyes, so identical to her sister's. "Why didn't you go for Claire first?"

"She's of more value to Christopher than you are to Turner. He won't hurt her."

Andy blinks dazedly. "You almost got shot for me."

The Marine responds with a slight lift of an eyebrow. "I was going to keep you safe no matter what." Her gaze drops. "You're safe with me. I'm not what they say I am. I'm really not."

Picking up on the distressed undertone Andy pats Ryan's arm. "Hey. He was just trying to push your buttons. You're not like that. Claire–" Her eyes widen. "Claire!"

"Easy, Andy. Sophie has it under control. If you can wait here for the ambulance with her–"

"No!" Andy Walsch struggles to her feet. "You're not going without me. I want to see my sister!"

Standing, Ryan quickly assesses the trembling blonde before she leans down to Sophia. "Can you get someone to take over from you? If Andy's there, I want you there for her. Okay?"

"Sì." Summoning one of her men with the two-way radio at her waist, Sophia waits until he arrives and takes over the pressure on Turner's wound before she gets to her feet. "Let's go."

Sierra stands on the balcony, his irritation level rising exponentially as he tries to contact Turner for the umpteenth time. When the phone simply rings and rings he turns away from the picturesque scenery and swears softly to himself.

"What's happening?" It's Alpha, standing alertly at the sliding door, his eyes never leaving the bound figure on the couch.

"Still no answer. Something's very wrong."

"Just don't get any fucking bright ideas, okay?" Alpha slips his fingers into his shirt pocket and pulls out a blue packet of cigarettes, slides one out and slips it into his mouth. "The last time you decided something was wrong, we lost the woman and Turner handed my ass to me on a plate."

"Thanks for reminding me about that." Sierra stares at Alpha, his dark eyes biting, until the other man turns away from his gaze, shaking his head. His nostrils flaring at the initial smell of sulphur drifting from the match, Sierra steps past the other man and approaches the still form lying on the couch.

"Hey."

His voice is low and neutral. No response. He presses two fingers against the pulse point in the woman's neck, monitoring the steady heartbeat for a moment. Judging by the dried blood and the dark bruise coloring her cheek, Melville had hit her once or twice, and she is still out, even an hour after they found the man and returned the favor with interest before leaving him in his study.

Quickly checking the knots around her wrist, he makes sure that she will be unable to move and then he rises to check the front door again. He is just returning to the living room when Alpha steps in through the sliding door silently.

"Company. Two Caucasian males and one Asian male, armed, west side of the street."

"Movement?"

"None."

Sierra steps out onto the balcony, putting his back against the side wall as he glances quickly around it to study their surrounds. With a nod to himself he steps back in and closes the glass door behind him. Alpha is already perched on the edge of a chair, his M16 on his knees as he checks the sliding mechanism. Sierra passes him, moving towards his own weapon. He reaches out for his rifle as he presses the redial button and waits for Turner to answer. When the call goes unanswered, Sierra slips the phone into his pocket, sits down, and begins to check his firearm.

The woman on the couch stirs, a low sigh escaping her throat, but beyond a glance in her direction Sierra does not respond.

When both men are prepared, Alpha takes up his station at the side of the glass door, his body still as he keeps quiet watch on activities beyond the balcony. Sierra stands against the wall, just inside the lounge, his rifle held competently in both hands. They do not have to wait long.

A knock sounds at the door, hollow in the silence. Motioning to Alpha to stay at his post, Sierra approaches the door on the balls of his feet. Another knock sounds loudly, and then a woman's voice rings out.

"Come on, Christopher, I know you're in there." Frowning, Sierra stays quiet. "You've got the wrong woman, you know. Don't be an asshole. She's of no use to Turner." Sierra glances back at Alpha, but the other man has his back towards the room, his posture stolid. "Turner's been found out, Chris. You have nothing to gain from this. Open up."

This time when Sierra glances back, Alpha is shooting the door a puzzled glance before he turns his back again. There is a moment of silence before the woman continues.

"It's Ryan, Chris. C'mon, let me in."

At the mention of the familiar name, both men freeze. Scowling, Sierra shares a perplexed look with Alpha and then steals towards the door to peer through the peephole.

Whoever the woman is, she definitely isn't Leah Ryan. Her dark hair cascades down her shoulders in unruly curls. As Sierra watches, the woman bites the inside of her bottom lip in quiet frustration and appears to look straight at him. Leaning back, Sierra peers through the doorway to the living room and shakes his head at Alpha, who nods once before he moves out of Sierra's sight, back to the balcony.

Alpha is standing alertly inside the sliding door just at the border of the concrete surface, his hands wrapped around his weapon, when a rustling attracts his attention. It seems to be coming from somewhere below the balcony and to the right. With a frown, he approaches and stops just short of the edge, aware that it may be a trap. He lifts his weapon, leveling it as he carefully sets one foot in front of the other. Drawing in a muted breath, he steps closer... and almost fires off a startled shot as one of the armed soldiers he spotted earlier bursts from the bushes below, scrambling towards an unmarked black van. Glancing up, the soldier spots Alpha and instantly drops down and rolls behind a small shrub. Ignoring the soldier's sloppy activities with a disdainful grin, Alpha carefully combs the area for signs of snipers before he steps closer to the railing to keep the amateurish soldier in view.

The grin is still on his face when Leah Ryan explodes up from absolutely nowhere and grabs the back of his head, yanking it forward so that the bridge of his nose meets the iron railing with a dull crunch. As his eyes roll back in his head, she levers herself over the rail to wrap her hands in the fabric of his uniform and lower him quietly to the ground. Crouched low, she checks his pulse and takes his weapon before she approaches the door.

A smallish stocky soldier is standing silently in the middle of the living room with a groggy Claire Walsch held tightly against him and the barrel of his rifle pointed in Ryan's direction.

He jerks his head in the direction of the door. "She's not you."

"And you're not Christopher." Lifting one hand in a gesture of submission, she leans down to put the borrowed rifle on the ground, though they're both aware that her compliance means nothing significant at this point.

He watches her carefully. "You killed him?"

From the direction of his eyes, she knows that he's talking about the soldier outside on the balcony. Apparently Turner's wellbeing isn't all that high on his list.

"No. Broken nose. Maybe a slight concussion." Her green eyes flicker to the bloodied blonde in his arms with a flash of anger. "Did you do that to her?"

"No. It was Melville."

"Where is he?"

Sierra cocks his head in the direction of one of the closed doors off of the living room. "He was an asshole."

"Agreed."

They keep eye contact, watching each other warily for any threatening movement.
"You know that Turner's gone down?"

"So she said." His head twitches ever so slightly in the direction of the door.

"It's true. Are you with him?" When he doesn't answer she gives a half smile. "Fine. She's telling the truth. How much do you know about what Turner was doing?"

Still he doesn't answer.

"Smart move. If I knew, I'd have to kill you." Her eyes slip back to the woman in his arms. "You hear you have the wrong one?"

"Doesn't matter to me. You know that."

"Turner's up shit creek. If you don't want to end up there with him... it matters."

"Is that right?" As quick as lightning he pushes Claire forward, and in the same instant his gun swings around.

Ryan grabs the blonde's arm and yanks her to the side as she jabs at the barrel of the rifle, pushing it upwards with the heel of her hand. The flash of heat on her flesh when the weapon discharges goes unnoticed as she catapults into the muscular man, her shoulder driving into his chest. His hands scrabble for control of the weapon as he lifts a booted foot and drives it into her shin, the force only slightly diminished by her rapid checking move.

She clenches her teeth against the sharp pain and drives an elbow into his stomach, flinching as his elbow hits the side of her jaw, even as the breath is forced from him in a painful gasp. Taking advantage of his momentary distraction, she wraps her other hand around the weapon again and uses her superior grip to lever it towards her.

Realizing her intention, Sierra quickly fixes his grip on the rifle as well. They stay locked in the struggle, and, to his surprise, Ryan holds her ground, the sinews in her shoulders and neck straining as she keeps the weapon forced towards the ceiling.

Her teeth are gritted in exertion and her words come out in a growl. "Do you really want to be involved in this?"

He tries to shift his grip, abandoning the attempt when his maneuvering seems not to have any effect. "I'm a Marine. You of all people should understand."

There is movement behind him, and Ryan shakes her head in warning at the rising blonde before she grimaces. "Look where obedience got me. You want to walk *this* road?"

"I don't choose the road." He kicks out in an attempt to connect with her bruised shin, but she blocks adeptly and delivers a quick, stinging kick to the bridge of his foot.

"If you don't choose your road, you'd better be mighty sure that the one who does the choosing won't throw you to the wolves. You think Turner gives a shit about you?" She sets herself against the renewed force of his thrust, pushing in so close that her torso is pressed against his. "You're on your own now, soldier. Grow some balls. Make your own decision."

He pushes harder, using his body weight to drive her backwards, and almost trips over his own feet when she twists around and lets his impetus move him past her. Their hands drop lower and she slams the heel of her hand into his fingers, forcing the barrel away from her. Surging forward, she drives a knee upwards into his groin, and though he tries to twist away the glancing contact causes an explosion of pain in his gut. Grunting, he tries to keep his grip, but the force of the second blow drives him to his knees. Clutching his crotch he ducks his head and steels himself against another blow. When it doesn't come, he glances up in puzzlement.

Ryan looms over him, her face stark, and the gun hangs loosely in her hand by her side.

"If you're the one who killed Victor, I really should snap your neck here and now, but I've had enough of that for a lifetime. Listen to me: Don't let him use you like he's done with me. You're not a part of this thing, and you shouldn't want to be. Believe me. I'm going to go into that room to check on Melville. If you're not here when I come back, I probably won't remember your face. Do you understand me?"

He nods dumbly, cautious. Ryan walks around him, extends a hand to the trembling blonde, and pulls her into a one-armed hug, tender and intimate. Then, limping ever so slightly, she leads the other woman towards the door. Her last glance over the blonde's shoulder at Sierra is one of unexpected kinship. before she disappears from his view.

Melville is dead. He did not suffer; Ryan can see that. The angle of his broken neck indicates that his life was taken expertly and very quickly. Shielding Claire from the sight, she says a silent prayer for his soul, hoping that it counts for something, and then leads the blonde back into the empty living room.

The two commandos are gone. Feeling Claire's knees beginning to buckle, Ryan lays the rifle on the couch and wraps her other arm around her lover, holding her close. Though Claire is not crying, her breathing is irregular and strained.

"Andy..."

"Your sister is okay, Walsch; just a bit battered. She's outside with the paramedics and anxious to check on you." Ryan drops a soft kiss on the blonde hair and then leans back to check the split lip and bloodied cheek with gentle fingers, apologizing softly when Claire winces. "You?"

"I'm fine." Claire stares at Ryan's face – the dried trail of blood running from her lip, the lurid bruise beginning to form at her temple – and her mouth begins to tremble.

With a shake of her head and a sharp breath Ryan pulls the blonde close. They stand like that for a long time, and to her mortification, Ryan doesn't notice Sophia waiting in the open door of the apartment until the other woman clears her throat pointedly.
"Is this a bad time?" She looks Ryan over uneasily. "*¿Estas bien?*"

Claire starts, twisting around to look at the dark woman, and when she glances up at Ryan her expression is heartbreakingly vulnerable. Shaking her head Ryan lifts a hand to touch Claire's face briefly. "It's not what you think, Claire. This is Sophia Ruiz. My cousin. She's with a government agency."

Claire looks at Ryan, and then back at the other woman. "FBI?"

Sophia shakes her head. "No."

It's pointed but not unfriendly, and Claire instantly understands that she won't field any further questions in that line. However, there is another question just begging to be asked. Frowning,

Claire tries to put it as delicately as possible. "You were... kissing your cousin?"

"I was not. I was actually just leaning in to block the camera's view, but she won't let me hear the end of it either," Ryan retorts drily.

Sophia lifts an eyebrow ironically, and suddenly Claire can clearly see the resemblance between the cousins.

"I was also hoping to make her connection to me a little more ambiguous, at the least," Ryan continues. "She's not easy to track, but Turner would have had the means, had he suspected anything other than what he did. He thought he knew me well enough to make assumptions. He was wrong."

"So, you kissed her." Claire's mouth twitches.

A muffled chuckle escapes Sophia's throat. "She really didn't. I would have clocked her." Her dark eyes move to Ryan. "¿Es ella?" *Is she the one?*

Ryan raises an eyebrow and looks at the dark woman intently for a moment before she nods. "Sì, prima. Es ella."

Sophia smiles, and it is such a beautiful smile, all vivacity and dimples, that Claire cannot help but smile with her, even though she has no idea what has just happened. Approaching the blonde, Sophia takes her gently by the arm, levering her from Ryan's hold.

"Come, chica, your sister is going insane with worry." She leads Claire towards the door. "And you're probably in shock. I'm taking both of you to the hospital." Shooting Ryan a quick look over her shoulder, Ruiz adds. "You too, prima. Unless you want to go out the way you came in."

Ryan grimaces. "If I never see a drainpipe in my life again, it'll be too soon."

A doctor is putting careful stitches in the gash on Andy's cheek as Claire looks on, holding her sister's hand tightly. Occasionally Andy squeezes Claire's hand, though neither is sure at this point whether it serves to reassure Claire or to remind her to loosen her grasp.

Ryan perches on a bed in the corner, in quiet discussion with Sophia, her face expressionless and her eyes intermittently shifting over her cousin's shoulder to the women sitting two beds over. The Marine did not want to come to the hospital, writing off her injuries as minor, but was persuaded by Ruiz's terse argument that the Walsch sisters needed attention and wouldn't come without her.

Ryan has already been checked out by a doctor, and the only visible sign of any discomfort is the ice pack she's pressing gingerly against her temple. She leans in close to say something and then shoots her almost-smile over Sophia's shoulder, gratified to see Claire's eyes crinkle in her direction before the other woman turns back to her sister.

Sophia smiles. "Oh, you've got it bad, Ryan."

The Marine snorts. "Nonsense, Ruiz. It's adrenaline and... whatever else. Stress."

Sophia mimics her snort. "Hah. If this is what stress does in our family then I'd better get another job before I start staring at my colleagues all goopy-eyed."

"You're funny. Not to me, though. Maybe to other people. Maybe." Ryan shifts the ice pack a little and yawns. "Damn. What a day."

Sophia is about to retort when her mobile phone rings. Ignoring the way Ryan's green eyes twinkle at the blaring tones of *The Animaniacs*, she flips open her mobile.

"*Sì.*" Sophia listens for a while, her slight smile fading. "*Sì. Sì.* Is he badly hurt?"

Ryan leans closer, watching Sophia intently. With a quick glance at her, Sophia turns her back on Ryan and listens for a while longer before she closes her phone and turns to her cousin. Even though she takes care to keep her expression impassive, Ryan has known her cousin long enough to notice the curbed signs of strain in the set of her generous mouth. "What? Soph?"

"It's Turner." She reaches up to rub her forehead abstractedly. "Somehow he's gone missing between the building site and the hospital. Ortega found the ambulance driver in the gutter two blocks down. He'd been hit in the head; can't remember a thing." Sophia notes the grim set of Ryan's jaw as the other woman carefully puts the ice pack on the bed next to her. "There was an agent in the back of the ambulance with him. Scott is now hurt... or he's a part of it. Either way, this goes–"

"...deeper than we thought." Ryan finishes the thought and shifts forward to slip off the bed, glancing in frustration at the hand now resting firmly against her shoulder. "Sophie, let me go. I have to check it out."

"No." The same touch of steel that was in Ryan's voice is now in Sophia's. The agent cocks her head and indicates the two blonde women behind her, one of whom is worriedly glancing over towards the obviously agitated Marine. "*That* is where you have to be, prima. With her. I don't think Turner will take the chance of trying anything else this soon, but if he does, and it endangers Claire *again*, would you be able to live with that?"

Ryan's jaw clenches and she locks eyes with her cousin. "That's why I have to go, Sophie. I have to find him. She can't be a part of this."

"What you're really saying is that you don't want her to be a part of *you*, prima." Sophie's voice is soft. "She already *is*. You always want to be the one who goes first. I know you, prima. You're trying to save her by running away so that she won't have to." She pats the tense shoulder under her hand affectionately. "Here's a thought: Why not give her a chance to decide for herself? She's a tough one, and she's stood with you this far. She must actually *like* your grumpy ass."

Scowling, Ryan turns away. "That's because she doesn't know what I'm like. And besides, it's not about that. Turner–"

"...is *my* business now. And she'll never know you any better if you don't give her the opportunity." Seeing Ryan's eyes shift past her for a moment, Sophia steps back. "Don't undervalue your worth, prima. I don't like when you do that to somebody I love."

She turns and shares a radiant smile with Claire, who has just stepped up behind her. "I have to go. Under better circumstances it would have been delightful to meet you, Doctor Walsch. I think we'll see each other again soon. Please take care of my cousin. She doesn't always do so well for herself."

"Thank you so much for finding Andy, Agent Ruiz." Instead of taking the proffered hand, Claire leans forward and places a friendly kiss on the woman's cheek.

Cocking her eyebrow jauntily, Sophia grins at her glowering cousin. "Adiós, prima. Be careful!"

Ryan frowns as she watches Sophia go. "I should be going with her."

"Well," Claire's face is carefully neutral, "if that's where you want to be, then you should go."

Sighing, Ryan smiles faintly and reaches out to tuck a strand of the light hair back behind Claire's ear. "It's where I think I *should* be, but it's definitely not where I *want* to be." Her thumb brushes gently over Claire's swollen lip, avoiding the painful cut. "How's Andy?"

Closing her eyes against the feather-light touch, Claire turns her head with the motion of Ryan's finger. "He hit her so many times, Ryan. Nothing serious, but she'll hurt for a while. I wish she hadn't decided to surprise me."

Closing her eyes, Ryan drops her head. "I should have killed him when I had the chance. He was a sickening man."

"You have more integrity than that." Claire strokes Ryan's forearm lightly, reveling in the feel of the warm soft skin for a moment. "Can I ask you something?"

"You can ask me anything."

"Melville?"

A corner of Ryan's mouth twitches upwards into a trace of a melancholy smile. "Ah, Christopher." Wrapping her hand over Claire's, she holds it for a moment. "I'm sorry I didn't tell you about him, Claire. I should have, I just never... I didn't... Anyway, I apologize."

She is quiet after the atypical hesitation, and it is only when Claire's hand shifts under her own that she continues softly. "I married Christopher in the mid-nineties, when I was still in the Marines. It was pure subterfuge. I was attracted to women, and the military didn't exactly encourage that behavior."

A bitter smirk flits across her face.

"No, let me be clearer, actually. I don't want to gloss over it. My behavior was terrible, nothing to be excused. I used women as I felt like it, without a scrap of decency. I screwed around, I lied, I cheated, and I didn't care who I hurt. That lasted until I became involved with the wife of a superior officer, and when the potential consequences of that hit me... Well, marrying Chris, a friend and colleague of mine at the time, was the easiest course of action. Or so I thought.

It was meant to cover me, to make it seem as if I'd learnt my lesson. Things were getting a bit thorny, and I would've done *anything* to cover my ass. I didn't stop to wonder what Chris was getting out of the deal.

We were married in name for about a year, but it felt like forever. Chris likes... liked to hit. I could defend myself, but when things got out of hand and I went to his commanding officer, any action on my complaint was blocked from above. That officer whose wife I screwed? Well, he had friends higher up than I did. Anyway, Chris continued to beat the crap out of me, and everybody carefully looked in the opposite direction. I suppose I thought I deserved their contempt for my sins. In any case, when they found out that he really liked his women just a tad too young to be legal, his transgressions finally outweighed mine and he was shipped off to a very small, very strict base in the northwest, and I was delicately reminded to keep my behavior in check."

Claire watches her closely. "I hate to think what you mean when you say 'delicately'."

"Well." Ryan shrugs. "Nothing overt. The reminders were certainly always... resourceful, but I took the point. I maintained a certain image, taking great care to keep my personal life personal. When I went into Fairwater, Christopher was still at his remote base, keeping his nose clean, but sometime after I committed myself, he completely lost it and messed with a captain's daughter - so Sophie told me. He has... had nothing but the Marines. His attempt at using you to blackmail Turner was probably just a completely delusional, last-ditch effort." Ryan frowns. "If he was helping to keep me in Fairwater, he might have had some connection with DEX. I can't even begin to think of how he was tangled up in all of this. It's just too much for my brain right now."

Ryan falls silent and stares down at their connected hands.

Claire watches her silently for a long while before she speaks. "Do you really think you deserved how your own commanders brutalized you? How they used you in ways you had no knowledge of?"

"I've hurt people. Should I expect better for myself?"

"That's a long time ago. If you keep judging yourself by your past, you might as well give up right now, and that's not something I'd expect from you. Ryan. It's not about just surviving, it's about thriving." Leaning forward, Claire kisses her lightly before she steps back. "Can we please go home now?"

Michael Enfield frowns at the ringing phone and slams down his pen, motioning for an aide to close the door before he lifts the handset.

"What?"

"It's Turner." The voice on the other side is faint. "There's been a breach."

Enfield pokes at the pink file on the desk in front of him with irritation. "Yes, I know. I hear everything; did you forget?"

"Whatever." Even Turner's physical distress isn't tempering his rudeness. "Reparative measures need to be taken."

"Already done. Will you be all right?" The question is cursory, without much real concern.

"Sure. That bitch Ryan..." There's a slight gasp; he must have shifted the wrong way and aggravated whatever injury he's received. "I'm keeping a low profile for a while, until I'm on my feet again, then I'm going after her myself."

"You will do no such thing, Colonel." Enfield's voice is smooth and soothing, an attribute that is an asset to his career. "Leave it alone. You've messed up time and time again with regard to the captain. We'll be watching her closely, and if she makes any move we don't like, we'll take action. In the meantime, the Marine Corps will arrange to have all charges – military and civilian – against

Captain Ryan dropped. You will be nowhere to be found. Oh, and one more thing, Turner: Make sure the loose ends are tied up cleanly. Make *very* sure. Technically, this experiment is *dead*. Do you understand me?"

"Loud and clear." Turner clears his throat. "That all?"

"Yes." Enfield reaches up and straightens his tie. "I'll give your regards to the senator. Goodbye."

Beyond exhausted, Claire lets a slightly limping Ryan lead her into the bedroom and settle her on the double bed. "Is your leg okay?"

"I'm fine." Ryan catches the doubtful look. "Seriously. You look worse than I do."

"Luckily I don't look half as bad as I feel."

Ryan slips off Claire's shoes and puts them to one side, then lifts Claire's legs onto the bed, gently coaxing her onto her back. "C'mon, Walsch. You need some sleep." The Marine is about to leave when Claire's hand wraps around hers.

"Ryan, can you sit with me for a minute?"

"Sure." She perches on the edge of the bed carefully, her eyes blank. "What's up?"

"What's going to happen next?"

"With Turner?"

"With us."

"Us?" Ryan returns Claire's gaze steadily. "Is there an 'us', Claire?"

"Well, here you are, and here I am, and together we're an 'us'." There's a shadow of aching in her eyes. "I thought you didn't play games, Ryan."

The Marine looks away. "I don't. But I also don't make promises I can't keep. That could hurt."

Withdrawing her hand, Claire takes a deep settling breath. "This is awfully close to hurting already, Ryan. I'm usually pretty good at reading people. Was I wrong this time? Can you honestly tell me that you don't feel anything for me?"

"We've just gotten back from the hospital, Claire." Ryan stands up and stretches. "Can we have this talk a little later?"

The blonde stands her ground. "Was it lust? Was that really all it was?"

Ryan turns around, her shoulders rigid and her hands clenched at her sides. "You're the one who said that. I don't know, Claire. I don't *know*. I've never *had* anything more! What does that even mean?"

"You don't want to stay to find out?" A sad smile flickered over Claire's mouth. "Do you think you've changed at all?"

"If you have to ask me that, then obviously I haven't!" Ryan drops her head and rubs her temples with clear frustration. "What is it that you want from me, Claire? I told you that I couldn't offer you anything."

Though Claire is trying hard to keep her face impassive, her rapid blinking transmits her distress. "I want to know whether you're going to be around when I wake up. It's an easy out."

They stare at each other for a long moment before Ryan answers. "No. I don't think I will be." She pauses. "I'm sorry, Claire. I don't think I am what you want me to be."

"Okay."

The sound of Claire swallowing back a sob almost impels Ryan to take the other woman in her arms. Standing ramrod straight, she forces herself to remain where she is, until Claire has pulled herself together enough to continue.

"It's not the answer that I wanted, but since I asked, I suppose I have to be content with the truth. Can't change that. You really don't lie, do you?" She pulls the sheet over her body. "I can't have you this close and not have any of you. I'm going to go to sleep, Ryan. When I wake up, you either need to be all here, or you need to be all gone. Okay?"

"Okay." It's a whisper.

"Okay." Gripping the sheet tightly with trembling hands, Claire takes a deep breath. "Thank you for everything, Ryan. There are parts of what we've shared that I regret, but most of it? I never, ever will. Take care of yourself. Tell your cousin I'm sorry I couldn't." Abruptly she turns and wraps her arms around the pillow under her aching head.

With a last glance at the tousled blonde hair Ryan turns and walks out. In the living room she stops and stares at the open sliding door for a long time before she approaches Andy out on the balcony. "Shouldn't you be in bed, too?"

"I can't sleep."

"Smoking won't help. It's a bad habit."

Andy takes a deep drag and exhales slowly, the pleasure apparently only marginally diminished by the aching in her face. "I've quit a few times – very successfully, may I add – but if any time's a good time to start again, it's now."

"Those things'll kill you."

"So will just minding my own business, apparently." Andy draws on the cigarette again, wincing at the pain in her lip and cheek. "So. You walking out on my sister?"

Ryan casts a wry glance at her before she walks up to the railing and drapes her forearms over it. "Well, yeah."

"Don't be a bastard."

The retort is so casual that it elicits a dismal chuckle from Ryan. Turning around, she leans against the rail and looks over at the other woman. "I'm trying not to hurt her any more than I already have, Andy. As her sister, you should be pleased about that."

Andy puffs a wobbly smoke ring into the air and then rolls her eyes dramatically. "As I remember it, you were the one *saving* all of us, Ryan. Flying through windows like fucking Batman. If it weren't for you, things would have been much worse. Possibly fatal."

"If it weren't for me, neither of you would have been in that situation in the first place."

"And yet, there we were!" Andy flicks the cigarette ash sharply over the railing and straightens up angrily. "It happened, Ryan. You can't take it back, no matter how much you may want to. But if it hadn't happened, Claire wouldn't have met *you*, and now you want to take away the *one* positive thing she found in all of this? What kind of fucked up logic is *that*!"

"I'm going to hurt her." Ryan stares down at her feet. "You think that it all stops with the end of Turner, Andy, but it doesn't. Not for me." She glances over. "You won't understand."

"No, I won't, especially if you don't even bother *trying* to explain!"

Ryan sighs. "When I was chasing Turner these last few months, tracking him down and setting him up for a fall, it was the sole focus of my life. I was fighting to survive. I thought that once I'd taken him down, things would be miraculously resolved, that my entire history would prove to have hinged on this, that I could sit back and say 'let's start again, this wasn't my fault'.

But my life has always been like this, Andy. People told Claire. They told her that I was wild, that I was bad, and other things worse than that. She chooses to see the good in me, but the other element is the bigger part of me.

I want to be different. So much that it hurts. I want these last few months to have changed me into something better than I was before... but wanting something is no guarantee of getting it. Deep inside? I'm not worth it. With or without DEX, I'm still the person who did what I did. It's written in my history; it's something I can't erase. For the want of a better cliché," Ryan grimaces, "she makes me want to be a better woman. But I don't think I have that in me. I don't want to hang your sister's hopes on a 'maybe', Andy. I've been strong enough to save her from everything but me, and I don't want to fail her at the last turn. She deserves so much better."

"Yes, she does."

Andy cups Ryan's chin and tilts it upwards, her blue eyes - so much like Claire's - taking in the tears forming in the Marine's eyes compassionately.

"For everything Claire's been through in her life, she deserves whatever the hell she wants, and that happens to be *you.*" When

Ryan opens her mouth, Andy shakes her head. "Quiet. Listen to me. And I mean really listen."

She waits for Ryan's faint and before she continues.

"Life is like a river that you're drifting down. In front of you may be waterfalls, or rocks, or the most peaceful waters you could hope for, but you can't know until you get there. Behind you is the wake you're leaving in the water. Yes, it's attached to you, a history of your passage... and yet it's not what moves you forward. Beyond being a transient memory, your past has absolutely no relevance to where you are drifting right now; it is only a reminder of where you drifted before to reach the here.

What you were once is *not* the driving force behind what you are now, Ryan. Blaming your past for your weaknesses is what people do when they can't take responsibility for the present. That's not you. You know who you are at this very moment, Ryan. You're someone strong and solid and devoted, being loved by someone wonderful who knows all these crazy things about you and still wants you for **you**. Grab on to that with both hands. Don't keep looking back; there's nothing left there for you."

A tear tracks down Ryan's cheek. "But how do I do that? How do I know that I won't backslide?"

Andy grasps Ryan's right hand and presses it gently. "You do that by keeping something extraordinary ahead of you that you can keep your gaze fixed on."

With her free hand Ryan wipes quickly at her eyes. "I don't know if I'm capable of that, Andy."

Leaning forward, Andy pulls Ryan into a tight embrace. "Hey, I've seen you do a lot more than that, Batman. I think you can do absolutely anything you set your mind to."

Ryan awkwardly rests her chin on the shorter woman's shoulder and just breathes, letting the unknown and the fear wash over her until the clamoring in her head dies down. Then, straightening up, she presses her cheek to Andy's in a rare unguarded expression of affection. "Claire was right. You're amazing."

She can feel the other woman's skin shifts against hers in a grin. "You're not so bad yourself, Captain." Stepping back out of Ryan's arms, she pushes her toward the door. "You know what you have to do."

"Yes." Ryan turns away and then pauses for a moment before she turns back with a questioning look. "Hold on a second. You called her Sophia... *before* I said her name."

There is a moment when Andy looks as if she is going to deny it before she cocks her head, her blue eyes cautious.

The Marine raises a dark eyebrow. "Care to explain?" A glimmer of amusement plays around her mouth. "Don't leave out the coincidence of arriving in town at just the right time. Sounds like a good bit."

Andy taps another cigarette out of the pack and slips it between her swollen lips. Taking a deep drag, she winces before she exhales. There's a slight smile on her face. "I'm sure that if you think back a little, you'll realize that you're mistaken, Captain Ryan."

They share a look of complicity before Ryan nods. "Now that you mention it, I'm sure I will."

Standing at the bedroom door, Ryan studies the figure in the bed, back turned towards her, the blonde hair she knows from experience to be so silky and the neck's she's seen bent in such an intimate arch. "Claire?"

Claire rolls over, hope flashing across her face for the briefest of moments before she manages to school herself into something more neutral. "I thought you'd left."

"I was very close." A halting breath. "I have to tell you something. I told you that I would never lie, but I realize now that I have."

Claire's eyes close sadly. "Don't."

"I lied when I told myself I could walk away from you. I lied when I told myself I was doing it for you. I lied when I assured myself that I'd make it out of this intact."

Ryan studies the blue eyes as they open in surprise; the red rings around them; the cut over the eyebrow and the gash bisecting the bottom lip.

"The demons inside didn't come from some chip, Claire; they came from me. All this time I thought I was fighting some injustice, trying to save the world, and what I was actually doing was just trying to save my sanity. All this time I thought the worst hurt would be the glass in my hands or the bullet in my shoulder, but it turned out to be the fight *against* letting go of my darkness. If I could have held on to that chip, I could explain away my whole history. I could say '*this is what I am, and this is what you get, and this is the way it will always be*'."

She shakes her head.

"But if I hold onto that excuse as tightly as I need to, I won't have a hand left to hold on to you."

Claire watches her unblinkingly. "Which are you going to let go?"

"Well," Ryan cocks her head, "I figure that if you still want to take me on, I'd like to let you be the force that pulls me forward instead of having the old demons push me. The view sure would be better." A self-deprecating grin flits over her face. "Not the most romantic proposal ever. I'm sorry - words aren't really my strength."

Sitting up, Claire swings her legs off the bed and looks up at Ryan, standing so uncertainly before her. "Have you ever heard the Chinese saying 'If you've saved someone's life, you're responsible for them forever'? Well, when those Marines were shooting at us at the hotel and you stepped in front of me and shielded me, that's when this stopped being your choice."

Stepping closer Ryan shakes her head. "You think I saved you, but you're wrong. It's the other way around. When I asked you to stop reaching out to me... and you didn't. When all the signs pointed to crazy, and you wouldn't let go... You saved *me*, Claire."

"Hmm." Claire raises her eyebrows. "So I suppose this means, for all intents and purposes, that we'll have to be responsible for each other for a very long time?"

"Yeah." There's a hint of uncertainty in the Marine's voice.

"I can think of worse things." Claire stands up, a grin spreading across her face. "Can you shut up and kiss me now? Would that be fine?"

Leah Ryan's face shifts into a radiant, whole-hearted smile as she opens her arms.

"More than just fine, Walsch. So much more."

Made in the USA
Monee, IL
09 December 2022